THE
FIRST LADY
Sleeps

Enjoy
Walloon Lake
2021

JOHN MULLALLY

All Novels Publishing, LLC.

The First Lady Sleeps

All Novels Publishing, LLC.

© 2011 by John Mullally

ISBN 978-0-9837808-0-9

Editing and typography: Richard Harris

Cover photo: Gerald Martineau

Cover design: Steven Demos, M.D.

Finished cover and text layout:
Amy Cole, JPL Design Solutions

Printed in the United States of America

Dedicated to Barb and our grandchildren:
Betsy, Sean, Brendan, Connor, Ethan,
Claire, Addison and Reagan.

May the depicted fictional events never
happen in your lifetimes.

I

As soon as he emerged through the well-worn gray double doors connecting the tarmac to the spartan waiting area at the Detroit City Airport's corporate fixed base operation, two burly uniformed Detroit police officers flanked him. One said, "Tom Gleason?"

Gleason turned to the cop who had spoken. "Are you boys my welcoming committee? Usually I get a limo."

"Are you Thomas Gleason?" the cop repeated.

"Yeah. I'm Gleason."

"Slowly hand your bag and briefcase to my partner, sir."

He complied. The second cop commented, "Pretty small bag for staying overnight. What's in here, I wonder? Cash? Drugs? With Canada so close we're really watching all the private jets for illegals or smuggling."

Gleason wasn't about to reveal that it contained his SIG Sauer P226 handgun. Instead, he said "Do you know who I am?"

"Thomas Gleason, or so you say."

"Special Agent Gleason of the United States Secret Service, to be exact."

"Not our problem. We'll check your story and ID later. Today you're a person of interest. Our boss has some questions for you."

Gleason let himself be escorted out the airport to a patrol car waiting at the curb. One of the cops pushed his head down and prodded him into the smelly, stained back seat. The car proceeded slowly out of the passenger pickup area. Instead of exiting to the freeway it veered off into the deserted far corner of the long-term parking lot.

"Aren't we going downtown?" Gleason asked.

"No, we're going right here. End of the line for you, special agent."

The patrol car pulled to a stop beside a big black Buick with darkened windows that was listing to the driver's side until the driver got out. He was a huge African American—six feet and several inches, built like a sumo wrestler with ponderous girth and no flab. His presumably shaved head gleamed. An unlit cigar protruded from his broad grin. "Gleason," he boomed. "I believe you've met two of Detroit's finest."

Gleason suddenly noticed that the uniformed cops were standing stiffly at attention, eyes straight ahead. The big man pulled his wallet from the inside pocket of his rumpled suit jacket and handed a $100 bill to each of the cops. They thanked him, calling him Chief, and he nodded, "Good job, officers. There's a sucker born every day."

"Okay, Jeff," Gleason said, shaking his head, "You almost had me this time. If it wasn't for my keen powers of observation and deduction, I'd been fooled into thinking they were for real. Fortunately I noticed that they didn't ask me for my ID, which no serious patrolman would ever do. Remember paybacks are hell!"

"They are my on duty cops, having a little fun. Once in a while we just like to yank the chain of arriving big shots, especially from Washington," Detroit Police Chief Jefferson Hawkins could hardly continue because of his belly shaking laughter. "Hey, hop in the front seat of my specially equipped Buick, a big upgrade from the back seat of the black and white. Where are you staying?"

"The Marriott at the Renaissance Center."

"As nice as it gets in Detroit. Looks like no cut back in the way you Feds spend the people's money. I hope you at least have a suite."

"Yeah, I've reserved the presidential suite, no less. We convinced the hotel that although the president wouldn't be here tonight, I needed to check it out before his visit next month."

"The top floor presidential suite overlooking the river, too expensive for a working man like me," the chief said, as his police-equipped Buick turn onto East East Jefferson that runs parallel to Detroit River busy with every type of boat from large ore carrying freighters to small rowboats with fathers and sons fishing with long cane poles, the garrulous chief put on his chamber of commerce tour guide hat. He pointed out Belle Isle, once considered the crown jewel of all of Detroit's waterfront assets. In a month the first family would be viewing the Gold Cup hydroplanes races there from their friend Azee's mega yacht during Detroit's annual floating mardi gras.

The chief ticked off past and present riverfront highlights to match his rocking and rolling Buick's excessive speed. The "from one beer lover to another" Stroh's brewery was located in the area where the rum running speed boats of the prohibition era used to unload their forbidden Canadian booze into the Purple Gang's waiting trucks and horse drawn vehicles disguised as milk wagons dripping melting ice water to make them appear truly authentic. Old-timers could remember when a tour of the Stroh's brewery included a sandwich and a beer in a souvenir glass. The Roostertail restaurant was the place to be for an unequalled view across the river to Windsor whether or not the often airborn hydroplanes, sliding around each turn at one hundred miles per hour, were throwing their roostertails heavenward to the applause of the engrossed spectators.

In spite of the chief's nonstop effort to put Detroit's best foot forward for Tom's edification, they were able to exchange the kind of getting-reacquainted chat that steers clear of remember-whens, even as Gleason watched Hawkins's face in profile and marveled that he didn't look like he'd aged a day since the two had first met in basic training at the Federal Law Enforcement Training Center near Glynco, Georgia, more than twenty years ago. By the time they had survived the ten week basic training course, Gleason and Hawkins had each other's backs, and at the end of a seventeen weeks at the U.S. Secret Service Training Facility in Laurel, Maryland, they were fast friends. It was no surprise that the two were both sent to the Secret Service Field Office in Detroit, where Hawkins had been born and raised.

After an initial mentorship with senior agents in the field office, Gleason and Hawkins were assigned as partners, a relationship that had lasted almost three years. Each man had saved the other's life at least once.

In the end, it was unsavory associates that broke up their team. The main business of the Detroit Secret Service office was to apprehend counterfeiters and other white-collar financial criminals. Along the Canadian border business was good and temptations were many. Two other special agents in the unit had devised a way to skim part of the bona-fide currency that changed hands during their investigations, diverting nearly $1.2 million into their own offshore accounts before they got caught. If they had been metropolitan police detectives, the scandal would have been in the news for weeks, but the Secret Service, charged with preserving the utmost public confidence in the U.S. money system, protected itself from even the hint of impropriety at all costs. Within days after the corrupt agents were secretly taken into custody, the Detroit field office experienced a staff turnover so complete that everybody in the unit was newly assigned there and everyone who could remember the crime was gone.

Gleason, who was starting to feel like a Detroit native with season tickets to the occasionally competitive Tigers and totally toothless Lions, was offered a special agent position with the Secret Service protective unit in Washington, DC. He accepted it with mixed emotions as a chance to return to his East coast roots and start a family if he could find a wife willing to accept his demanding Secret Service lifestyle. Hawkins was offered a job in the Los Angeles field office. Instead, he resigned from the Secret Service to take a detective's rank in the Detroit metropolitan white-collar crimes division. Now, after fifteen years, the men were still proud to call each other friends—something Gleason didn't have many of.

They pulled under the porte cochere at the hotel entrance. Hawkins unnecessarily flashed his police chief shield as he was recognized by everyone in downtown Detroit. He handed his keys to the valet with the warning that they would be right out so the car didn't have to be moved unless a fire truck had to access the drive. The valet nodded and bowed to the chief signaling that the car would be just fine where it was. Gleason checked in, being treated like a Motown rock star for whom nothing was too good.

The presidential suite was impressive from the five-foot-tall, carefully manicured potted plants in the entryway to the plush red carpet and its oversized bath gleaming in marble and brass. From the 70th floor of the tallest hotel in North America and the highest skyscraper in Detroit, the suite's floor-to-ceiling windows spanned the full length of the living room and master bedroom, looking out over the fast moving Detroit River, the international border separating Windsor and Detroit. Hawkins took in the view while Gleason showered quickly and traded his shiny black shoes, dark suit, subdued necktie and white shirt for a red sport shirt and casual slacks. Twenty minutes later both men were back down to the unmoved Buick, where Gleason slipped the valet a $20 bill for watching the illegally parked car.

The thirty day prior meeting gives the Secret Service a chance to coordinate with local authorities prior to a presidential visit. Gleason elected to personally handle the meeting in Detroit because of his longstanding personal and professional relationship with Chief Hawkins.As head of the White House Secret Service advance planning team and traveling detail, Gleason knew the political importance of the Motor City Blitz as the White House staffers were referring to the upcoming pre-election visit to Detroit.

Relations between the United States and Canada had become strained over environmental issues such as export restrictions on fresh water and timber since the signing of the North American Free Trade Agreement ten months before. Gleason's instructions were to let his Canadian counterparts have as much input in the local arrangements as possible to mollify their discontent. The president had suggested landing at Windsor's airport and then motorcading with the Canadian Prime Minister through Windsor and across the Detroit River to the Renaissance Center for the noontime NAFTA luncheon. The Canadians would be honored to have the President of the United States on their soil even for a brief drive-through visit, generating positive media coverage while building international good will between the United States and its largest trading partner.

The thirty day prior visit is twenty-four hours of whirlwind activity filled with stressful meetings and fast-food dining. Although Gleason's main focus was presidential safety, he also had to be aware of the president's entire entourage. Emergency disaster teams, police and fire units, National Guard, and FBI were routine partners of the Secret Service in planning a safe presidential visit. The Royal Canadian Mounted Police, the U.S. Coast Guard and the customs and immigration services of both countries also had to be brought under Gleason's Secret Service umbrella. Since the first lady was accompanying the president, and they were going to be separated for two hours while the president left to open the Judeo-Arabic Forum in suburban Detroit, dual security preparations were needed.

In sharing some of the decision-making with the Canadians, the one non-negotiable item was that the president must ride in his usual limousine, affectionately nicknamed the Beast by the Secret Service, and not a Canadian government limousine. The Beast, another identical Cadillac backup presidential limousine and several heavily armed Chevrolet Suburbans would have to be flown into Windsor International Airport the day before the president arrived. Gleason would recommend that the Motor City Blitz be scuttled if the president couldn't motorcade through Windsor in the comfort and security of his 10,000-pound armored Beast.

Gleason's job was to package the eight-hour presidential visit into a neat little bundle that would be discarded when Air Force One lifted off at day's end for the return to Andrews Air Base.

"Jeff, can we drive the route of the presidential motorcade so it is fresh in my mind for tomorrow's meeting?"

"Sure can. As you know, your local government is always at the service of you big shots from Washington. Let me just flip down my flag to start the meter so I don't overcharge."

"I have to warn you, I'm not authorized to tip a fellow law enforcement officer performing his duty. But I can buy dinner for anyone who cooperates with the White House."

They slowly circled the fortress-like Renaissance Center until they were on the service drive separating it from the Detroit River. The river reflected the modest skyline of Windsor. "The presidential party will come out this rear exit after the NAFTA luncheon," Hawkins said. "Then the first lady will board the yacht *Aqua Mole*, which will be docked behind us. The presidential motorcade will form up between the parking structure and the Renaissance Center."

"Nice and tidy, just the way we like it." Gleason said, referring to the proximity of the Renaissance Center's exit to the first lady's host yacht and the departing motorcade. The president would be exposed only for the short walk escorting the first lady to the *Aqua Mole*. There were no overlooking office buildings that could provide cover for a sniper. "I don't see the river as a major threat unless terrorists have a submarine. The Coast Guard and Navy SEALs will be able to cover us from any threats on the water. We'll have to secure the parking ramp making sure there's nobody with weapons hiding in trunks or under cars. Let's drive the motorcade route before it gets dark."

Hawkins nosed the Buick left onto busy Jefferson Avenue to begin the motorcade route. "There's the tunnel to Canada on the left," he pointed out as they merged with the heavy traffic.

Gleason made a mental note that the customs service would have to hold all traffic from the tunnel so the presidential motorcade could clear the entrance.

Passing under Cobo Hall, the Lodge expressway began its northwesterly trajectory to the suburbs. The Lodge was built as a ditch for much of its length, with fifteen-foot-high walls to shield the surrounding urban neighborhoods from the noisy traffic of the fleeing downtown workers. The walls of the Lodge ditch would be problematic for an emergency escape by the presidential motorcade. "Is there an alternate route the motorcade could use to get the forum?" Gleason asked.

"Not really, unless we take surface streets through some areas of Detroit where I for one am afraid to go."

"Great! The police chief's afraid to travel streets in his own city. Ever since Kennedy's assassination more than thirty years ago, the Secret Service worries about motorcades as if a second assassination with the same modus operandi would be worse than a different method like a bomb or grenade." The fact that the motorcade's sixty-mile-per-hour speed in the Lodge ditch would make a formidable target for any but the most experienced marksman offered little solace to the paranoid Gleason. "By the way, how many cross-street overpasses and walkways are there?"

"Man, how do I know?"

"Aren't you supposed to know things like that?"

The chief replied, "We put up Cyclone security fences on all overpass bridges and walkways after two people were killed by somebody dropping cement blocks. Now there's no worry about someone dropping a bomb into the president's lap. Tell me Mr. Secret Service academy honors graduate, how many spikes are there on top of the wrought iron fence around the White House grounds?"

"Two thousand seven hundred sixteen. I counted every last one."

"I'll have detailed maps at our morning meeting. You can count every last overpass bridge and walkway as well as the entrance and exit ramps." At the Eight Mile exit the chief put on his chamber of commerce hat again and pointed out the signs to Northland Shopping Center, which was the first suburban mall built, drawing shoppers away from the big downtown stores like

Hudson's. Detroit unwittingly contributed to the demise of the once prosperous downtown areas by its automobiles and suburban shopping malls.

The black Buick turned off the Lodge expressway at the Ten Mile exit to get onto Lahser Road where the Temple B'nai Joseph was located. The Jewish community had gradually moved to this northwest suburban area of Detroit where they established numerous temples and synagogues. The perpetual Mideastern turmoil had caused many non-Jewish nationalities to immigrate to this same side of Detroit, so it indeed was a mini United Nations, a fitting place to host the president's first Judeo-Arabic forum in thirty days. "This will be the end of the road for the presidential caravan. Do you want to go inside and check the meeting facilities for the forum?"

"Not really. We'll do that tomorrow with the whole entourage."

As they made the return trip into the city through waning rush-hour traffic, the brilliance of the setting sun was barely muted by the Buick's deeply tinted windows. Hawkins suggested, "Since you've got the White House credit card, what say we make it an international affair? We can do a little nightlife recon on the Canadian side of the river. I know a quiet little place in Windsor..."

"It's your call, chief. Just keep in mind that we have a meeting right after breakfast tomorrow."

"Hey, man, that's many hours away."

"And I'm not exactly the life of the party at strip clubs these days."

"Yeah, I was meaning to talk to you about that. You haven't smiled once since you got here. Not when seeing your old partner for the first time in years. Not once. What's that about? In my experience, a man who never smiles is a man you can never be sure of."

"We all have our own problems, mostly self-induced, I might add." Gleason tried not to let himself drift back into his past. His divorce was still too painful to explore. When in Washington, at the end of the day he would go home to an empty condo that was all too conducive to bottomless introspection and guilt trips without a destination.

Arriving back downtown, Hawkins turned onto the Ambassador Bridge, which links Detroit and Windsor downriver from the Renaissance Center. Hawkins slowed down near the 150-foot-high midpoint of the gently swaying center span. The lights from Detroit and Windsor were starting to wink on as the magenta sun slid into the darkness of the river. "Want to get out and admire the million dollar view? I'll turn the flashers on."

"Not necessary. I can see it from here."

"My oh my! You do have a bad case of the glooms. Can't be bothered to stop long enough to admire a first-rate sunset."

"My mind is someplace else. I was just wondering about security on the bridge. Our customs and immigration buildings are at our end and Canada's are at the other end. When the motorcade is here in the middle of the bridge we've already left the United States and we haven't reached the 'Welcome to Canada' sign yet. So whose soil are we on?"

"Neither country. It's no-man's-land. The toll bridge is privately owned by an international corporation. As a matter of fact, my wife is on the board of directors."

"So if there's a traffic accident in the middle of the bridge, who sends the cops?"

"My policy is to send Detroit's Finest, let them argue it out with the Mounties. If our guys get there first and there are no Michigan plates involved, they might drag the victims across the center line into Canada."

"Well, when the president comes, I'm going to need total control of the bridge, regardless of who owns it. It worries me that some crazy with a weapon could stow away under the roadway only to appear when the motorcade is exposed like we are now."

"Surveillance cameras at both ends record every vehicle coming and going. This bridge has tighter security than the publically owned tunnel near the Ren Center, which we'll take back to Detroit." They quickly cleared the perfunctory check at Canadian customs, where the border agents seemed to be on a first name basis with Chief Hawkins.

As they were driving along the Windsor shoreline of the Detroit River, the chief asked Gleason if he recognized the company name on the large marble pedestal sign they were passing.

"Maybe if you slowed down I could read the name."

"It's the newest and largest office building on the river—Global Construction Technology. See that yacht docked behind their main office tower. That's the *Aqua Mole*. I think you'll be talking about it tomorrow."

"Why didn't you just say that in the first place? That's a prime subject of tomorrow's meeting. If we know the first family is being hosted by foreign interests, we tend to be a little more careful, even though Azee—the name he always goes by—is the president's biggest campaign contributor and a close friend to the first lady, the vice-president, and just about everybody in the White House. Except servants like me, of course."

"Azee owns everything we just passed. Azee is as American as you or me. He recently moved his company headquarters across the river to save taxes and to bid on Canadian harbor projects that require Canadian contractors. He still lives outside Detroit on a huge estate surrounded by a wildlife preserve and a moat."

"A moat? Are there alligators in it?"

"Probably. I've never gotten close enough to see. Azee is reclusive and rich enough to get away with it. The rich live by different rules than we do, and the super-rich don't seem to live by any rules."

II

The chief's car appeared to be on automatic pilot as it came to a stop in the "handicap only" parking space nearest the Casino Windsor's front door. "They save this parking place just for me," he said.

Owned and operated by the provincial government, the Casino Windsor was the first legal gambling establishment in Ontario, Hawkins explained. It had opened earlier in the summer in this temporary location, a former state-run art gallery, while its glitzier permanent home was being built down the street. The favorable currency exchange rate lured serious Detroit gamblers to pack the place every night, and the steady flow of American dollars went a long way toward funding Ontario's ten-year-old, free universal health care program.

"Good evening, Chief Hawkins," the doorman smiled in greeting. "Good luck at the tables tonight."

"Here's the keys, Andrew, in case you need to move it." The chief hurried toward the richly polished doors. "Unlike Vegas, we have to close the casino doors to keep out the cold and snow and sometimes a few ruffians from the States."

Gleason never remembered seeing Jeff as agile and fast as now, dodging and sidestepping the one-armed bandits and overcrowded blackjack tables like an NFL running back. The chief obviously was on a mission. The smell of food lured him straight to the candlelit dining room. Gleason followed him to a corner booth with a small reserved sign. It was obvious that the chief could have found his booth blindfolded.

"Chief Hawkins, sorry I missed you at the door. You know where to go," the hostess winked.

"Now, Misty! Please don't bother yourself about us. I'd like you to meet my old friend, Tom Gleason from Washington."

"You don't look all that old, Tom. Pleasure to meet you," Misty purred as she handed him a menu, pointing out an entree called the Chief's Choice, a pound-and-a-half porterhouse steak.

Gleason noticed the item right below it, an eight-ounce sizzler called the Deputy's Duty. "Don't tell me they named the big one after you, Jeff. There's no way I'm having the Deputy's Duty."

"American macho, eh? Your waitress will be over right away." Misty glided away, the hem of her black silk dress brushing her legs at mid-thigh.

Watching her go, Gleason raised his eyebrows and commented to the chief, "you sure get around."

When the waitress came, both men placed their orders for pound-and-a-half steaks with all the trimmings. As soon as she left, the chief excused himself to go to the men's room. He struggled to dislodge his large belly from the impinging table top. He was still gone when the Caesar salads came. Gleason continued to wait pensively, idly spinning his gold plated suite key on the polished oak tabletop.

Misty startled him by trying to gracefully slide into the booth next to him. "Hey, Tom! I see you're staying in the Ren Center Marriott," she whispered taking the heavy key away from Tom's playing hands. "The chief told me you're even staying in the presidential suite. Is that really true?"

"Well, yeah. My job does have some perks. One night only, though." His tongue found itself momentarily tied, and he belatedly retieved the suite key from Misty to more closely exam it under the dim candle light. He saw that it was embossed with the presidential seal.

Misty leaned over for a closer look, grazing Gleason's chest. "Can I see it?"

He handed the key back to her. She took it delicately, as if it were made of gold. Her smile turned a little wicked. "No, I meant the suite. I've never been in a presidential suite before."

This time Gleason was too dumbfounded to say anything.

"The kitchen stops serving at ten," Misty said. "I can probably be out of here by eleven and over there fifteen minutes later if the border crossing isn't jammed up with American gamblers returning home."

"Wait," he protested. "I have to take charge of an important security meeting in the morning."

"Oooh, a *security* meeting. Sounds exciting. What time does this security meeting start?"

"Nine-thirty."

"Sounds like plenty of time to me. Matter of fact, we've known each other five whole minutes, and it seems like we've talked about nothing but time."

"What? Oh, you mean like money?"

"Tom, don't even go there. Working girls don't work in restaurants. An old friend tells me he's got a friend I should meet— tall, handsome and works for the president of the United States. Money isn't part of the deal. You'll understand better when you've been single longer."

"You mean Jeff told you about my divorce?"

"Speak of the devil ..." Misty slid out of the booth just as Hawkins returned and the inch-and-a-half-thick slabs of steak arrived. "Eat that red meat," she winked. "You'll need it."

"Wait... The key."

She realized it was still in her hand and gave it back. When she was gone, Hawkins shook his head. "You gave the presidential suite key to a woman you just met?"

"Well... I'm new at this game."

"There may be hope for you yet." They bantered back and forth while their main mission was devouring the Chief's Choice. "What do you say to a couple hands of blackjack before we head for the tunnel?"

"Chief, I'm tired and have paperwork to do for tomorrow," Gleason said. "Let's skip the tables tonight and return to the good old USA."

"Fine with me. Sorry you couldn't finish all your steak. Next time you should probably order the Deputy's Duty, unless you go into training to keep up with the big guy!"

Gleason knew when to cut his losses with silence. The chief's huge frame was in overdrive again as they skirted around the hostess desk and back out through the noisy, smoke-filled casino.

The return route to Detroit using the tunnel reminded Gleason of his earlier ride in the Lodge expressway ditch: there was no way out. For someone who needed to be in total charge of his own destiny and that of the president, the claustrophobia caused by being trapped beneath a river of water was unthinkable. He wanted to see and anticipate his own demise, not be the helpless victim of a terrorist bomb and a tunnel collapse. He was slowly sinking into the dark abyss of his alcohol-affected mind, so the tunnel exit juxtaposed to his hotel entrance was a welcome sight. "Thanks for the great evening, Jeff. See you in the morning."

Elevators sometimes gave Gleason the same uneasy lack of control feeling that he just experienced in the tunnel. Fortunately, the mirrored, high-speed Otis deposited Gleason at the top floor presidential suite before the alcoholic glow totally overwhelmed his psyche. Seated at the ornate writing desk trying to arrange his stacks of papers for the morning meeting, he heard a gentle tapping on the door. A squint through the peephole confirmed that his guest had arrived.

"We were slow at work after you left, so I came early," Misty whispered, quietly closing the door.

"Early's good. I left you money for a taxi."

"I hitched a ride in a friend's limo so I owe you a refund."

"I should have friends like that with a limo to run me about town. Let me take your jacket."

"Quite some pad you have here." Misty opened her handbag and organized a row of miniature liquor bottles on the end table. "What's your pleasure?"

"Surprise me." It wasn't that much of a surprise. She poured them both Canadian Club whiskey from Windsor's venerable Hiram Walker Distillery. "Let me give you that tour I promised." Gleason raised his glass in a ceremonial toast. They wandered from room to room, each more opulent than the one before, laughing and giggling like two teenagers on their first date. The view from the undraped windows of the glistening river and the sparkling city lights of Detroit and Windsor fading into the distant horizon would bring out the romance in a cloistered monk. Misty found the dimmer switches for the lights above the bed and whirlpool so that the full moon in the floor-to-ceiling windows was their only illumination. The circular, pillow-strewn bed adjacent to the oversized whirlpool playpen was almost too pretty to disturb with casual lovemaking.

"I need to clean-up from the smoke and grime of the casino. Will you scrub my back?" Misty asked as she adjusted the water filling the whirlpool. Its ripples reflected from the mirrored ceiling and walls.

"I hope I can do more than that." Gleason enjoyed Misty setting the stage for romance by lighting candles she found in a closet drawer. His clothes hit the floor simultaneously with her frilly underpants.

The romp in the whirlpool and the adjacent round bed was a first for Gleason since his divorce—or for that matter in his whole life. During the final year of his disintegrating marriage, spiritual faithfulness was not as easy as physical faithfulness. He often fantasized about moments like this. Paperback novels extolled the virtues of communal whirlpool bathing. Gleason's memory of these literary fantasies was turning as foggy as the mist rising above the bubbling waters of the whirlpool. All the accounts he recalled were wrong. They had underplayed the alternating excitement and serenity engendered by these gurgling waters. For a few amnesiac moments, he was not responsible for the life of the president of the United States. He was only responsible for his own life, and he was enjoying it to the fullest. As the whirlpool water cooled, he blew into Misty's moist ear, "Does your back need more scrubbing?"

"No, it's just perfect. Are you returning to this high-rise heaven in a month? I'd like to visit you again. You give the nicest back rubs."

"Sorry, Misty." Gleason was jolted back to the reality of his ever-present responsibilities. "Next time back, I'll be working full-time, like you. Maybe some other time, some other place."

"You can always reach me through the chief."

Gleason's mind immediately went into overdrive. He'd never wanted his private life to be a matter of public knowledge, as it apparently was now. While Misty gathered her scanty belongings and repacked her greatly diminished bar, Gleason retrieved his money clip and peeled off a $100 bill. "Is this enough for the taxi ride back to Windsor?"

"Please, Tom, I should pay you for the pleasure of visiting the presidential suite. You left too big a tip at the casino, and I told you before, this has nothing to do with money. I owe the chief a favor or two. Besides, I'm sure my limo is still waiting."

Misty quickly departed.

With a plush oversized towel cinched around his waist, he stood at the window overlooking the moon lit river and the hotel entrance far below. He could see a white limousine pull under the porte-cochere, pause momentarily and then quickly leave, immediately turning into the tunnel entrance to Canada. He thought of his father's dictum: "If things seem too good to be true, they usually are."

He could only remember one previous time that he had such foreboding as he now felt after Misty's businesslike departure. He felt a profound urge to talk to his ex-wife, Cindy to get his feet back on the ground—or was it to confess the dumbest thing he ever did to the woman he still loved. Looking at his gold Omega Seamaster, a wedding gift from Cindy, he realized that the hour was much too late to call her as she always retired early to be fully rested to face the questioning minds of her college philosophy students.

III

If all the agencies involved perform their pre-assigned tasks, the thirty-day prior meeting should run like clockwork, even with Gleason in a less than normal state of preparedness due to last night's recreation.

Chief Hawkins arrived with his contingent of uniformed police officers taking front-row seats. The small, surprisingly austere meeting room at the otherwise opulent Renaissance Center was nearly filled by the 9:30 starting time. When the chief caught Gleason's eye on the elevated dais he gave him a thumbs up, which Gleason ignored by quickly turning his head to acknowledge the presence of the director of the Detroit FBI office, Maria Visconti. She was seated next to a well-tailored businessman, who was chatting with a highly decorated military office seated beside him.

Gleason panned the lively audience over the top of his reading glasses, a reluctant concession to middle age. "Let's begin. We have a lot to coordinate since we have our Canadian counterparts with us. The tendency at these advance planning meetings is for everyone to relax, knowing that there's still a month left to prepare for the president's visit. To stir you out of this complacency, I'm going to ask two related questions. "Who's Leon Franz Czolgosz? What's his connection to Detroit?"

The one raised hand he recognized as belonging to Secret Service agent Sandra Kozial, seated in the front row. "Pardon me, but I should have prefaced the questions with the disclaimer that Secret Service agents couldn't provide the answers." No other hands were raised, so after a few seconds, Gleason broke the stalemate. "The easy thing would be for me to answer these two questions. You would then immediately forget about them and the reason that I posed them. For your first piece of homework, I want everyone to look up Leon Franz Czolgosz and his connection to Detroit. Commit the answers to your memory as an incentive to stay focused for the next thirty days."

Gleason continued with a little edge in his voice, "everyone has today's agenda in their packet. We will not deviate from it. We have found it to be the best method to prepare for a safe, productive presidential visit." Gleason started the tedious but crucial task of reading through the pre-visitation checklists for each agency represented. The slightest hesitation of anyone responding to Gleason's staccato questions elicited an instant request for clarification.

There was a method to his madness in everything he did. Gleason found that the establishment of the chain of command, with himself at the top, was critical to the success of a presidential visit. When the local Secret Service agent in charge of the first lady's menu for the NAFTA luncheon replied that the chef had not yet submitted his menu recommendations, Gleason theatrically appeared on the verge of losing control as he publicly dressed her down. "You know that the first lady is seven months pregnant and is eating more than pickles and ice cream. Give the supplied menu to the head chef. Tell him to prepare it without deviations. None! Is that clear, Agent Kozial?"

Mortified, Agent Kozial slumped into her seat. Her, "yes, sir," achieved Gleason's desired effect of establishing an authority pyramid with himself at the top. Gleason's apprehensions about the Canadian law enforcement agencies making unreasonable demands to establish their participation in this rare presidential visit were unjustified. They seemed placated when he announced that each country would supply the necessary modes of transportation for their own country's contingents. The fact that the president was landing in Windsor on Canadian soil and was going to take the short motorcade ride from the airport through downtown Windsor was honor enough for them. Marine One and an armed helicopter would be airborne during the motorcade from Canada across the Ambassador Bridge to the end point at the Renaissance Center to assist in any unplanned emergencies.

The public reason given for the river crossing on the bridge rather than in the tunnel under the river was to allow maximum media exposure of this bi-country visit, since both the president and prime minister were facing elections in a few weeks. Gleason generally recommended bridges over underwater tunnels whenever there was a choice because of the lack of alternative escape routes for the motorcade from the confines of the tunnels.

"Quiet please," Gleason commanded. "In a moment we'll form up the motorcade with police escort to simulate the presidential travel route to the site of the Judeo-Arabic Forum. I'd appreciate everyone being observant of any potential trouble areas on the motorcade route. Since the Kennedy assassination in Dallas, motorcades have been a special concern. By the way, General Hodgechis, how many National Guard troops will you have positioned at the railings overlooking the Lodge expressway?" It was obvious that Gleason was still concerned about the security above and down in the Lodge expressway ditch.

A trim, distinguished uniformed military officer stood up. "We'll activate five thousand troops for the president's visit. Not all of them will be at the railings overlooking the Lodge expressway, though. Some will be stationed at other locations like our command center in the Henry Ford Hospital parking lot, about the midpoint of the motorcade route. My guess right now is that about four thousand troops will be available to guard the elevated perimeter of the Lodge expressway."

There was a sudden silence in the ballroom. Chief Hawkins

saw Gleason silently struggling to control himself as his face began to flush. He knew that the general had used the wrong word, "guess," when stating how many of his troops would be guarding the top of the expressway wall. "Now, general, I must emphasize that we don't guess when the president's life is at stake. Your assignment is not to be treated as a para-military drill or weekend militia campout. The president's safety is not a guessing game. By the way general, how many of your troops are members of this Michigan Militia that we've been hearing so much about?"

The general stiffened and came to a near-attention stance. "Sir, we do not keep statistics on that type of membership. It's never an issue unless a soldier's job performance is adversely affected."

Not giving the general time to continue, Gleason attempted to push his metal folding chair away from the table. The rubber-tipped chair legs didn't slide on the elevated temporary stage, but a front card table leg collapsed, and the table slipped off the front of the platform with a resounding crash, scattering neat stacks of papers into the front rows of the audience. He walked to the edge of the platform, glaring at the rigidly standing general. "You mean to tell me, general, that you could have fully armed anti-government Michigan Militia members guarding the president?"

The general took one step forward and came to full attention. "Mister Gleason, I have just stated that we do not and will not keep records of our National Guard troops who are militia members. All our troops will be fully armed according to our standard operating procedure manual. We cannot issue live ammunition to only non-militia members." A trace of a smile elevated the corners of the general's mouth as he assumed an at-ease position awaiting the reply from on high.

Chief Hawkins was too embarrassed for Gleason to look directly at him rocking and teetering on the edge of the platform as if deciding whether to spring like a hungry lion to devour his prey. Jeff recognized that his friend was in a tight spot that the Secret Service Academy did not prepare him for. Only Gleason could extricate himself from this insidious trap as he commenced an intense monologue. "General, you put the president in a difficult position. You are proposing to use armed militia members with questionable patriotic motives to form the perimeter around and above the presidential motorcade. As a matter of fact, with your cavalier attitude about the troops under your command, what is there to stop fully armed terrorists, dressed in camouflage fatigues like your troops, from simply slipping into the voids along the railings above the Lodge expressway? General Hodgechis, your disinterest in monitoring the suspicious activities of your troops will be brought to the attention of the proper military authorities. It would be prudent to have your resignation or retirement letter prepared to submit. Be seated, general. This dilemma we are facing is unprecedented in the history of the Secret Service where uniformed armed forces of the United States cannot be relied on to defend their commander in chief. A presidential executive order will be forthcoming to resolve this serious problem. We will continue the day's planned activities."

The governor's representative, flanked by two burly uniformed state police officers, rose and reminded the now-retreating Gleason that two hundred reliable state police officers would be stationed on the sidewalks at the top of walls. Gleason nodded to show his acceptance of this offer, but it provided little solace to the Michigan Militia dilemma. It seemed certain that the protective cocoon of the high walls was a barrier and not a facilitator to presidential protection.

The morning's drive through from the riverfront Renaissance Center to the Judeo-Arabic Forum site in suburban northwest Detroit elicited the same visceral feeling in Gleason as during the chief's tour last night. The vulnerability and inescapability of the presidential motorcade traveling for miles in the Lodge ditch fifteen feet below the surface streets was a continuing major concern. Those that control the high ground throughout the macabre history of war usually rule the day. The possible inclusion of anti-government fanatics from the Michigan Militia in the National Guard units guarding the motorcade was a political quagmire that could possibly scuttle the presidential visit or at least drastically alter the day's agenda and travel plans.

The final agenda item of the busy day involved the inspection of the *Aqua Mole* and meeting its owner, Azee, back downtown. Gleason became animated as he stepped aboard the *Aqua Mole* docked at the Renaissance Center bulkhead after it was moved across the river from its Global Construction Technology berth.

"We saw the yacht at your office building last night." Gleason stepped aboard to shake Azee's outstretched hand. Gleason instinctively retracted his hand as he felt a pinching sensation when Azee tightened his handshake. Too many rings, he thought. The large gold ring bearing the letter P on Azee's right pinkie had been given to him personally by the pope in appreciation of Azee's firm, Global Construction Technologies, stabilizing and leveling the foundations of some of the Vatican's ancient buildings that were sinking and settling after many centuries of supervised neglect. One of Azee's European subsidiaries had secured this prestigious contract through its well cultivated Sicilian contacts that had an inside tract on the Vatican bidding process. The pope even blessed the ring before giving it to Azee with the comment that the blessing can also help non-Christians as well as Christians. Vatican officials obviously had not performed a background check on Azee or they would have discovered that Azee was baptized in the Eastern Rite Catholic Church. Azee thought better of correcting the pope. It suited his business needs worldwide, but especially in the oil-rich Middle East if most assumed he was non-Christian, as his name and appearance indicated.

It wasn't until Azee was sitting across the desk from Cardinal Pavlowski, the unsmiling prefect of the Vatican treasury, awaiting final payment, that he was told the significance of the letter P on the ring. Azee had assumed that the letter P stood for pope until he was informed by the stern Cardinal Pavlowski that it stood for the Latin word "Pontifex," which he unnecessarily translated for Azee to mean "bridge builder." Azee felt especially honored when the cardinal told him that the pope had personally only given out one P ring previously, and that to the saintly Mother Teresa. Azee drew more comfort from the ancient symbolism represented by the ankh ring on his right ring finger than from any formal religion. The ankh was an Egyptian hieroglyph for life that symbolized earth, air, fire, and water, the basic building blocks of Azee's construction firm. The hieroglyphs were known as "the words of the god," and the P ring from the pope was the newest addition to his manual religious shrine. Gleason then remembered that it was the well-dressed Azee who was seated beside Agent Maria Visconti at the morning meeting.

"You could have stayed on the *Aqua Mole* last night in the owner's stateroom. Many of my visiting business clients enjoy the serenity of spending the night on the Detroit River. I always return home to my estate at Orchard Lake when in Detroit. I'm out of the country so much that I enjoy spending whatever time I can at my Cripplegate estate," Azee concluded.

"Thanks for the offer. I was quite comfortable at the hotel. I had to do paperwork for today. You're already doing enough for the White House by hosting the first family for the afternoon Gold Cup hydroplane races. Maybe at a later date we can get together for a little R-and-R. By the way, Azee, how did you arrive at the boat's name, *Aqua Mole*?"

"The name reflects the early struggles of my company. Most of our early construction jobs involved doing subsurface tunneling and trenching using my newly patented laser alignment instrumentation. We were usually working underground, so we called ourselves moles. At the suggestion of the first lady, we arrived at the name *Aqua Mole*."

"Now the name makes sense. You certainly have worked hard to achieve what you have. The *Aqua Mole* certainly will be satisfactory for the first family's visit. I'm sure they'll be pleased."

"The first lady has been aboard the *Aqua Mole* many times. Most memorably she brought her mother with her for a Greek isles cruise two years before the president's election. She reasoned that once her husband was on the national stage, campaigning

for the presidency, she wouldn't be able to enjoy such a trip with
the Secret Service hovering about. No offense, Mr. Gleason. The
Secret Service does a terrific job, but I think that she wanted "one
last fling," as she put it. Of course I have my own security people,
but they don't compare with the Secret Service. I still have her
handwritten note saying that the Greek Isle cruise was the best
vacation she and her mother ever had."

"I remember reading about their trip right before her husband
announced for the presidency. It must have been quite an adventure."

"It certainly was. We tried to retrace Homer's sagas of the
Iliad and the Odyssey. The *Aqua Mole*'s sturdy hull and creature
comforts like air conditioning and microwaves gave us a distinct
advantage over those hardy Greeks, sailing on no more than lashed
together logs and rafts. Have you studied the classics, Tom?"

"Some. I proofread my wife's doctoral thesis on Plato's *Republic*.
Her thesis was written in English, not the Greek or Latin that you
and the first lady share."

"Our knowledge is of classical Greek, not modern Greek. Our
Latin's much better than our Greek, thanks to a drill sergeant who
taught us for all four years in high school."

"*Veni, vidi, vici*, is the only Latin I remember from my time in
high school Latin," Gleason proudly proclaimed.

"Well spoken, Tom, like a true linguist. This famous quota-
tion of Caesar is my favorite classical saying. It's inscribed in
Florentine marble over my office's main doorway to motivate our
employees. Every time I pass under that archway, I think of what
a terrible fate Caesar suffered, dying at the hands of his trusted
friend, Brutus. The first lady and I enacted this tragic death scene
in our drama class's presentation of Shakespeare's *Julius Caesar*."

"It sounds like politics hasn't changed much in two thousand
years. There'll always be a Brutus to destroy our own heroic leaders like Lincoln and Kennedy. I suppose that's why we need the
Secret Service and I still have a job."

"It really makes you wonder why anyone in their right mind
would want to be president. Their life isn't their own. It's very

lonely for their wife and children. The presidential salary doesn't adequately compensate them for the constant risk to their life and the toll on their privacy."

"I suppose I'm too close to the forest to see the trees that come crashing down on the president and his personal life. Most of us in the Secret Service protective units feel that keeping the president alive is our only job."

"If it's okay with the Secret Service, I've scheduled the *Aqua Mole* for refurbishing next week," Azee commented, anxious to change the subject to a more mundane matter as they were concluding the tour. "Mainly cosmetic touches: carpet, drapes, furniture and a fresh paint job. I want everything shipshape for the first family."

"You really don't have to do that. Your yacht is more than adequate for the first family. Are you planning on hauling the *Aqua Mole* to repaint the hull?"

"No. I had it repainted in the spring. I can have it put on the hoist if you need to inspect the hull."

"That won't be necessary. We'll have Navy SEAL divers inspect the hull the morning of the cruise for bombs. As a matter of fact, armed Navy SEAL divers will be aboard a closely trailing navy launch during the cruise for any water-based emergency. Of course the air will be covered by helicopters and F16 jets from nearby Selfridge Air National Guard Base"

"It appears the Secret Service has land, sea and air covered. We can all sleep well knowing that nothing can happen."

"We'll do our final security check and seal off the perimeter the day before the first family arrives. We need to request that your captain refrain from using electronic devices during the cruise so as not to disturb the secure communications network staffed by our White House technicians. Will this be a problem for him?"

"My boat captain is also my airplane co-pilot. He can't start his car without first activating a dozen electronic gadgets. He'll have to resort to simple oblique cruising and the old naked eyeball method of navigation. Sure he'll manage."

"As you know, we assume total control of the vessel. There will be armed naval officers in our party who will be competent to captain the *Aqua Mole* should the need arise. There will be Coast Guard cutters forming a one-hundred-yard perimeter. Only the navy launch with the Navy SEALs will be within this secure moving perimeter. After two hours of cruising, the *Aqua Mole* will return to this same Renaissance Center dock to pick up the president on his return from the Judeo-Arabic Forum. Knowing him as I do, he'll be ready for a little relaxation. Are there any questions before we conclude our tour?" Not hearing any questions from his bureaucratic cohorts, Gleason motioned to the ramp for all to disembark.

He stopped Maria Visconti, the head of the Detroit FBI office, and directed her to a far corner of the large stern deck for a quick tete-a-tete. He quietly asked her to discretely find out who in Windsor owned a late-model white Cadillac limousine. He also needed to know from the Immigration and Customs records at the tunnel if any of them used the tunnel late last night. She could leave him the answers on his secure office voice mail as soon as possible.

When everyone was on the dock beside the *Aqua Mole*, Gleason stayed on the slightly elevated stern to make a final announcement. "Thanks for your work today. We all have an important role to play in the president's visit. Please be in touch with me if any problems develop. We will cancel this visit if any situation compromising presidential safety develops. It's everyone's job to assure that this doesn't happen. If there are no questions, we'll see you in thirty days."

The group broke up immediately because as government employees they weren't being paid overtime. Gleason's eyes followed General Hodgechis until he entered the adjacent parking ramp. He hoped that this would be the last time he would see the general in uniform. Gleason had to be careful not to obsess over this one issue and overlook something else in his meticulous preparation leading to just another routine presidential campaign visit.

Chief Hawkins pulled his car up near the gangplank to pick up Gleason for his return ride to the airport. However, Gleason again retreated to the far corner of the stern deck to apparently make a phone call. The chief turned off his idling car and opened the windows to savor the heat and humidity of an early fall day when Gleason made a second phone call that was running much longer than his first call. Gleason was smiling when he slipped the phone into his belt clip and approached Azee who lingered with his boat crew to be sure that Gleason was done with the *Aqua Mole*.

Azee understood all the necessary contingencies connected with the presidential usurpation of his yacht starting with today's walk through inspection. As they were going ashore, he told Gleason that he would be aboard the *Aqua Mole* for the cruise since he no longer had to ride in the motorcade to the forum with Vice President Taylor. Gleason knew that the vice president was scratched from the Motor City Blitz because of his recent knee replacement surgery. However, he was unaware that Azee had planned to ride in the vice president's limousine. The Secret Service was always relieved when the president and the vice president were not at the same place at the same time.

Azee had his own private reasons for avoiding the motorcade and the Judeo Arabic Forum. He preferred to keep a low profile in international politics because at least one of his businesses had offices or construction projects in almost every Middle Eastern country from Israel to Bahrain. Azee's forte was politicians that could foster his international business interests, so he had to keep everyone happy. His multinational companies were apolitical with the desire to work anywhere there was "black dirt, wet water, and lots of green," as he was wont to tell his employees, new and old.

Gleason and Azee exchanged a cordial goodbye with the promise to stay in touch if need be before the presidential visit in thirty days. Gleason collapsed into the chief's soft leather passenger seat with the simple proclamation, "thank God today's over."

Looking at his impressive fake Rolex, Hawkins suggested that they have a drink and a quick dinner to let the rush hour traffic thin out before heading to the airport. He suggested another high spot in Detroit that they could see down Jefferson Avenue from their location at the Ren Center dock. The Top of the Flame was a four-star restaurant atop the Michigan Consolidated Gas company office building where the maitre'd was an old friend who owed the chief a favor or two.

Gleason looked down the street and could see a blue neon glow atop one of the tall office buildings that he figured must be the gas company building. He thought to himself, just what I don't need— to sit up there looking down the street at the top floor presidential suite where I literally screwed up last night. The chief was stopped at Jefferson Avenue waiting for Gleason to decide on dinner so he knew which way to turn. When their traffic light turned green Gleason said, "I called the pilots from the boat and told them to file a flight plan for take off within the hour."

The disappointed chief nodded his acceptance and headed up Woodward to avoid the traffic leaving downtown on East Jefferson Avenue. He again assumed his tour guide role and pointed out that world-famous Vernors Ginger Ale was bottled for years at a glass-front building on lower Woodward. As kids he and his friends would ride their bikes over to watch the fast-moving bottles being filled and spinning their way to end of the line. Occasionally a kind worker would sneak them a sample bottle out the side door with the admonition, "Don't tell anyone," and of course they went home and told all their friends of their lucky day.

The chief tried to ignore the block long boarded up Hudson's department store, but Gleason commented, "Too bad Hudson's couldn't still survive downtown."

Hawkins quickly cast an even heavier pall on their conversation, "I'm afraid that it isn't the only thing that can't survive downtown. The riot areas of 1967 aren't far from here and still look much like a war zone. Maybe the prez can bring a plane full of federal money when he comes in a month."

"Good luck with that, chief. Next time I think I'll land at Detroit Metro Airport and not the small Detroit City Airport. Are we taking the fastest way to the airport? I also called Cindy from the boat and asked if we could get together when I get back."

"No wonder you didn't want dinner with me! I guess I know

where I stand, ex-wife over your best buddy."

"Don't take it personally, Jeff. You did enough for me last night."

Fortunately they came to the traffic light at Grand Avenue and Woodword that gave Hawkins an excuse to ignore Gleason's remark about last night. Before turning to head to the Detroit City Airport, he pointed up to the traffic signal with the explanation that this corner was the location of the first traffic signal in the world, a fitting recognition of the many automobiles in the once prosperous auto capital of the world. Neither of them seemed like they wanted to get into any thing heavy, after their whirlwind twenty-four hours, so they kidded and joked like neither had a care in the world for the rest of the trip to the airport.

Aboard the jet back to Washington, Gleason felt an atypical mixed reaction about the preparations for the Motor City Blitz. Like Azee, he tried to stay clear of politics unless it was beneficial to his own job of providing increased security for the president. Politics aside, Gleason had to alert the international anti-terror-ism sector of the CIA because of the Canadian connection with the Motor City Blitz. The Detroit presidential visit represented a broad spectrum of diverse international political interests, and thus potentially more problems than a visit to Paducah. Gleason drowsily smiled himself to sleep for a short nap doubting that he would find anyone like Misty in Paducah.

IV

Gleason stopped by his White House office to clear his desk and check phone messages accumulated while he was in Detroit. Everything appeared routine except the message from Maria Visconti, the head of the Detroit FBI office. Even that message would appear routine to anyone except Gleason, who had personal reasons for needing his questions answered. She reported that there were three late model Cadillac limousines registered in Windsor. One was still in the name of a limousine service that had closed over a year ago and was without a current Ontario license plate tag. The other two were registered in the name of a company called Global Construction Technology.

The customs office at the tunnel doesn't keep records of each passing vehicle. There are 24/7 daily videotapes, saved for three months, which can be reviewed after paying an administrative fee. However, she interviewed one of the second shift attendants, who remembered a white Cadillac limousine headed back to Canada before her shift ended at midnight. The darkened windows didn't allow her to see who, if anyone, was in the back seat. Gleason decided not to thank Maria so she wouldn't think this limousine detective work was any big deal, and hopefully she would soon forget it.

On the short walk over to his boss's office, Gleason decided that this limousine information and its implications wouldn't be shared at this time. On a flow sheet listing governmental agencies, the Secret Service is under the Department of the Treasury's bureaucratic umbrella. Gleason, as chief senior agent of the White House Secret Service protective detail, had reporting responsibility directly to the Secretary of the Treasury, Bart Jameson, who made it clear four years ago on his first day on the job that he didn't want to be bothered with the mundane, everyday workings of the White House Secret Service operation. Gleason happily complied with Jameson's laid-back management style.

His request for a meeting after his return from Detroit surprised Jameson. Gleason opened the meeting by outlining the results of the Detroit preparatory meeting and the amicable working relationship with the Canadians. The main area of concern that he wanted to run by his "paper boss" before he presented it to his "real boss," the president, was the political quagmire of fully armed National Guard troops, who might include hostile Michigan Militia members, guarding the president. Like a good bureaucrat, Jameson suggested that Gleason should drop this dilemma onto the desks of the military brass at the Pentagon. With less than thirty days until the Motor City Blitz, Gleason knew that there wasn't enough time for the Pentagon to study the question and render a decision. Their decision-making time table was usually six-month minimum unless someone just detonated a bomb at their door step. Jameson and Gleason agreed that the president, as commander in chief, should be informed. If he wanted to order the Pentagon to make a quick decision, that would be the ideal solution.

Gleason was pleased when coffee was brought in and they moved from the cluttered desk area to a comfortable corner seating arrangement. The secretary had been head of a large Wall Street firm before he was called by the president to be secretary of treasury. His banking relationship and friendship with the president were a matter of public knowledge. Gleason didn't want to be the man in the middle between these old friends, so he was always deferential to both his bosses. He was somewhat thrown off guard by the secretary asking him what he thought of Azee. "I wasn't aware that you knew Azee," Gleason said.

"I don't admit it to everyone, but we've known each other for years. Everyone on Wall Street knows Azee. Wall Streeters don't like him because he moved his banking to Switzerland and off-shore tax havens. When he was starting his company, I went out on a limb to arrange loans for him when he couldn't get backing anywhere else. The rest is history."

"That's interesting. His continuing friendship from high school days with the first lady certainly keeps him well connected at the highest levels. The vice president also seems to fit into his circle of influence."

"As you've surely noticed, the president gives Kathy free reign when it comes to Azee. I guess the president is smart enough to not rock the boat, especially in an election year. The president, as a first term congressman, introduced me to Azee at a Yale–Harvard football game that Azee was attending as Kathy's guest."

"You certainly have a long relationship with the first family and Azee. He was almost too helpful and condescending at our meeting. It's like he wants too badly for this cruise to happen."

"That's probably so. Azee's always seeking to get some reflected glory off his friendship with the first lady and even the vice president. Originally I was going to be in Detroit for the NAFTA luncheon and cruise. However Azee called and said that I should skip it. Whether he wanted more time alone with Kathy, I don't know—or for that matter care. Thankfully, as a result, my wife and I will be at our place in the cool Hamptons while you're sweating out a campaign stop in Detroit."

"That's funny. The vice president also was scratched from the Detroit trip. At least he had a good excuse."

"Be careful, Gleason. Don't lump me together with him." They both had a good laugh at the mutually disrespected vice president's expense. "By the way, Azee called first thing this morning. He was pleased the way you handled the meeting and of course the acceptance of the *Aqua Mole* for the cruise, as if there ever was any doubt. Gleason, let me give you a little man-to-man advice: Don't let Azee force you into doing anything you don't want to. He can be very invasive without you even being aware."

"I know what you're talking about. He offered me the *Aqua Mole* for my nighttime use. I didn't need it as I was headed back to D.C."

"In those circumstances, the *Aqua Mole* always comes with a crew of one, usually a dancer or a hostess from one of the strip clubs or casino." The mention of hostess set Gleason's blood boiling, as he had already linked Misty's hostess job with Agent Visconti's limousine information. Azee already had gotten to him. "Thanks for the advice. I'll be on guard as we work our way though this Motor City Blitz." Gleason rose and shook his boss's hand, thinking, "Now you tell me," as he hurried out of the office.

Needing to clear his head, Gleason elected to take an outside path from the Treasury Building to his White House office. He didn't want to say the wrong thing when he met with his real boss, the president. There was a wrought iron bench in a hidden little garden area overlooking the manicured south lawn of the White House.

The summer flowers had faded, but the first lady's rose garden was still perfuming the heavy Washington air with subtle fragrances. Often the first lady would have morning coffee in her secluded garden before the day's heat became too oppressive with the always inspirational Washington Monument soaring heavenward in the distance. She wasn't there this morning, so Gleason sat for a moment on the bench to contemplate what was unfolding around him. Like a trapped helpless insect he felt caught in the center of an ever enlarging spider's web. On the periphery of the web were the first lady, the vice president, the secretary of the treasury, Detroit's police chief and the president. Azee was the spider spinning the web, and Gleason wondered if he was using Misty for the fatal sting.

His office was just down the hall from the first lady's modest, homey work place. He noticed that her door was a few inches ajar, which was the signal that she was in and it would be okay to enter. Gleason knew that at this time of day after she got the boys, eight-year-old Jason and six-year-old Eric, off to school with their perpetual Secret Service companions, she would be working on her diary or answering her endless correspondence.

Gleason always got a psychological lift from a short visit with the first lady. He gave a single knock as he pushed open the door. "Good morning, Kathy. I hope I'm not disturbing you." When he first met the first lady, she insisted that he and everyone in the White House call her Kathy. It has taken him nearly all four years of the first term to get comfortable with this informality, and he was hoping for another four years for it to become second nature.

"Good morning, Tom. Come in and have a seat. Why don't you close the door so we aren't disturbed. Did you have a good trip to Detroit?"

Too late, he thought that he should have checked the White House switchboard log to see if Azee had also called the first lady. "Yes, everything went according to plan, except for a small problem with the National Guard that the president can address. Mr. Azee's yacht will certainly make for a nice afternoon cruise. I tried to dissuade him from repainting and redecorating just for your visit, but he seemed pretty intent on doing it."

"That sounds like him. I'll talk to him in the next couple days, but I'm sure that he'll still go ahead with it."

"He really seems to be looking forward to hosting you for the cruise."

"You know, Tom, some of the president's advisers, I won't mention their names, have questioned Azee's and my relationship. I told them, mind your own business! We were special friends in high school and college. We were two poor inner city kids trying to make their way in a foreign and sometimes hostile environment. I'd say we've done pretty well for ourselves, although the journey is far from over."

"No question about that and you have been responsible for

much of the president's success."

"Trust me, if my friendship with Azee was harming the presidency, I would terminate it. I tell everyone that really needs to know, and that's a very short list, that our friendship is strictly platonic, based on many common interests from our school days. I feel comfortable around Azee, unlike many of the new friends you make because of who you are politically."

"I certainly can relate to that on a much smaller scale. When people would somehow find out that I am in the Secret Service protecting the president, we'd get random dinner and party invitations from people we hardly even knew, so I can only imagine what you go through."

"That's what I love about you, Tom. We're a lot alike. I've been thinking that just in case political enemies or the media ever decide to make my friendship with Azee look like a scandal, I want to trust you with the password to my computer diary files. There are no deep dark secrets in my diary, so don't feel that you are prying into my personal life. Hopefully someday, everyone will be able to read the diary in book form. I usually bring out the diary on the boys' birthdays and at the holiday times to remind us of the fun that we've had. I hope the boys never get too old to want to hear these family stories. It keeps them grounded in the real world where they'll be living when our White House days are over."

"Raising normal kids in the White House has to be the hardest and most important thing you do."

"We get a lot of help with the boys from wonderful people like you. If something happens to me, at least the boys and the baby will have the memories in the diary."

"Nothing's going to happen to you, Kathy. Nevertheless, thanks for your trust. I'll keep you informed on the Detroit plans." Gleason accepted the small slip of paper with the password, "Melody1994."

Gleason must have looked confused as Kathy smiled. "You're the first person to know the baby's name. Don't spill the beans to the president until I've had a chance to tell him."

Gleason held his finger to his mouth indicating his promise of silence. His eyes misting at the first lady's expression of loving trust caught Kathy's similar eyes, and he nodded his assent. He needed to leave immediately before they collapsed in each other's arms.

V

"Move that limousine away from the president's path to the yacht," Gleason barked to no one in particular. He was more surly than usual because of his gut feeling, based on his many years of protecting presidents, that this Motor City Blitz was not the tightly scripted visit he had tried to plan. He felt powerless at this late hour to alter any unplanned event as simple as moving the vehicle out of the arriving president's way.

"Sorry, but our limo has a flat tire. We didn't want to make a commotion towing it away," said Royal Canadian Mounted Police agent Jacques LaPres, Gleason's Canadian counterpart, charged with protecting the Canadian prime minister. "This is one of our backup limos. We had to put it in service on short notice."

"Don't worry about it, Jacques. The entourage is coming out the door."

Unlike his ever-serious Secret Service protectors, the president was ebullient as he greeted friends and the media while departing the joint United States–Canadian NAFTA luncheon to escort the first lady to the *Aqua Mole*, docked at the steel bulkhead on the Detroit River. Architect Portman's moat-and-castle design of the concrete fortresslike Renaissance Center was ideal for the needs of the Secret Service charged with protecting the safety of the president. That is, if all pre-planned instructions were meticulously followed without exceptions, such as removing the immobilized Canadian limousine.

The gently bobbing *Aqua Mole* was shielded by the towering Renaissance Center from other downtown office buildings and the busy traffic on Jefferson Avenue. Any and all protesters were relegated to Jefferson Avenue beyond the sight and hearing of the presidential party. The radical demonstrators sympathetic to the Quebec Sovereignty Movement were unusually spirited because of the presence of both the Canadian prime minister and the president of the United States. A ten-second video clip on the evening news would give the desired credibility to their cause as they "interrupted" this meeting of the two countries trying to bolster support for the NAFTA agreement.

Canada was feeling like the proverbial stepchild of NAFTA as most of the United State's business focus was south toward Mexico. The president and the Canadian prime minister were so mutually laudatory in their luncheon remarks that their respective countries' elections in a few weeks would appear to be mere formalities. "Sure glad all that ass-kissing is over," the president quietly mumbled to Kathy, struggling to keep pace with him on their short walk to the docked *Aqua Mole*.

"Keep on smiling, Archie, the cameras are still rolling. You've only two more hours at the Forum to be nice. Then you can relax with us on Azee's yacht," his wife said.

"You know I never relax on your friend's yacht. After the election, I won't need to humor Azee by taking anymore damn cruises."

"Archibald, you really need to lighten up. We still have a month and a half before the election, which is our last as you've promised. I'm the one who's supposed to be moody. My pregnancy can only carry you so far in the polls." Kathy, when particularly frustrated, always used his given name, Archibald, to get his full attention.

"Sorry, Kathy. I guess this damn campaign is taking its toll," the duly chastised president replied as they approached the throng of reporters gathered at the stern of the *Aqua Mole*. "Behave yourself with your old buddy, Azee, 'til I get back."

"Thanks to you, Archie, I can't get any more pregnant," Kathy fired back, patting her protuberant stomach, choosing to ignore for now the jealousy and innuendo behind her husband's cutting remark about Azee.

Transcending all the high-powered political rhetoric of the president and the Canadian prime minister were the two first ladies. The president wisely became a shrinking violet whenever the media approached them. Most of their interest was in the first lady's pregnancy. She was greeted by randomly shouted questions from the waiting press. "How are you feeling?" "Are you really going out on the rough water in your condition?" "What will you do until the president returns?" The first lady let her winning smile and warm eye contact be her answers.

Privately, the White House medical staff was not overjoyed with her mid-forties pregnancy, but as the political polls were increasingly positive, these skeptical advisors publicly feigned their happiness. The president privately joked that he should keep Kathy pregnant for his whole term of office to ameliorate the downward drops in his approval ratings.

The first lady, in spite of and indeed because of her pregnancy, struggled to maintain a real life for herself and their two young sons while the president was perpetually preoccupied with his responsibilities. The long-anticipated cruise on Azee's yacht was one such attempt at having a life.

The president was aware of his wife's need for a life removed from politics. He wholeheartedly encouraged her to skip the next stop on the day's political bandwagon, the opening of the first Judeo-Arabic Forum at Temple B'nai Joseph in suburban Detroit. Although he personally didn't enjoy the company of his wife's oldest friend, Azee, he couldn't afford to alienate him because of his large campaign contributions and his worldwide business and political contacts. The Secret Service timetable called for the president to rejoin his wife aboard the *Aqua Mole* two hours after his opening address at the Forum.

The president gave his wife the proverbial political peck on the cheek. "See you in a couple hours." He handed his wife off to the obsequiously smiling Azee like a nervous father surrendering his daughter to the waiting groom and briskly walked to the Beast to begin the motorocade to the Forum.

"Hello, Quinn. How lovely of you to entertain us on this beautiful afternoon." The first lady greeted Azee by his high school nickname, as she gingerly stepped aboard the stern of the gently rocking *Aqua Mole*. She bent to hug and kiss her shorter, longtime friend, as well as a nearly eight-month-pregnant woman could.

Azee was pleasantly embarrassed when Kathy greeted him by his old nickname. He referred to himself as Quinn only when sending a coded message to select business associates or a private message to the first lady. Now she used Quinn as a term of endearment, whereas during their high school years Quinn was a term of derision, masking disdain for Azee's Middle Eastern origins.

"Now please be careful, Kathy. In your condition we surely don't want to relive the infamous Cass Tech backstroke." Like a teenager on his first date, Azee held Kathy's hand, transferring a coin like object with the simple pronouncement, "Bath." He promenaded her across the expansive rear deck toward the narrow ladder leading to the yacht's flying bridge. Azee prudishly cast his eyes downward toward the dockside television cameras near the still unmoved Canadian limousine. He deferentially followed the first lady up the narrow ladder to the flying bridge, where he guided her to a white wicker deck chair near the outer railing. "Kathy, I'm honored to again have you aboard the *Aqua Mole* for this Gold Cup spectacle."

"I noticed that your Mati eye on the bow looks larger and more brightly painted than during our cruise of the Greek Isles," the first lady commented as she carefully turned toward Azee, seated beside her.

"You're observant to notice that I had the *Aqua Mole* repainted for your visit, even though Agent Gleason said it wasn't necessary. The artisans complained about having to graphically surround the hawseholes where the anchor lines go into the hull."

"You're always so thoughtful and gracious to the president and me. There's no way we can ever repay you. I know why you had the two blue Mati eyes enlarged. They perfectly match your own eyes, which I've always admired."

Azee smiled, wondering if she remembered from their classical studies that only blue-eyed individuals were considered capable of casting evil-eye spells. "Thank you for your kind words. Just seeing you enjoy yourself on this short cruise is reward enough." His eyes locked on her two-karat topaz Mati eye amulet hanging from a slender gold neck chain, his Grecian cruise gift after their final and most spectacular stop at Santorini. "I thought it fitting that the Mati eyes be enlarged to ward off any evil spirits lurking in the murky Detroit River water. The Aegean waters were so clear we could see the rocky bottom in thirty feet of water."

"Hopefully, today's cruise will provide equally fond memories. My mother, God rest her soul, spoke of the Greek cruise just hours before she died. You'll have to explain to me the rules of hydroplane racing."

"There isn't much to know. The fastest hydroplane, if it stays afloat 'til the finish line, wins. I hate to mention it, but sometimes there are fatal accidents with boats somersaulting through the air in end-to-end flips."

"I hope we don't witness anything like that. I wouldn't sleep for a month."

"Don't worry, Kathy. The cockpits of the hydroplanes have built-in safety features just like race cars. Everyone who's anybody in the Detroit social scene will be aboard their yachts for this Gold Cup championship race, so we probably won't be able to get close enough to see any tragedy."

"I hope and pray you're right. Although when Archie comes aboard, he'll want to get as close to the action as possible."

"That must be a male thing. You'll have to let him know who's boss, and we'll keep our distance. The Gold Cup races are Detroit and Windsor's Mardi Gras on the river, so we'll have a great time without a close-up view of any accidents. The view of the Detroit-Windsor skyline is always inspirational. Excuse me for a minute, Kathy, but I need to go below before we cast off." Azee proceeded over to the narrow stairway, pausing to let Agent Gleason get to the top, where he whispered, "need to hit the head before we sail."

The first lady slowly opened her hand, examining Azee's small boarding gift. The bright noonday sun reflected off the dull gray metallic surface of the dime-sized object. She could feel rough, slightly elevated edges of an inscription. She thought it was an antique coin until she read the simple inscription: BATH. The engraving on the small piece of lead was like a thunderbolt, awakening ancient memories.

Marianne Dufoe, the Canadian prime minister's wife, seated next to the first lady, detected Kathy drying tears from the corners of her eyes. "Are you okay? In your condition you don't need to proceed with this cruise."

"Thank you for your concern, Marianne. This cruise is very important to me. It may be the last fun thing I'm able to do before the baby comes. This bright sun is making my eyes water. I need my sunglasses." An aide immediately produced her prescription Ray-Bans, which she put on to cover her tearing eyes.

Her heart was heavy as she again quickly glanced at the priceless two-thousand-year-old present with the recently engraved name of the place where she had become a woman. It was now clear why she had insisted they take this cruise. Even though her husband could dispatch a flotilla of naval ships, he was powerless to deny his wife this sentimental cruise with her fawning friend whom he privately loathed but publicly cultivated. She knew that her husband would rationalize, as in every decision he made, that this two-hour cruise would serve as continuation of the day's pre-election political agenda, the Canadian prime minister serving as a valuable public relations pawn.

Only Kathy and Azee knew the significance of Bath in their lives. In the summer before their senior year, Cass Tech's Latin Department sponsored a field trip to Bath, England. They had uncovered this small piece of lead from the ancient Roman baths in an archeological dig. Azee had saved it all these years. She felt warm all over in the noonday sun as she squeezed her priceless gift. Some things power can't buy, she thought to herself as she wiped away another tear.

After the presidential motorcade departed for the Judeo-Arabic Forum, Gleason was being briefed on the afternoon's emergency plans by a White House communication technician at the wheel on the flying bridge of the magnificent 100-foot Stephens yacht. His ever-vigilant eyes, straining against the bright noonday sun, noticed a stalled vehicle on the center span of the downriver Ambassador Bridge. "Where's a pair of binoculars?" Before he could bring the binoculars to his eyes, the center span of the Ambassador Bridge jumped and danced. Gleason saw the distant fire and smoke before the crescendo boom of the exploding van pierced the festive atmosphere on the flying bridge.

His years of Secret Service training kicked in. He dropped the binoculars and rushed to protect the first lady while shouting, "Down! Everyone down!" The futility of this command on the exposed flying bridge became apparent as the *Aqua Mole* seemed to become airborne by its own violent explosion. Gleason arrived at the first lady's side but did not wrestle her to the deck because of her pregnancy. Instead he gently held her elbows as she tried to slide from her chair to the deck of the flying bridge. Hovering above the first lady, Gleason was catapulted into the Detroit River as the *Aqua Mole* rolled violently from side to side.

While airborne, Gleason realized that a much closer and more powerful explosion had occurred. The dark coolness of the Detroit River gave him an unneeded second rush of adrenaline. He surfaced beside the bobbing hull of the *Aqua Mole*. Frantically dogpaddling to the swim platform at the stern where Agent Peter Yance was preparing to dive in to offer assistance, Gleason determined that he wasn't injured. "How's the first lady? Is she in the water?" Gleason hoisted himself onto the slippery swim platform.

"She's still on the bridge. I don't know her condition. We're rescuing everyone in the water first."

Gleason was relieved to hear that the first lady hadn't been blown off the flying bridge. His sloshing leather wingtips hardly impeded his ascent up the narrow teak ladder to the side of the unmoving first lady.

"What happened?" Azee shouted as he emerged from the head below deck. "Someone tell me what happened!" Then he saw the barely distinguishable Canadian limousine shrouded by dark smoke and bright flames.

Sirens pierced the air's acrid explosive residue as emergency vehicles rushed to the distant burning center span of the Ambassador Bridge and to the *Aqua Mole*, rocking against its Renaissance mooring.

"Quick, everyone inside, down below," Gleason ordered. The danger of further attacks was very real. He wanted everyone off the exposed flying bridge, not realizing that the yacht's main salon was an amalgam of shattered rubble from broken windows, dishes and splintered furniture. It would provide little protection against another attack. "Agent Yance, notify the motorcade to go to level ten security immediately."

Standing in a pool of blood beside the motionless first lady, Gleason observed her frosted blond hair turning red from a large cut at the top of her skull. The president's physician was with the motorcade, so a White House naval nurse, Monica Mason, had been assigned to remain with the first lady. Kneeling beside the first lady's traumatized head, Mason's starched white uniform was becoming as bright a red as the first lady's hair.

"These scalp wounds bleed more than you think." Mason continued to compress an already saturated towel on the first lady's injured cranium.

Gleason bent down and gently retracted the first lady's closed eyelids revealing her fixed and dilated pupils. "Has she moved at all?"

"No, but the bleeding seems to be slowing down. Based on the size of this scalp laceration, we probably have a fractured skull or a broken neck. We can't move her until her head and neck are fixed on a stretcher."

Gleason could see strands of blond hair on the bowed-out railing above where the first lady was lying. The propulsive force of her head striking and bending the 3/4-inch chromed railing pipe must have done more damage than the hemorrhaging scalp laceration, Gleason surmised. "Agent Yance, get that damn medevac helicopter! We have a major problem here! Did you reach the motorcade? Did they respond?"

"Take it easy, sir! Medevac helicopters are on the way. Marine One is coming from Selfridge Air Force Base," Yance replied.

"Get the motorcade back on the radio. Tell Marine One to proceed for a presidential pickup. There's nothing they can do here."

"We have the motorcade on the secure open line. They have momentarily stopped to go to level ten security, Yance reported.

"Stopped! For God's sake, order them underway! That damn Lodge expressway ditch is the last place we want the president. He's a sitting duck." Gleason envisioned the motorcade under full-scale attack with high-powered rifles and bombs from treacherous Michigan Militia members of the National Guard on the walls above the Lodge.

Azee quietly knelt at the love of his life's side across from Mason. His hands were holding Kathy's limp right hand as he slid his fingers to her wrist. "She still has a pulse!" He gently placed a trembling hand on her rounded abdomen, "But the baby's not moving!" Viewing the first lady's condition, he thought of his grandmother's Gibranian sophism: "The storm can destroy the flowers but can't harm the seeds."

"Please, Mr. Azee," Mason sternly cautioned. "Our main concern is keeping the first lady alive to transport to the hospital. You can't tell if the baby is alive by feeling the stomach."

The humbled Azee tightly grasped Kathy's unresponsive hand while quietly murmuring a prayer for her and himself. "Kathy, you can make it, please don't give up." Azee could feel the edge of the lead memento she still clutched. He considered prying it loose. Kathy had originally found the lead memento on their high school Bath dig, so it was hers to keep for eternity. With the gravely injured first lady at his knees, Azee's tear-filled eyes strained to look across the Detroit River to his concrete office complex on the Canadian shore. He fantasized striking a deal with the devil, gladly trading all for a healthy Kathy. This vista reminded him of the two young lovers' view across the Bath hot springs, where they had invoked the Roman gods and goddesses of love. He wanted to whisper in Kathy's ear his final anthem, "The things which youth loves are grasped by the heart until life is no more."

Gleason's eyes darted around the land and water perimeter of the *Aqua Mole* for any additional trouble. The curious pleasure boats were more closely surrounding the *Aqua Mole*, each with its own video camera recording this piece of morbid history. Gleason felt comfortable that the situation was stabilized until the first lady could be transported to the hospital. "Azee, go below and check for any hull damage. We have to stay afloat until we remove the first lady. Get on your marine radio and tell the Coast Guard cutters to enforce the no-wake zone. All this rocking isn't helping the first lady."

Azee gave one last squeeze to Kathy's limp hand as he left to carry out Gleason's orders. Azee's sentiments were like the turbulent water engulfing his once-proud yacht, ebbing and flowing between hope and despair.

The roar of the descending medevac helicopters made it nearly impossible to talk on the flying bridge. Agent Yance was shouting directly into Gleason's ear, "We've lost radio contact with the presidential motorcade after hearing two explosions."

Gleason feared the worst, but he couldn't control a foreboding situation miles away any more than he could change the disaster at hand. "Keep trying to reestablish contact." Gleason moved aside, making room for the arriving paramedics. "Let's evacuate the first lady as quickly as possible. Where are you taking her?"

"Henry Ford Hospital, less than ten minutes away," the first of the arriving paramedics replied.

"For God's sake, Yance! All our lines can't be down. Notify them that we're transporting the first lady to Henry Ford Hospital!"

The constant bobbing and rocking of the *Aqua Mole* against the Renaissance Center bulkhead was making it difficult for the paramedics to treat and stabilize the unresponsive first lady. At Gleason's not-so-subtle urging, the decision was made to immediately transport the first lady, as her condition was worsening by the minute. Gleason's final order to the police before boarding the medevac helicopter with the first lady's stretcher was, "Seal off the *Aqua Mole* so that no one goes aboard. No one!"

As they were lifting off, Gleason was trying unsuccessfully to elicit a response from the presidential motorcade on his secure White House phone. His worst fears flashed back to that hostile encounter with General Hodgechis at the confrontational meeting when the general said that armed National Guard troops would be stationed above the submerged Lodge expressway. These troops, possibly members of the subversive Michigan Militia, would have an unblocked line of sight for shooting at the presidential motorcade below.

The president had instructed the Secret Service to drop the issue of the National Guard being armed or disarmed. General Hodgechis was one of the few people who had ever played chicken with the Secret Service and won at least a partial victory. His troops would still carry their unloaded rifles. However, there was no way of preventing anyone from secretly loading their rifle. Now Gleason's vexing question was, "Did the president lose this high-stakes game of chicken?"

"Medevac One to Henry Ford Hospital trauma center," the pilot implored on his radio. "We're inbound with a comatose, critical head and neck trauma patient who's nearly eight months pregnant. We will need all life support systems activated. E.T.A. is less than ten minutes."

Gleason's efforts at contacting the motorcade were futile. While descending for the landing at the trauma center, he looked northwesterly in the direction that the Lodge ditch raced toward the suburbs. He was in a free fall from the mountain where all dreams turn into one hope and all thoughts into a single prayer. He momentarily closed his tear-filled eyes in prayer while squeezing the first lady's unresponsive hand. "Who's alive? Who's dead?" he wondered as the medevac helicopter mercifully sank to its landing on the big red cross atop the roof of the trauma center.

VI

The presidential motorcade departed from the Renaissance Center after the first lady and the other invited guests were aboard the *Aqua Mole*. As the armored Suburbans and limousines accelerated onto Jefferson Avenue and under Cobo Hall, the president turned to his back seat companion, Jethro Barkley, the mayor of Detroit. "Jethro, thank's for the kind words of welcome at the NAFTA luncheon. Kathy and I are always pleased to return to Detroit. It's special when Kathy can come home and renew some of her old friendships."

"Indeed, *we're* the ones honored when you come to Detroit, Mister President. I'm sure you can count on a victory in Detroit this election, especially with the goodwill generated by the Judeo-Arabic Forum that we're headed to. Whose idea was this forum? It's brilliant!"

"I think Azee thought it up. Detroit was selected to host this first Judeo-Arabic Forum because of its large and diverse population of immigrants from everywhere in the Middle East. Azee's worldwide business and political connections also were a significant factor in this initial forum meeting in Detroit. Azee's role, by his own volition, was finished after landing this history-making forum for Detroit. He's willing to let politicians from around the world convene to garner their headlines. What do you think, Mayor?"

"Are you sure you really want to know?"

"Why not? But in case you don't want to answer that, I've got another one. As mayor of Detroit, do you have much dialogue with your counterpart, the mayor of Windsor? I got the feeling at the NAFTA luncheon that there is a little friction between Detroit and Windsor."

"I can answer both questions with the same train of thought. It used to be just the fun ceremonial stuff that Detroit and Windsor shared, like the fireworks for our Fourth of July and their Dominion Day celebrations. Now two things have happened to strain our friendly cooperation."

"Let me guess what those two things are. One has to be the opening of casino gambling in Windsor, right?"

"You're well briefed on our local politics, Mister President. As you know, we're hopefully going to have our own casinos, so we can fight fire with fire—or should I say sin with sin."

"I understand from my Secret Service protector, Agent Gleason, that his friend, your chief of police, is doing a great undercover job monitoring the casino in Windsor for future police and criminal implications that could affect your own casinos. It's always nice to have dedicated public servants like your police chief trying to stay ahead of the curve. Your casinos should help him fill up any slack time in his department."

"His undercover work at the Windsor casino has produced some interesting information we're trying to assimilate and apply across the border here in Detroit as we get ready for our own casino problems. Your host for the afternoon cruise, the brilliant Azee, seems to have some involvement with the Windsor casino, but we don't think it's anything illegal."

"That doesn't surprise me. Any time there's a possibility of making money, he usually can be found nearby. As you know he's an old friend of my wife from their high school days here in Detroit and their college days at the University of Michigan. She's known him longer than she's known me, so I give her plenty of latitude in their friendship, unless of course he's involved in something illegal that could harm my administration. I hope that you encourage your chief to continue his undercover casino work."

"Sir, I don't know if you've ever meet Chief Hawkins, but his large size and outgoing demeanor preclude any typical incognito undercover work. He mostly has friends and contacts that share information with him over dinner and an evening at the gambling tables."

"I certainly hope your police budget doesn't fund these evenings at the casino. The voters might have a hard time with that expenditure! I've no guess on the second problem you and the mayor of Windsor share. My briefing people have let me down on this."

"I've already alluded to it. Did you notice at the NAFTA luncheon that I didn't introduce Azee as the owner of the boat you will be partying on after the forum?"

"I did, but I assumed we were pressed for time."

"Thank you, Mister President. I try to be aware of how valuable your time is. That's why I've never bothered you with this second problem, which is mainly Detroit's but it does have international importance. Windsor and Detroit waged a bitter struggle over Azee relocating his company headquarters from Detroit to Windsor. The great patriot that Azee is, he still moved his company headquarters to a foreign country. We lost. They won."

"Sounds like an election campaign. Win some, lose some."

"I wish it was that simple. Azee played one town against the other for more concessions than General Motors would have been entitled to. It got real personal at the end between the two mayors and Azee. I admit that I'm not a graceful loser. I've worked myself up from the slums of Detroit to be mayor. Azee has done the same to become a billionaire. But he's forgotten his roots, as his company's relocation to Canada shows."

"Sounds like you're taking this a little too personally."

"Pardon me, Sir, for being so frank. Everyone knows of your

wife's longtime friendship with Azee. They both grew up within
a few blocks of where we're now driving. Azee was and still is a
problem for all the law enforcement agencies here on the border,
including Canadian and United States Customs, INS, FBI and all
the local police departments. He's always ferrying foreign dignitaries across the border and around both Detroit and Windsor in
his helicopter, limousines and boats. Now with his headquarters
across the border, heaven only knows who, from where, is freely
visiting both countries. Windsor's airport is achieving international status with all the arriving private jets carrying foreign
leaders and corporate big shots. It's easy for anyone, friend or
foe, from anywhere in the world, to be just across the Detroit
River from us or even cross the border for a little R and R in our
country. Azee, as I'm sure you know from your wife, has a large
estate out in the suburbs that he's proud of and likes to show
off to dignitaries. They can get on his helicopter in Windsor and
fly to his suburban estate without going through customs like
everyone else."

"Kathy has never mentioned Azee's estate here in Detroit.
However, she's mentioned that Azee is building a retreat compound on an island somewhere in northern Michigan."

"That's what I understand. It's on Drummond Island and it's
also close to Canada. It's out of my sphere of authority, so I don't
worry about it. I have enough problems here in Detroit without
seeking more trouble three hundred miles away."

"Sounds like you should welcome the increased business and
excitement that all these foreign visitors generate."

"Should be so, but not if Azee operates above the law. There have
been a couple times when his entourage has been stopped at the border or in their limousines on our streets for some minor problem.
Passport and visa paperwork issues get forwarded to Washington,
and nothing ever seems to happen. The word in all our local agencies
is that Azee has powerful friends in the White House, so don't bother
him unless he kills someone, if you know what I mean."

"Mister Mayor, let me assure you that none of this has ever

come to my attention. I'll speak with the first lady when I rejoin her later today on Azee's yacht to make sure that she isn't providing him with undue protection. Are you going to be able to join us on the cruise?"

"Under the circumstances, I think it best that I skip the cruise. It sounds more like a personal time for your family and Azee."

"I appreciate your candor. Most of the advisors around a president tell him what he wants to hear. Your have to leave Washington to find out what's really happening in the country."

"The fact that I'm so honest is what makes Azee's corporate move across the river so difficult to stomach. In the negotiations, he used every trick known before he finally stabbed Detroit in the back. There has to be more to his move than the publicly announced better business climate in Canada. The really strange paradox is that in the last couple months we have seen more activity by Azee back in this country than when his headquarters were still here. You figure it out."

"Let me assure you that the White House will not interfere with any matter that you deem illegal concerning Azee. But as a personal favor to me and especially to the first lady—a diehard Detroit native, as you mentioned—I would ask you to delay any adverse publicity until after the election. Is this a problem for you?"

"No problem. I've nothing pending against Azee or his company. I just hate to see anyone, I don't care how rich or powerful they are, operating above the law."

"Speaking of law, I need to review my speech for this Judeo-Arabic Forum, which will help bring law and order to the Middle East. How much time before we arrive at the temple?"

"Twenty minutes at the most."

"Thank you," the president replied and turned his attention to the text of his opening remarks to the forum: "It is my distinct honor to open this first Judeo-Arabic Forum in Detroit. It's fitting that this first forum is being held in Detroit, where we have the largest population of Middle Eastern people outside of the Middle

East itself. Hopefully the beneficial results of this dialogue will be felt on the turbulent shores of the Mediterranean, thousands of miles away. Since the days of my youth growing up in the South, I've always believed that if prejudice and hate are to be overcome in the world, they must first be eliminated in every village, town, and state of this, our own great country. Our government in Washington can pass laws, the United Nations can enact resolutions, the World Court in The Hague can adjudicate differences between nations, all to no avail until we individually make peace with our own neighbors. That is what's so wonderful about this first Judeo-Arabic Forum: We're primarily making peace at home with ourselves. All of us here in Detroit must set an example for the world. The olive branch will prevail over the howitzer."

Just then the president glanced up from his manuscript as the motorcade passed under the Ford expressway and commented, "Strange that democratic Detroit would name an expressway after a Republican president."

The mayor tried his best to suppress his mirth. "Sir, there were automotive Fords in Detroit long before Michigan's Gerald Ford became president. I think that President Ford has an airport named after him over in Grand Rapids, his home town."

The mayor quickly pointed out the towering billboard for the Henry Ford Hospital to their left above the top of the Lodge expressway. From the speeding motorcade, they could not see the mobile National Guard headquarters in the parking lot of Henry Ford Hospital. General Hodgechis had chosen this location near the midpoint of the motorcade in consultation with the Secret Service and the governor's office.

The report of Gleason's confrontation with General Hodgechis over the use of armed National Guard troops, who might be members of the Michigan Militia, had reached the oval office. It kept getting buried deeper and deeper under more urgent papers until one day Gleason pulled it to the top of the pile and told the president that it needed immediate attention.

Being the master of compromise, an ability that had propelled him into the oval office, the president had issued an executive order allowing the troops to continue to carry their rifles but mandated that they must not be loaded. The public wouldn't be informed of this effective disarming of the troops guarding the president unless there was a leak to the press. Pistols and ammunition were not to be issued or carried by the troops. The Secret Service, at the president's request, had researched this subject and recommended that there was no genuine need for 5,000 armed National Guard troops to help provide primary protection for the presidential visit. These troops were to be present for crowd control and to monitor the high ground above the Lodge expressway.

General Hodgechis took this federally mandated partial disarming of his troops as a personal insult and a sign of distrust of his leadership. At the urging of his Michigan Militia friends, he was determined to submit his letter of resignation as Gleason had suggested at the thirty-day meeting. But after a quiet afternoon cruise on Lake Saint Clair aboard the *Aqua Mole* with Azee, he agreed to delay his resignation until after the presidential visit, if for no other reason than to deny Gleason the satisfaction that his resignation would bring.

The general, in what might be his final act of defiance, wore his own loaded sidearm as he nervously paced around the hospital parking lot command center with his two-way radio chirping on his belt.

The brakes of every vehicle in the speeding presidential motorcade locked as the restricted radio frequency from the Secret Service's downtown control center squawked, "The sparrow is landed, the sparrow is landed."

Instantly the presidential limousine was surrounded by Uzi-toting Secret Service agents who rushed from the black Suburbans. Nathan Rothchild, the agent in charge of the motorcade, quickly appeared at the partially opened window of the Beast and told the president, "Sir, will you and the mayor please put on the protective overcoats? We're returning downtown. There has been an incident at the boat while still at the dock. We have no additional information."

The presidential flags were retracted into the fenders, while identical flags were raised on the decoy limousine. Rothchild ordered the decoy and another trailing limousine ahead of the president's vehicle so that fully armed Suburbans could be in front of and behind the now-incognito presidential vehicle. The motorcade quickly regained speed in a desperate search for an exit from the Lodge expressway. The National Guardsmen at the railing overlooking the Lodge seemed to stiffen at the mini-drama being enacted below them. Rothchild's lead Suburban accelerated at the highly welcomed green sign: "Exit one mile." The National Guard's green camouflage uniforms became a blur as the motorcade lurched forward to escape the restrictive confines of the Lodge. The president and the mayor started to perspire under the weight of their heavy Kevlar lined overcoats.

VII

After they went aerial from the roadbed explosives, the catapulted lead Suburban and the decoy limousine somersaulted back to the destroyed pavement in a catastrophic crush that spared none of their occupants. Suburbans and limousines can fly, but they don't land very well. Dismembered occupants were indiscriminately disgorged like broken dolls on a smoking junk heap.

The hood of the presidential limousine was jackknifed up at 90 degrees when it struck the uprooted concrete roadbed in its path. The bent hood prevented the presidential limousine from rolling over onto its roof, so it came to rest on the driver's side with the wheels still racing. The driver, Agent George Johnson, was calling, "Mr. President! Are you alright? Sir! Please answer!"

The president, seated on the passenger side, was suspended by his shoulder harness like the World War II paratrooper on a French church steeple. In shock, unable to free himself from his shoulder harness and seatbelt, the president mumbled back, "The mayor is bleeding. Quick, save him."

The president could see the face of the unmoving mayor below him turning bloody red. Johnson, immovably wedged behind the steering wheel, could barely reach his secure radio and utter with the last breaths from his crushed chest, "The eagle is alive, the eagle is…" No sooner had Johnson uttered his last woods than a violent series of explosions reverberated above the concrete walls of the Lodge. The limousine did not shake or vibrate from the deafening blast because the sunken expressway was shielded from the concussion wave of the explosions. Its precarious position wasn't worsened by the blasts from the surface street.

The shoulder harness was cutting painfully into the suspended president's neck. He continued to dangle above the stunned, bleeding mayor. Even if he could find the harness and seat belt releases, he was reluctant to open them for fear of depositing himself on the injured mayor below him.

The president heard the click of the car's power door locks activated by an agent's remote opening device. The now-horizontal rear passenger door was pried open. Agent Philip Ryan carefully lowered himself into the bowels of the once proud Beast. "Mister President, are you injured?"

"I don't think so. Just my elbow hurts. Check the mayor. His bloody face looks serious."

"Sir, your left elbow is bleeding!" Ryan could feel a sharp projection through the blood-soaked overcoat. It was painful to the touch. "You have a broken arm, sir. We must get the bleeding stopped. Your elbow is dripping blood on the mayor's face."

Gingerly the agents unstrung the president from his perch above the mayor and lowered him to sit on the smashed window. They gently up-righted the mayor. Much to their surprise, he wasn't bleeding. "How do you feel?" Ryan asked.

"Fine, but I can't stop shaking. Can you believe we're still alive?" The mayor used his white breast pocket silk handkerchief to wipe the president's blood from his face.

"The mayor and I will need time to gather ourselves," the president said. "What the hell happened? What were those explosions we just heard? Is the attack over?"

"Excuse me, sir. I'll stand and look out the door to assess the situation." The distinctive smell of spent explosives many times stronger than after Fourth of July fireworks was settling into the protective cocoon of the destroyed Beast. At the sight of advancing National Guard troops with rifles at the ready aimed at the limousine, Ryan drew his revolver. Most of the Secret Service's more powerful automatic weapons were in the demolished lead Suburbans. There were two assault rifles in the trunk of the Beast, but that wasn't going to help the immediate crisis. He frantically waved his pistol in the air like a general ordering his troops to stop. Ryan was not privy to the fact that the National Guard was shouldering bulletless rifles. His stopping them with one measly pistol told him that they were friendly troops, or they would have blown his head off.

"What's the problem, Ryan?" the president demanded. "Do I need a gun too? Where are those damn National Guard troops we squabbled with over their loaded rifles? I wonder if the Michigan Militia is a part of this?"

Ryan tried to fathom the deadly destruction as he did a 360-degree evaluation of the security situation. There was an eerie silence, as if awaiting another explosion, except for distant sirens racing to the scene. "Get a medevac helicopter. The president's injured," Ryan shouted to the nearest agent outside the limousine.

Ryan sat beside the president compressing the bleeding elbow. "These last explosions were a gas station and an old house overlooking the expressway. After-the-fact distractions, I'd say. Our motorcade is another story. It seems that the roadbed exploded when the lead Suburban and the decoy limousine with the raised presidential flags were over the explosives. A spotter, possibly a National Guardsman, must have been watching and activated the explosives when he saw what he thought was your limousine directly over the bombs hidden in the sewer pipes under the road. We're lucky to be sitting here talking. If we hadn't changed the order of the cars in the motorcade, it would have been you in the lead limousine, where there probably are no survivors."

The president's head dropped at the realization that people had died in his place. "Do we know anything about the incident at the boat?"

"No, sir, we don't. The two incidents happened nearly simultaneously, and we lost radio contact. I hear a medevac helicopter coming in. Maybe they'll know what happened at the boat."

The president started to laugh sadly. The absurd isolation and helplessness of the most powerful man in the world sitting in a pool of his own blood, encamped in his overturned limousine without knowing if his wife was dead or alive, was numbing to the depths of his being.

"Please evacuate the mayor first," the president ordered as the paramedics peered into the limousine. A ladder was lowered, and the rescue crew aided the mayor in his ascent. An air splint was quickly applied to the president's left arm in preparation for his leaving the vehicle. "What do you know about the incident at the boat?" The president's simple question took all his strength to ask and brought tears to his eyes as he expected the worst.

"Nothing definite, Mister President. Another medevac helicopter, transporting the first lady, is landing at Henry Ford Hospital. She's reported in stable condition."

"Thank god, she's still alive. Are we going there?"

"Just as soon as we can get you out of this smashed sardine can."

VIII

The secure red phone in the White House office rang only once before being answered. Everyone, including Vice President Hubert Taylor, was riveted to the large screen television watching the live CNN reports on the Detroit bombings.

Calling from Detroit, Gleason asked to speak to Agent Hector Lopez, who was in charge of the vice president's security. Not knowing the full scope of the plot against the leadership of the United States Government, Gleason decided that keeping it short would be in everyone's best interest. "The eagle and sparrow have been grounded and are receiving medical care. The president has activated Section Three of the Twenty-fifth Amendment for an initial twenty-four hour period. Inform the vice president that he is acting president for this time period. Raise his security and those in the line of presidential succession to level ten."

Lopez hung up the red phone without saying a word. The voice scrambler gave Gleason's staccato orders a surrealistic aura like a message from on high. He felt awestruck as he approached the new president, who was starring expressionless at the television. "Vice President Taylor, I just talked to Agent Gleason in Detroit. You are acting president under Section Three of the Twenty-fifth Amendment for at least the next twenty-four hours. Not knowing the extent of this terrorist plot, we request that you stay in the White House tonight for security considerations and the morale of the nation."

"Give me my damn crutches," Acting President Taylor barked. It was his first presidential order. He struggled to extricate himself from the overstuffed oxblood cordovan leather chair that had swallowed his feeble body. "Just what the country needs," he grumbled—"a wounded president in Detroit and an infirm acting president in Washington. I shouldn't have had this damn knee surgery. I could at least inspire more confidence and vigor in the country without these crutches. Pardon me, Agent Lopez, but I've some phone calls to make." Just that quickly, Hubert Taylor reluctantly became acting president of the United States.

Taylor retreated alone with his secure cell phone to the corner opposite the dismaying television coverage. His first call was to Azee, who was walking across the parking lot of Henry Ford Hospital to locate General Hodgechis's command headquarters. He told Taylor he couldn't talk now, not even to the acting president, but they could talk later.

"Let him pass," the booming voice of General Hodgechis ordered the young MP guarding the entrance to the trailer headquarters. "Good to see that you appear unscathed by the attack at the *Aqua Mole*."

"The first lady was not so lucky. She's unconscious, as I'm sure you've heard. What are the reports on the motorcade? There was a breakdown of the Secret Service's communication network while the first lady was being prepped for the medevac helicopter, so we had no information about the motorcade."

"My main source of information is from my spotters' walkie-talkies above the Lodge, reporting on the progress of the motorcade passing below them. I thought it strange when one of the first reports had the motorcade stopping unexpectedly and amid a flurry of activity, changed the order of the vehicles to move the presidential limousine toward the back of the motorcade. The Secret Service must have figured that an attack would come from the front and not the back of the moving vehicles."

"I suppose that makes sense. The Secret Service has a contingency plan for everything."

"The next spotters observed that the motorcade quickly got up to speed when the road suddenly exploded and lifted up in front of the speeding lead car and the trailing presidential limousine, at least the one with the fender flags up. The obviously increased speed caused the closely following cars to run head-on into the elevated roadbed and the other crashed vehicles. Only the presidential limousine and two trailing black Suburbans, although now flipped over on their sides, avoided total annihilation."

"What's the president's condition?" Azee wondered.

"He was able to walk with assistance to the medevac helicopter. The president was seen holding his bloody left arm that apparently was in a splint. The mayor, riding with him, appeared uninjured."

"The paranoid premonition of the Secret Service certainly saved the president. We weren't so fortunate with the first lady. We had no warning. I was in the head below. A single explosion rocked and nearly capsized the *Aqua Mole* at her bulkhead mooring. Everyone on the flying bridge, except the first lady, was thrown into the river. She would have been much better off going for a swim in the Detroit River."

"Azee, don't torture yourself with 'what if's. We have to deal with the reality of what happened and who did it."

"I should have been up on the flying bridge. I might have been able to protect her."

"Enough, Azee! Excuse me, but I have to go meet the president's incoming medevac helicopter."

"I'll call when I return from my family vacation in Beirut," Azee replied as he headed into the hospital to visit the first lady for what he assumed would be the last time he would see her alive.

IX

Against the doctor's and Secret Service's advice, before having his own broken left arm attended to, he insisted on being brought immediately to his wife's bedside. The sight of the unconscious first lady's freshly shaved head and motionless body was a terrible shock to the partially sedated president.

From their first meeting while protesting at the base of the Washington Monument many years ago, he had been captivated by her long blond hair. He would often whimsically twist and tease it with his fingers when they were sitting in the movies or, more recently, in the back of the presidential limousine. "Kathy must have enjoyed it," he thought to himself. "She never stopped me." Although in later years she wore her hair shorter to speed up the morning's get-ready-to-face-the-world ritual, he still pictured Kathy as when they first met, with her long, flowing, windblown hair.

"As ordered, sir, we have enacted the Twenty-fifth Amendment," Gleason whispered above the hum of the surrounding life-support equipment. The solemn president nodded, sitting in his wheelchair with his right arm gently resting on his wife's protruding stomach.

He was no longer president, and the weight of the world was removed from his shoulders. He stared silently at his comatose wife. Memories flooded his mind in Niagaran cascades. Their serendipitous first meeting at an anti-Vietnam-War protest march on the Washington Mall obscured all other thoughts. Kathy's tense, shouting mouth, with perfectly straight teeth, was ameliorated by the softest, kindest eyes that the young Southern law student had ever locked on. Must be from a wealthy family that could afford orthodontics, he thought to himself, based on the dental demographics of his small rural hometown where only the well-to-do parents could afford braces.

Fortunately he was too much enamored with Kathy's blond hair and perfect teeth by the time he learned that she got free orthodontic treatment as a dental hygiene student at the University of Michigan Dental School in Ann Arbor. It was too late for her lack of family money to dampen his deepening love. A painful smile elevated the corners of his lips as he remembered Kathy's pseudo-disgust when, after a few drinks with friends, he would recall his favorite uncle's sage but unheeded advice, "You can make more money in five minutes at the altar than in a lifetime of work."

The reflection of the Washington Monument had followed the boisterous marchers the length of the reflecting pool toward the Capitol. Spontaneously they held hands and playfully tickled each other's palms with their fingertips. Their spirits soared higher than the five hundred fifty five foot-five inch tall white obelisk shadowing them.

The message of the march became subordinate to the hormones of the moment, and it took all the young soon-to-be-lawyer's will power to continue the public protest when he was fully primed for a private tryst. He could not remember if it was the second or third time marching around the base of the Washington Monument that he pointed off toward the White House and boldly proclaimed that someday they would live there. He loved her snide retort, "Yeah, maybe as butler and maid." That was how he proposed marriage and she accepted—before they even knew each other's full names. He promised himself that this would be the first thing he would ask Kathy when she awoke from her coma: Was it the second or third time around the Washington Monument that he proposed to her? Certainly she would remember.

That first night together was like a continuation of the march as she protested that she hardly know him. His insistence that she would have the rest of her life to get to know him now obsessed him. The memory of their providential protest encounter was now tragically cut short by another act of protest, vicious, far removed from their home in the shadow of the Washington Monument.

Looking at the wife he could hardly recognize threw him into an unaccustomed, introspective frame of mind. As happens in many political marriages, love becomes a business—the business of getting elected and then reelected. If he could roll back the clock to that happy, fateful first meeting, erasing the current trauma and all the intervening years of power and glory, would he? His answer was ambivalent, and that didn't surprise him. Had politics so consumed and destroyed his soul that he was willing to accept his wife's current pathetic condition rather than give up the years that made him the most powerful person in the world. He could not remember when he first realized that the power of politics had consumed his soul.

"Thank you for calling the White House, Gleason," he finally replied. "Washington and the world can wait. Let Taylor have his twenty-four hours of glory. Where have all the doctors and nurses gone?"

"They wanted you to have a few private moments with the first lady," Gleason explained. "I'll buzz for them."

The doctors quickly reviewed Kathy's medical condition with the president and her prognosis was dismal. Being comatose with serious closed head trauma and a possible broken neck, there was the high probability that Kathy would never recover. The condition of the eight-month-old fetus seemed uncompromised for the present, but that diagnosis was also guarded.

"Mr. President," Gleason interrupted the president's state of drug-induced nirvana, "is there anything you need before going into surgery?"

"Yes, have the White House round up Jason and Eric. I need to tell them that everything is going to be all right. Also tell the staff not to let them watch TV so they don't become upset. Is Taylor going to spend the night at the White House?"

"He has been directed to stay at the White House tonight. I'll get the boys on the phone."

X

After awkwardly waiting beside the pay phone in the first lady's corridor, Azee was allowed to visit the first lady at the president's order. The president was wheeled from the curtained privacy of Kathy's enclosure into the hallway. Azee's bejeweled right hand instinctively reached out to greet the preoccupied president. "Mister President, I am so sorry about today's events."

"I appreciate your concern, Azee. Fortunately you look unharmed," the president commented as his wheelchair was being turned in the direction of outpatient surgery.

"I was below deck when the explosion occurred. Luckily the first lady wasn't blown off the flying bridge into the water, or she might have drowned. How is the baby?"

"The doctors say that the baby appears unharmed. At least there is some good news." The president turned in his moving wheelchair and called back, "Go in and see Kathy. You've known her longer than I have."

Azee's gaze locked onto the back of the president's wheelchair with cruise missile accuracy until it vanished into an elevator for its descent to the surgical area. His tanned, dark complexion turned crimson as he struggled to contain his anger at the president for another of his jealous references to his long-term friendship with the first lady. Azee had never tried to publicly upstage the president, yet he always detected bad vibrations from him.

He had no way of knowing how much Kathy had told her husband about their relationship in their student years. He assumed that she was discrete; otherwise the president probably wouldn't have allowed them to get together for today's cruise. Then again, the fact that Azee was the top donor to the president's reelection campaign probably encouraged the president to overlook the obvious baggage that many of his big campaign contributors carried with them.

He approached Kathy's bedside with years of suppressed passion as he asked the attending nurses if he could have a moment alone with her. He was totally unprepared for what he saw when he parted the curtain. The noisy machines and beeping monitors were to be expected. But the sight of his now-comatose first and only love was devastating. His gaze fixed on Kathy's closed eyes to avoid having to look at her shaved head and motionless body.

Like many of his Middle Eastern friends and associates, Azee was starting to view life in philosophical and poetical terms devoid of the scientific certitude of Western culture. Even though he was dying a thousand deaths, he took great comfort in knowing that Kathy could not see herself and that she was pain-free.

He was eternally grateful that the two of them had once expressed their true feelings in Bath. They had sensed that their teenage romance had no future, but they had tasted paradise once. His fondest high school and college memories were intertwined with Kathy like a multicolored ball of string that kept growing layer upon layer as the years relentlessly advanced. He did not want to unravel this kaleidoscopic love affair for fear that when all the strings were unwound the central core would be found devoid of any real meaning. Azee needed the illusion as much as the reality of love. His profound psychological need motivated him through all the intervening years to periodically attract her attention if not her latent affections.

He tenderly stroked her freshly scrubbed, once-vibrant face, now bruised and swollen. Tears filled his eyes for what was and would never be. He inserted his stubby finger in her clinched palm. He could still feel the rough edge of what would be his final gift. The medical staff was too busy inserting needles and tubes to check her closed hands. Again Azee was momentarily tempted to pry his final gift free, but he thought it fitting that the Bath lead memento should stay with Kathy as long as she had life to grasp it.

His emotions became all-or-nothing, realizing that Kathy was going to die. He hoped the same for the baby, conceived out of political need by a husband who did not deserve to have this final reminder of a wife he never truly loved or fully appreciated as much as Azee did. The baby was just another piece in the political puzzle for the president. Azee's death spiral of self-pitying hatred into the murky netherworld of glorified past and nonexistent future was interrupted by a nurse's urgent request that she needed to attend to the first lady.

XI

Gleason had the White House on the phone when the president was brought into the prep area. "The president needs privacy to talk to his children," Gleason announced to clear the immediate area around the most famous compound fractured arm in the nation. As the president talked to Jason and Eric, tears filled his eyes. He realized what the boys had already lost and how fortunate it was that he survived relatively unscathed compared to their mother. After sensing his young sons' concerns about their mother, the president knew that he had to return home to the White House as quickly as possible to minimize their trauma.

The orthopedic department of Henry Ford Hospital was mobilized to treat the most powerful person in the world. The hospital had been ordered to level 10 maximum security. Per routine procedure an armed Secret Service agent had to be with the president at all times. Gleason overheard the chief surgeon, Dr. Walter Hellman, request that two units of blood be available for the surgery. "Excuse me, Dr. Hellman. Is the president going to need blood during the surgery? How much blood has he lost already?"

"The patient's hematocrit is below twenty-five, and he'll lose more blood during surgery as we drill and pin his bones. We'll need at least two units of blood at the start of surgery."

Gleason approached Dr. Hellman beside the narrow Stryker litter that the sedated president was now resting on. "Our Secret Service protocol requires that two agents with the same blood type always travel with the president. I am one match, and unfortunately the other was killed in the explosion. I will give two units of my blood for the president, and you are to use your own blood bank only in the direst emergency. Is this clear?"

The instantaneous silence in the surgical suite struck like a bolt of lightning. World-renowned surgeons like the volcanic Dr. Hellman were not accustomed to taking orders from anyone, especially a lay person with little medical background. "Are there any other special requests before we set about saving the president's arm and possibly his life?"

"Yes, just one more. It is ..."

"Mister Gleason, wait just a minute. I will have to order the lab to treat your two units of blood by a process called apheresis so that you don't go into shock. We even can collect a third unit of plasma, safely for both you and the president, by this process in case we need it. You were starting to say?"

Gleason dreaded finishing his train of thought now that Dr. Hellman was starting to thaw his frigid demeanor, but he felt obligated to have the president's operation proceed by the book — the Secret Service manual. "Dr. Hellman, Secret Service protocol requires that an armed agent be with the president at all times, and that includes being present in the operating room."

Dr. Hellman backed deliberately away from the president's litter. "Perhaps you can find another surgeon to perform this rather delicate surgery. I absolutely will not operate under the gun. Our hospital policy forbids firearms where explosive anesthetic gas is being used, specifically in operating rooms." Dr. Hellman ripped off his rubber gloves and threw them at the waste container in the far corner of the room, missing it by his usual three feet.

Dr. Hellman's steely eyes met Gleason's icy glare. Fortunately, the sedation had taken the president into never-never land, so he didn't have to referee this childish turf war. Gleason knew from

his years of high-level Washington skirmishes that you only fight
battles that you can win, and this was a no-win situation for the
president. "The Secret Service can make an exception to our normal operating procedures due to the gravity of this particular situation. The armed agent will be posted in the hall outside the operating room door. However, we will still have an unarmed agent
observing inside the operating room. Does this meet with your
approval, Doctor Hellman?"

Gleason could see the wheels in Dr. Hellman's brain slowly go
into reverse gear. "I can operate under those conditions," the doctor replied contritely. "Can we get started? I was planning to play
golf sometime before dark!"

"The final detail is that you and I will have to sign our
Secret Service form EXNOP—Exception to Normal Operating
Procedure—to cover our agreement."

"Agent Gleason," the newly exasperated Dr. Hellman bel-
lowed. "Is that all? This operating room is my office, and I usually make the rules. Perhaps you could have the terrorists sign an
EXNOP. Better yet the negligent Secret Service agents responsible
for allowing this disaster to happen should sign an EXNOP. Go
give your blood, Agent Gleason, so we can begin."

Dr. Hellman burned Gleason to his bureaucratic core, but the
doctor was correct. He himself, as the agent in charge of presidential security, should sign a file cabinet full of EXNOPs, because
the tragedies in Detroit were exceptions to every know rule of
civilized society. "I agree, Doctor, let's get going." Gleason hoped
to placate the irascible surgeon and forestall another cyclonic out-
burst as he left to find the hematology clinic for his gift of life to
the president.

XII

Azee's elevator ride down to the hospital lobby was like decending into mythical Hades. Breaching the media phalanx outside the revolving doors was more difficult than crossing the River Styx. The curious media, banned inside the hospital, encircled the main entrance like sharks in a feeding frenzy waiting to pounce on anyone, known or unknown, entering or leaving the hospital. Everyone coming and going was interrogated by the reporters as if they were major participants in this modern Greek tragedy as it unfolded.

Azee's loyal driver, Abdul, had the limousine's oversize back door open asAzee hurried past the media. He ducked and tucked, diving clumsily into its cavernous lambskin interior , which cushioned his four-point landing as he summarily ordered Abdul, "Go." The familiar plethora of switches, phones, electronics and computer equipment was calming to Azee after the traumatic experiences of the day. He picked up the black intercom phone after the limo had cleared the mass confusion of the hospital entrance. "Has there been any activity on the yellow phone today?"

"It rang four times. As instructed, I did not answer these calls." Azee strictly forbade anyone to use the yellow phone. Even with the alpha numeric activation code known only to himself, Azee was totally paranoid about anyone else having access to this phone. It was quietly rumored during coffee breaks at the GCT headquarters in Windsor that calls on the yellow phone could be rerouted through multiple satellite hookups to avoid tracing. Azee and a brilliant young electronics wizard, after putting substantial cash in the right technicians' hands, could access untraceable international satellite phone service on the yellow phone. Azee bragged that not even the White House had such a sophisticated system. He reserved this ultra-secure phone for his most sensitive projects.

"Thank you, Abdul, for being attentive to the communication systems. You know we depend on these coded calls to stay in touch around the world. Drive past the Lodge expressway bombing site if it isn't cordoned off."

Azee busied himself with the yellow telephone, entering coded numbers that retrieved the unanswered calls. As he expected, the calls came from Quebec City, Shannon, Damascus and Washington D.C. The first two calls were refueling stops on his impending flight to the family's fortified Beirut seaside villa. The *Flying Mole* had been recently retrofitted with additional fuel tanks that extended its range to include the capability of non-stop transatlantic flights. Azee had business contacts at Quebec City and Shannon that would meet him during these unneeded refueling stops to exchange information.

The calls from Damascus and Washington D.C. were also expected, and Azee would deal with them as soon as possible. The short three-ring calls were his modern Morse Code signal that a meeting was urgently required. However the hypersensitive areas of his diverse business dealings were best communicated by his own personal pony express traveling at forty thousand feet.

Azee was oblivious to the boarded up, dilapidated haunts of his childhood days in northwest Detroit as they plied the pot holed, refuse-laden surface streets. Approaching the Lodge expressway and the Six-Mile Road overpass, multiple childhood memories flashed across his mind. His attendance at Cass Tech High School was the pivotal point in his dreary inner-city youth. It afforded him a superior high school education and opened the door for him to attend the University of Michigan School of Nuclear Engineering on a full academic scholarship.

His short stocky non-swimmer physique allowed him only modest success on the competitive Cass Tech swim team. Kathy's presence on the team muted his lack of success in the pool. He was legitimately occupied with the vigorous honors academic requirements. His counselors even suggested that he could finish high school in three years. However, the swim team and the extra curricular Latin Club—and Kathy's presence there also—were like anchors holding him in high school. Kathy was elected Latin Club president, and Azee was elected vice president in charge of programs. This second-place status took an adjustment of his male ego. The Latin Club's after school meetings provided Azee with more contact with Kathy than if they were going steady, which wasn't an option for them.

His crowning achievement as V. P. in charge of programs was a formal scholastic debate about Gibbon's classic work, *The History of The Decline and Fall of The Roman Empire*. Azee fixed the selection of teams so that he and Kathy were defending the affirmative side that modern America was headed down the same path of self-destruction as the Roman Empire that Gibbons described. He smiled as he remembered this first fix to get on the same team with Kathy. Better yet, he thought, she never suspected this team fix. The debate preparation, like the swim team, allowed him to spend time with Kathy that he ordinarily wouldn't have.

They researched with passion how America's moral decline paralleled that of the once-proud Roman civilization. While studying for the debate, he found Kathy especially attractive after swim practice with her still damp blond hair falling nearly to her shoulders, framing her delicate facial features like a gold-leaf picture frame.

Once in such a mood of rapture he asked if she would go to the prom with him. Now, years later he still could vividly picture her glowing smile disappear. She spoke, with a tinge of sadness in her voice, a parentally planned, rehearsed answer, "it wouldn't be right." From that moment his debate preparation was less intense.

However, his preparation for life was jump-started at this early age. He vowed never again to allow himself to be so vulnerable when pursuing something he wanted and loved.

Nevertheless, debate night arrived sooner than he wished because he knew that after the debate he'd have less contact with Kathy. After spirited presentations by the affirmative and negative sides in an auditorium filled with proud parents and bored fellow students, a vote was taken to determine the winner. Their affirmative side won the debate by a narrow margin, and he instinctively gave Kathy a feet-off-the-floor hug that brought a guffaw of jealousy from his fellow students. Instantly he knew that he'd be chastised by his parents for his on stage exuberance. Yet the memory of Kathy being held tight to his chest for this fleeting embrace would make any parental reprimand meaningless. He hoped that Kathy wouldn't be subject to the fifth degree by her parents, anxious to know what was going on between her and her short, dark complexioned debate partner. Azee wished he could've been like a mouse in the Mideastern saying, "the walls have mice and the mice have ears."

The counterpoints of Kathy's prom rejection and winning the debate were profoundly germinal to the rest of his life. These conflicting vignettes had been permanently imprinted on his brain like a red-hot branding iron. When the tigers came at night, he continually reassured himself that all his strivings and the ultimate success of his multi-billion-dollar business empire were not a subconscious attempt to prove that he was good enough for Kathy. Azee's single-minded obsession with making it big had alienated all his high school friends except Kathy.

The view of the ravaged Lodge roadbed from the Six-Mile overpass bridge was a testimony to the efficiency of modern explosives combined with incisive knowledge, daring, and cunning. The war-torn wastelands of Beirut, where Azee met his wife, Hasnaa, were like a duplicate postcard of the spectacle Azee was viewing from the overpass. Already bulldozers and cranes were systematically stacking rubble at the fringes of the bombed out areas without removing it from the premises. Video cameras were recording every fragment.

Fire inspectors were shifting through the ashes of the bizarre house conflagration and the leveled gas station. Walking back to the limousine with Abdul, Azee felt fettered with unseen chains and controlled by an invisible power. He had become a ghoulish gawker over a madman's handiwork. He reminded himself that the president was still alive and that the love of his life was unattainable.

Azee's drive to Cripplegate, his suburban Orchard Lake estate and wildlife preserve, was a series of hushed phone calls around the world to check the status of his many construction projects. Azee was a master consensus builder, as witnessed by the fact that his corporate conglomerate crossed all national borders as well as all religious and ethnic differences. When bidding on and ultimately winning multimillion dollar contracts, Azee was the ultimate corporate mogul. His word and handshake were better than an attorney-drafted contract the size of a phone book. His Fortune 500 construction firm specialized in difficult international projects that everyone else backed away from. Azee's background in nuclear engineering allowed him to consult on the construction of nuclear power plants when it was still politically feasible to build them. His patented laser alignment instrumentation was a sine qua non for the critical accuracy needed to build safe nuclear power plants, where price considerations took a back seat to safety. Azee's firm profited beyond his wildest dreams on these early projects.

The changing political climate following the 1986 Chernobyl disaster brought a trend away from building nuclear power plants and toward tearing them down. Azee's skills were equally useful and profitable for that purpose as he was wont to say, "the pays the same whether you build them up or tear them down." Along the way, he developed contacts with independent arms merchants who roamed the globe seeking to buy, sell, or barter for any "refuse" from a dismantled nuclear plant.

Azee had just hung up the yellow phone only to hear its distinctive high-pitched ring. Few of his friends and high level business associates had this secure phone number, so he knew that the call was important. "Hello. Azee. President Taylor here."

"Hello, Mister President. Where're you calling from?"

"From the White House. Baby-sitting Jason and Eric. I can't believe that my first official duty as president was to break up a food fight. How are you doing?"

Azee, quickly remembering his boast that he had a more secure communication system than the White House, decided that he should still be guarded in his response to a call from the White House. "Physically okay. I was in the head below deck, safe from the explosion. The president will be okay except for his broken arm. Wish I could say the same for Kathy and the baby."

"Things could be worse. The president could have been killed. The media and the people on the hill will make political hay out of this tragedy. There'll be a new Warren-style commission appointed to investigate this whole damn thing."

"How long do you expect to be president?"

"Thank God I should only have to baby-sit these kids for twenty-four hours. Forty-eight hours max. No one mentioned baby-sitting in the vice president's job description."

"Assuming the president survives in good health, this tragedy should help your re-election. There'll be a lot of sympathy votes for you and the president in November."

"Sympathy? Who the hell wants sympathy? I agreed to be on the ticket for this second term only if I could resign after two years. Archibald knows that I don't want to be president, even for these twenty-four hours, and that I plan to go to work for you, as we've discussed. I need to make some serious money for my retirement years."

A startled pause filled the phone line between the acting president in the White House and Azee in his limousine as he approached his estate's guardhouse at the start of the long, serpentine driveway. "Now Mister President, don't be making long range plans like that. Let's just survive the next few days. The future always takes care of itself."

"I'm just a little overwhelmed by today's events. What are your plans?"

"I'll be returning to Beirut tomorrow. It's Jamal's ninth birthday.

I'll return in a few days via Damascus. Perhaps I can stop in D.C. for lunch with an ex-president on my return."

"I sure hope I'm an ex-president by then. My goal is to have the shortest presidency on record. Whoever's responsible for my acting presidency should be shot for the grief it caused an old bureaucrat who wants nothing more than to accumulate a few more years on his federal pension. Sure, let's do lunch at Sequoia. The Potomac will be spectacular with the fall colors."

"I'll call when I know my final travel plans. Good night, Mister President." Just as Azee hung up the yellow phone, Abdul braked to a stop at Cripplegate's impressive guardhouse.

"Mister Azee, we were so worried when we heard about the *Aqua Mole* blowing up," Aadam, the uniformed guard, said as he peered into the partially opened window of the limousine.

"As you see, I am alive, a very lucky man. Anything unusual happen here?"

"Nothing except for a pushy television reporter who demanded to do a live broadcast from inside Cripplegate. I sent him away, but maybe next time I won't be so nice. The yellow phone rang four times, but I ignored it. Your line from Beirut is activated. Ring from the house if you need anything."

Azee was pleased to find Aadam, his chief of security at Cripplegate, on duty after such a pressure-filled day. A former special forces commando, Aadam was forever indebted to Azee for rescuing him from his heroin habit on the streets of inner city Detroit. Azee insisted and verified with random drug testing that all his security personnel practice complete sobriety as a condition of continued employment. Aadam's new home was the guardhouse, which was like the control room of a modern high-tech prison with bulletproof walls and windows. A bombproof armory in the basement of the guardhouse, though at present only modestly stocked, was off limits to everyone in Azee's employ except Aadam and Abdul, who had contingency plans for every emergency. Waving goodbye to Aadam, Abdul slowly drove up the estate's tree-lined twisting driveway and across the draw bridge to let Azee get out under the covered portico protecting the massive, hand-carved front door. "I'll be available in the transportation garage apartment tonight, Mister Azee," Abdul reassured Azee as he stepped out of the limousine.

XIII

The president was usually a fitful sleeper with the hot line at his elbow, but the surgical sedation and the 25th Amendment provided the surcease of duties needed for a restful night's sleep.

"Good morning, sir. How are you feeling?"

"It's nice to start the day with your familiar face, Gleason. Someone who isn't going to poke me with a needle. I slept pretty well, but this damn cast kept me from moving around. I understand that I received your blood at the time of surgery. How are you feeling after this donation?"

"No worse the wear, sir. It's the least I can do for you." Guilt engulfed Gleason for breaching his sworn responsibility to see that such tragic incidents never happened in the first place.

Fortunately the president quickly asked, "How's Kathy this morning?"

"I was just in her room. Unfortunately, there's been no improvement, but she apparently had a stable night. A nurse gave me the first lady's personal effects, including her wedding ring."

"Just leave them with her secretary when we get back to the White House. I doubt she'll ever wear the ring again."

"They also found her squeezing this small piece of lead. Do you have any idea what it is?"

"I sure as hell don't recognize it. What are those marks on it?"

"I don't have a clue. I wanted to check with you in case it was something personal between you and the first lady before I send it to the FBI lab. Her doctors want a conference as soon as possible this morning."

"I'm not going anywhere, for God"s sake! How long is the 25th Amendment in effect? I feel pretty good right now."

"Twenty-four hours is the first request. Taylor apparently didn't sleep well in the White House last night, either. When you get older you always seem to prefer your own bed, so I'm sure he'll be happy to return home tonight."

"Of course. The old fart hates to put himself out unless I directly ask him. You remember that engraved plaque the staff gave him at our first Christmas party in the White House? 'Sauve Qui Peut'? He thought that personalized plaque was so nice, until Kathy translated it for him:'Every Man for Himself.' If he didn't have such strong ties to the money people on Wall Street, I'd have kicked his ass off the ticket this second time around. I'll live with his self-centered senility for a couple more years before he resigns to go to work for Azee. Notify Washington that I will reassume the presidency when this initial twenty-four-hour period expires this afternoon."

"The nation will be grateful to have you back in the oval office, Mister President. Taylor called an emergency cabinet meeting late yesterday, more for public relations than to discuss the three bombings."

"Three?"

"There was a third explosion of a stalled van on the Ambassador Bridge just seconds before the dockside explosion at the yacht. On seeing that explosion from the flying bridge, I started to help the first lady get down to the deck from her chair when the Canadian limousine exploded, catapulting everyone except the first lady from the bridge into the river. She would have been better off being thrown into the water than hitting her head on the railing."

"Let's not go there, Gleason. You were doing your job trying to get the first lady into a safer position. I'm grateful that you were there to attend to her."

"Thank you, sir. I will spend the rest of my life to my last breath righting this terrible wrong."

Gleason didn't see the need to inform the president of Taylor's first and hopefully last cabinet meeting, where he essentially fired Secretary of the Treasury Bart Jameson by asking for his resignation. Jameson had been the president's friend and personal banker on Wall Street. Gleason knew that the president would be upset to hear that Jameson was being blamed for the tragedies in Detroit simply because the Secret Service is under the Department of the Treasury's control.

Gleason's information on the firing of his boss was fragmentary, but his imagination filled in between the lines. Taylor, in front of the entire cabinet, humiliated Jameson by asking, "How could you allow the president and the first lady to be bombed?"

A deadly silence impaled the cabinet room as Jameson slowly stood up at the far end of the polished cherrywood conference table to address the acting president: "Brownie, Eis Aidou." Only he and Taylor would know what his parting shot meant. The Greek phrase had been their old fraternity password. It meant "Go to hell." During Jameson's freshman year in college, Taylor had been his almighty fraternity president and he the lowly pledge. Taylor, to Jameson's knowledge, was always called Brownie because he was known for "brown-nosing" his professors.

"Jameson, I am sure the president will want your resignation on his desk when he arrives back in Washington."

Rather than take the tunnel back to his Treasury Building office, Jameson elected to walk down the long White House driveway to Pennsylvania Avenue. Leaving the White House grounds, probably for the last time as Secretary of the Treasury, he saluted the Marine sentries in the Pennsylvania Avenue guardhouse. They returned crisp military salutes. He briskly crossed Pennsylvania Avenue to find a bench in the far corner of Lafayette Park, a democracy-by-protest billboard enclave that used to be part of the

White House's formerly expansive front lawn. It was his favorite spot in all of Washington. The always-present boisterous protestors with their hand-lettered card board signs contrasted starkly with the governmental flamboyances of power all around them. Pausing in the shadow cast by the statue of Andrew Jackson wearing his stove pipe top hat, sitting on his majestically rearing horse, the view of the White House through a field of multi-message protest billboards was always the reality check Jameson needed.

The weathered inscription at the base of the Jackson memorial, "Our Federal Union Must Be Preserved," many times had been the catalyst that brought him back to continue serving his long-term friend, the president. Now the Federal Union was tarnished and fragmented by the vindictive acting president. This time, thanks to Taylor, bridges were burned, imploded like Detroit. The president had Jameson's undying loyalty, but Taylor always brought out the worst in him.

XIV

Azee called his Windsor office on arising and learned that both the tunnel and the Ambassador Bridge connecting Canada and the United States were closed by executive order of the acting president. Azee requested that his corporate helicopter be dispatched to pick him up at Cripplegate for his usual airborne commute to the office. Waiting for the helicopter, he made a number of phone calls around the world to check on the progress of his diverse projects. Azee's project managers were always, at any time of the day or night, to be available to talk to their boss. Since Azee usually called during his normal business hours, his managers had to expect most of their calls would be in the middle of the night half way around the world. Global Construction Technology functioned on Azee's time clock, and pity the employee who was unavailable when the boss called.

Azee took such good care of his key people that no one had voluntarily left the employ of the company in recent memory. There were occasionally deaths and forced retirements of some formerly "important partners," as Azee liked to refer to his workers, but those who stayed were promised and given remuneration substantially higher than the industry average.

While boarding the helicopter at the estate's helipad, Azee

instructed Aadam that no one was to be allowed on the property for two weeks while he was gone. Aadam nodded his assent, knowing that he would need to cancel school field trips and senior citizen tours that were already scheduled for the next two weeks.

Azee ordered his pilot to take a flight path over the Lodge expressway. He could see numerous video cameras recording the tediously slow removal of debris. Backhoes were unearthing a long concrete storm sewer line from the destroyed roadbed toward the bombed-out house overlooking the catastrophe below.

There seemed to be more activity at the site of the house explosion than there was in the demolished roadbed where the president had been within feet of eternity. As they flew away from the Lodge bombing zone toward the yacht, Detroit's autumnal splendor unfolded below them, masking the terrorism that had seared the area only yesterday. Armed guards cordoned off the charred limousine frame and the bobbing, windowless *Aqua Mole*. He was surprised at the size of the large crater where the Canadian limousine had been parked. There had been so much confusion and hysteria yesterday and he had been so thankful to be alive and unharmed that he had failed to notice the four-foot-deep bomb crater, which was impressive when viewed from the air.

The flight near the center span of the Ambassador Bridge revealed a scene in stark contrast to the previous picture at the Lodge expressway. Cement and blacktop trucks worked feverishly to put down a new roadbed in the area of the explosion so the vital international link could be back in service when the border was reopened. The sheer weight of the heavy construction vehicles on the bridge indicated a lack of serious structural damage to the bridge from the exploding van. It was obvious that much less explosive power had been deployed in the van on the bridge than in the limousine beside the *Aqua Mole*. Azee guessed that most of the van's explosive forces were harmlessly dissipated into the air 150-feet above the Detroit River and not onto the bridge structure.

When the headquarters of Global Construction Technology moved from Detroit to Windsor two years earlier, the news commentators explained that the more favorable tax structure and the newly liberalized workman's compensation laws in Canada would allow GCT to grow more rapidly. GCT was also bidding on some major construction projects along the Saint Lawrence Seaway, especially at the port of Montreal, that required the bidding company to be Canadian. The Canadian government embraced the relocation of GCT with unbridled enthusiasm and adopted a laissez-faire attitude toward all projects not directly affecting Canada itself.

Azee welcomed the corporate relocation to Canada as a chance to escape the increasing scrutiny of the United States government, especially the omnipresent IRS and the ever-inquisitive State Department monitoring Azee's foreign contacts. GCT's contract through its independent Lebonese subsidiary with the Iraqi government to build a large underground grain storage facility near Baghdad probably would not have been possible if GCT was still an American company.

Timing is everything in business and politics, and Azee moved GCT to Canada at the most propitious time. With a separate corporation running each one of his foreign construction projects, the paper trail leading back to GCT and ultimately to Azee himself was serpentine at best, and the relocation to Canada would create a few more dead ends for snooping investigators and overzealous regulators.

Azee wasn't prepared for the public outcry in Michigan opposing his corporate move to Canada. He doubled his personal public relations efforts to counteract this new negative corporate image. His desire to be well perceived inspired him to open and expand his Cripplegate wildlife preserve to the public as well as to host the first family aboard the *Aqua Mole*. Azee decided he must try to distance himself as far as possible from the *Aqua Mole* bombing, even though it happened on his yacht, to avoid rekindling the old negative publicity about GCT's move.

After a brief stop at GCT headquarters to retrieve documents he would need during his two-week absence, Azee planned to leave immediately for his villa in Beirut, removing himself from center stage while the international drama unfolded. The helipad on the roof of the GCT headquarters was a testimony to Azee's newfound Canadian political clout. The neighbors in the adjacent highrise condominium buildings on the Detroit River had objected vehemently to this intrusion on their airspace by the roof top GCT helipad, but Azee had held firm in insisting on the rooftop location instead of a conventional ground-level location because of the prominent world leaders that visit GCT headquarters to review their construction projects.

Azee and his staff of engineers had elevated the science of building security to a new level in their GCT office complex. The austere poured-concrete exterior, resembling the Renaissance Center across the river, belied the star wars technology on the interior. Every inch was monitored by motion and sound detectors as well as video cameras.

The terrorist-proof building's control room resembled the pentagon's war command post in every way except the ability to launch nuclear weapons. Seated at the control console, surrounded by the banks of blinking lights and glaring monitors, Azee could instantly span all time zones worldwide to contact his workers, or he could identify anyone entering the lobby downstairs. The array of antennas and satellite dishes on the rooftop would do the CIA proud, though they called for an extra measure of skill from the helicopter pilots who had to take off and land there.

Abdul landed with surgical precision, and Azee jumped from the helicopter while the main rotor was spinning slowly to a stop. Ducking his head needlessly below the still-moving blade, he hurried to the roof top entrance and inserted his photo ID card into the electronic slot that would summon his private elevator.

Once inside, Azee punched in a sequence of numbers that told the elevator to descend to the subterranean vault that was his private, personal domain. Azee had insisted during construction visits to the Bloomington, Indiana, Otis Elevator factory that he and his staff would do the secret programming necessary for this subterranean descent. Otis officials reluctantly agreed to let him configure the elevator "any damn way he pleased," as long as he paid the exorbitant special order invoice before installation. Beside the usual integral combination locks on the glistening stainless steel door, for which only Azee had the combinations, a high-tech pupillary scanning device verified that indeed Azee alone was seeking access to the ultra secret vault.

Turning on the light switch inside the vault also activated a time-delayed bomb and incendiary device that would destroy the intruder as well as the inside of the vault unless it was deactivated within ten seconds by entering the proper code into an alphanumeric pad. Azee could also activate the doomsday system remotely via satellite and a built-in seven-day self-destruct feature would automatically destroy the inside of the vault if it wasn't reset within the seven-day period. Azee felt secure in knowing that if he was detained anywhere or met an untimely demise, his personal memorabilia would become charred history. Azee tried not to dwell on this apocalyptic scenario, but he felt compelled to either protect or destroy the contents of his secret vault no matter the cost.

When he entered the vault after deactivating the doomsday system, his eye caught a yellowing newspaper on top of a pile of cardboard filing boxes that had the headline, "DISFIGURED CORPSE FOUND." It brought back a recollection of the weekend two years ago when he and a single technician, Pierre, had installed and activated the vault security system.

For the only time in his adult life, he was totally cut off from the outside world. Azee was so paranoid that he had all phone lines disconnected for the installation weekend. Pierre also reluctantly surrendered his cell phone to Azee when he arrived that Friday afternoon. He did not let Pierre out of his sight, even for bathroom breaks. Over the two days they worked, ate and slept inside the new GCT office without contacting another soul.

Pierre had supervised many of GCT's most sensitive projects around the world. He grew restless if he stayed too long in his frigid bachelor home north of Quebec City. His involvement with the upstart radical wing of the Quebec Separatist movement started as a pastime between overseas assignments for GCT.

Azee had imported Pierre and some of his more radical confreres on midnight speedboat runs from Canada to his Drummond Island property in northern Michigan. Their job had been to test explosives. He had permits to do blasting on his property to build roads through the unforgiving dolomite so local suspicion wasn't unduly aroused. Over their nightly beers at Suny's, the main Drummond Island watering hole, the bored locals questioned Azee's sanity when he had a hundred-yard-long stretch of one-foot-thick reinforced concrete road poured on top of three-foot-diameter cement drainage pipes and then blown up for no apparent reason.

Pierre was viewed as a *grandpere* of the increasingly violent separatist movement and found himself being asked to give live demonstrations on the deployment of explosives. Azee became concerned that these live demonstrations would come to the attention of the Royal Canadian Mounted Police. After the Drummond Island road demolition tests and the office vault project were completed, Pierre had become expendable.

As Azee struggled to carry three identical black briefcases out of the vault to the elevator, he was startled by the stacato sounds of bouncing marbles hitting the concrete floor. He saw that they were actually white, silver and gold teeth that had been knocked from their plastic jewelry box atop a wooden file cabinet. Not bothering to pick them up, he absent mindedly pushed them into the corner with his foot without wondering why he had morbidly saved Pierre's teeth. Except for paper clips, the gold and silver teeth were the only incombustible materials in the vault.

All storage boxes were cardboard, and the one file cabinet was of the antique wooden variety. To quench his insatiable paranoia, Azee had inserted a sealed one-liter plastic bottle of gasoline into each file box so it would melt down in the doomsday conflagration and ignite the contents of the box from the inside. Before securing the vault door, he opened each briefcase to verify its contents.

In each one, rubber bands held neat bundles of Canadian, Irish or Iraqi currency. Azee put the three briefcases on the polished marble floor of the elevator while he reset the vault's doomsday security system.

The short elevator ride back to the rooftop helipad gave Azee a few seconds to recall this secretive weekend operation with Pierre, whom he liked to remember by his depersonalizing nickname of "Double E," denoting his experise in electricity and explosives.

When Azee and Pierre had boarded the *Flying Mole* after their intensive weekend work session to drop Pierre back home at Quebec City, Azee gave his pilot a fatal thumbs-down hand signal. Azee did not like to exercise his *"ius gladii,"* as he chose to call the power of the sword, for he knew the immutable fact of history that those who live by the sword, die by the sword.

The elevator deposited Azee and his three briefcases on the rooftop helipad for the short flight to the *Flying Mole* waiting at Windsor International Airport. The pilot, Taajud-Deen, had already filed the flight plan: depart Windsor, refuel Quebec City, refuel Shannon, arrive Beirut.

XV

"Mister President, we have spent the night consulting with medical experts around the world on our two patients," Dr. Willard Mann said, standing at the foot of the president's bed.

"What do you mean two patients? I'm feeling fine. As a matter of fact I'll be reassuming the presidency this afternoon. Let's leave my condition out of the discussion."

"Mister President, I am referring to the first lady and your premature baby." Dr. Mann, the world-renowned trauma surgeon, had been brought in from neighboring Ann Arbor to coordinate the first lady's medical care. As with most doctors dealing with instantaneous life-and-death decisions, forbearance and patience were in short supply.

"Of course, of course. Please go on."

"We wish we could limit this discussion to your wife, but that's not possible, unless you elect to terminate a still-healthy pregnancy. Our options are quite limited. First, we could do nothing and let nature take its course. This would result in the certain death of both patients. Second, we could perform a C-section to deliver the premature baby. The first lady's condition is so precarious that she probably would not survive this procedure to save the baby. Our third and final option is to try to maintain the first lady's vital functions as long as possible to allow the baby to mature more."

The morgue-like silence in the room was interrupted only by the beeping of the president's heart monitor. Dr. Mann's concise summary of the crisis reminded the president of a security council briefing in which all the options are bad. "Is Kathy essentially dead?" was the only question he could get out.

A different, less authoritarian voice answered from the opposite end of the semi- circle at the foot of the bed. "Your wife still has vital life functions necessary for the continued nourishment of the baby," Dr. Cecelia Robinson said. "In many severe trauma cases there is what we call the lethal triad: hypothermia, acidosis and coagulopathy. We are fortunate with the first lady's case that..."

"Excuse me, doctors," the president interrupted, "but I'm too out of it with my pain medication to understand all the medical terms. My basic question is, will Kathy ever wake up from her coma?"

The doctors in the room all silently looked at each other until finally Dr. Mann took a step toward the bed and rested his hand on the president's casted left arm. "I assume, sir, you want the absolute truth about the first lady's condition. She has no brain wave activity, and her breathing is being assisted by a respirator. She has a Glascow Coma Score of three. The longer she remains comatose without brain wave activity, the less chance there is for even a partial recovery. But we're less than twenty-four hours into her coma. With the baby present, we cannot use our usual medications to minimize brain swelling."

Dr. Robinson noticed the president's eyes glazing over. She handed him a tissue. "Damn," the president thought to himself, "if I ever need someone to help me decide to drop a nuclear bomb, I must contact this Dr. Mann. He is all business." Finally the president broke the silence. "You mean if the baby wasn't present, Kathy would have a better chance of recovering from the coma?"

"Theoretically the answer is yes. We could use sedating medications to decrease her brain swelling beyond the surgical decompression we did yesterday. But the basic question remains whether she's also too traumatized with high spinal cord and brain stem injury to recover at all."

"No buts about it. Let's abort the baby and give Kathy every possible chance to recover," the president hopefully spoke.

Gleason nervously shifted his weight from one leg to the other as the next round of silence became as oppressive as a funeral pall engulfing the room. Gleason had learned not to respond immediately to the president's impulsive decisions. He prayed that the doctors would keep their silence and allow the president to talk his way out of the corner he'd backed himself into. Gleason remembered a quip President Reagan had made during an important strategy session, "There are simple answers. There just aren't any easy ones."

The president was obviously struggling with the ramifications of his rash answer. Then, as Gleason expected, he broke the paralyzing silence. "Doctors, I have always practiced the politics of the possible. You are asking me to deal with the impossible, where there are only bad answers. My re-election is only weeks away, and I don't think the majority of Americans would be sympathetic to a late-term c-section or abortion without any assurance that it would help and not harm the first lady. And just between us, the baby was Kathy's reward for letting me run for re-election. I cannot allow anything to happen to the baby this close to the election. Is that clear to everyone in this room?"

Gleason smiled imperceptibly, realizing that the true president was back in charge. Dr. Mann, still touching the president's arm, stated matter-of-factly, "We are right back where we started. The first lady's body has been maximally traumatized resulting in coma and paralysis. We must arrive at some treatment decisions."

"Paralysis?" the president exploded as he bolted upright in his bed. The startled Dr. Mann instinctively retreated a step from the bedside. "Why wasn't I told of her paralysis?"

"I'm very sorry, Mister President," a conciliatory Dr. Robinson replied. "We assumed that someone last night mentioned the possibility of paralysis anytime there is such severe head and neck trauma. It does not change anything in our treatment plan except for one possibility."

"What the hell is that one possibility? Are there any other surprises?"

"We spent most of last night searching for even the most obscure treatment that would offer hope," Dr. Mann said, nervously rocking from side to side." The only treatment suggestion that would be harmless to the first lady and the fetus and yet still offers a glimmer of hope for improving her comatose condition comes from doctors at Bethesda Naval Hospital. There are no guarantees that their treatment will be effective. Our group opinion is that we have nothing to lose by trying their suggestion."

"Does this treatment have a name, or is it stamped 'top secret' by some promotion-hungry navy medical officer?"

Relieved smiles crossed the faces at the foot of the bed. "No, sir, there is no secret about the treatment. It's called hyperbaric oxygen therapy. It has been used for a number of years on stroke victims. The patient is put in a pressurized environment while oxygen is forced into her whole body, hopefully resulting in increased oxygen saturation of the red blood cells," Doctor Mann said.

The pensive president was trying to absorb this single ray of hope. "Is she stable enough to transport to Bethesda?"

"Yes, we could move her back to Washington. I will personally accompany the medevac flight."

"That's very kind of you, Doctor Mann. Will this hyperbaric oxygen treatment be safe for the baby? With the election so close, we have to be careful not to do anything the media can construe as hurting the baby."

"They will certainly use fetal monitors and other tests to be sure the baby is safe. All of us in this room will have to defer to your navy doctors as the experts in this treatment. Only you can decide on the political timing and consent to this procedure for the first lady," Doctor Robinson said.

The silence threw the issue back to the president, who brought his right arm over his abdomen to help move his heavy cast to a more comfortable position. The semicircle at the president's bedside silently rocked back and forth in unison waiting for his decision. "This tragic incident has caused a groundswell of support for my re-election campaign," he announced. "I've always believed that preserving the status quo is an admirable position when the alternatives are unclear."

"Certainly no one would fault you for rejecting this somewhat unknown treatment," Dr. Robinson interjected. "Perhaps a perspective somewhat different than the political one might be, what do you think your wife would want if she could talk? Better yet, what would you want for yourself if you were comatose?"

"I have no doubt that I myself would want any treatment that offered even the slightest chance of a cure. I am certain that Kathy would feel the same way. Can we start making arrangements to transport her?" The reinvigorated president again sat upright in bed, but his morning orthostatic hypotension forced him to quickly recline before he fainted.

Everyone in the room nodded in relieved assent as they filed out. Gleason was last in line. He smiled, conscious that the president had made a medical decision with political overtones. "Is there anything you need for the return flight home, Mister President?"

"I don't know where my clothes ended up. I will certainly need clean underwear. Maybe I should just wear this damn hospital gown with my ass hanging out. You had better find me some clothes. Especially underwear."

"We can certainly find some clothes for you, Mister President."

The president tried to sit up in his bed as he shouted at the departing Gleason, "What about Jason and Eric? How are they doing? Do you think we should have them meet us when we land at Andrews or at the Bethesda hospital?" He collapsed back onto the bed as if inundated by a tidal wave of guilt at his lack of consideration for his two young sons.

"The boys are fine, Mister President. But they keep asking how soon before their mom and dad are coming home."

"Poor kids. They're too young to understand what it means

to be president. All they want is their mom and dad back home. I really don't want them to see all the commotion connected with unloading Kathy off the plane. I would like to see them as soon as we land, though..."

The brief silence reminded Gleason of what he liked most about the president. There was a sensitivity buried deeply in the man's publicly masked soul though it always took a major event to spring it free from the recesses of his perpetually political psyche. "We could have them come up the front steps into the plane's forward cabin, while the medical people bring Kathy out the rear cargo door."

"Good idea. We have to be careful with the press. I don't want to ban them completely. Don't forget that in this election year everything we do faces double scrutiny. How would it look if I deserted Kathy, even to be with the boys?"

"I've requested that the bare skeleton press pool continue to cover the story. So far the press has cooperated with our requests. They are preoccupied with the bombings. I'll ask that the White House staff take all the necessary steps to get ready for your homecoming."

XVI

Hushed calls on the yellow phone usually filled Azee's short helicopter commute from the riverside GCT offices to the Windsor International Airport. Today, though, he pensively concluded his only call as the chopper was touching down on the tarmac beside the *Flying Mole*. It ended with Azee's assurance that he would be arriving alone in Quebec City for a layover that would be only long enough to refuel and use the restroom. Although the *Flying Mole* was retrofitted with auxiliary long-range fuel tanks that made nonstop transatlantic flights possible, Azee often had business to conduct along the way that allowed for refueling stops.

Disembarking from the helicopter, Azee gave one of the identical briefcases to Taajud-Deen, the pilot, to stow in the exterior luggage compartment of the *Flying Mole*.

Azee, ascending the narrow steps to the elegant but confined cabin, gave Taajud-Deen a subtle thumbs-down signal, indicating the fate of the passenger who was already seated in his oversized recliner seat.

He shook the man's rough, calloused hand. "Henri, it's nice of you to join me on this short flight to Quebec City," Azee said as he sank into his seat to the right of his guest.

"*Mais oui.* Your offer is a welcome gift of time. Returning home by boat would have taken days, especially with the unpredictable fall storms on the lake. And all the highways and railroads out of Windsor are roadblocked to look out for the bombers."

"Have you told anyone of this new travel arrangement?" Azee asked with apparent nonchalance. "Your people are expecting you home in a few days, as usual after an operation?"

"I've told no one of this sudden change in my return plans, as you instructed. My main concern is that my fellow motor pool workers in the Ottawa garage will miss me after my two week vacation is over. Then they'll start piecing things together faster than they ordinarily would."

"Toward the end of your two week vacation call them with some story about needing to extend your vacation due to a death in the family. This will give you additional time to disappear before they focus on you as a suspect."

The Bombardier Global Express's take-off was like a rocket launch as the passengers were quickly thrust back into the plush seat backs of the oversized chairs. "I forgot how much fun this sled ride is—especially the takeoff," Henri commented as the *Flying Mole* began to level off.

"Almost as much fun as your snowmobile racing days with the Bombardier Ski Doo team," Azee quipped.

"Better than that," Henri mused, one corner of his mouth lifting in a tentative, unaccustomed smile. He was remembering the 1984 Soo 500 Enduro, a big snowmobile race held annually in Sault Ste. Marie, Michigan, where Azee had found him sabotaging the rivals' racing sleds. Recognizing the rare combination of mechanical talent and flexible ethics, Azee never alerted the race authorities. Offered a clandestine position on the construction tycoon's cash-only payroll, Henri was still among Azee's top operatives after ten years.

Azee unfastened his seat belt, stood and surveyed the passenger cabin. If it had been fitted out with airliner-style first-class seating, it would have carried up to 19 people, but in its custom club configuration it could seat nine, including three on a long divan that could fold out into a king-size bed. Each seat had its own table and electric plugs. Built into the wall to the right of the cockpit door was a revolving fine art gallery, where Azee could select from a range of paintings to suit his clients' preferences. From the current selection, it was obvious that the *Flying Mole* had just made or was about to make a trip to Japan. It was a depiction of the despair and desolation of bombed-out Hiroshima—a study by the mid-20th-century artist Iri Maruki for one of the 22-foot-tall murals in an anti-war museum in Saitamna, Japan. Despairing lovers lit by an eerie pink-orange glow contrasted with the pristine beauty of Lake Ontario below. The cabin filled with an oppressive silence.

In a low, calm voice, Azee mused, "You're a dinosaur, Henri. Perhaps I am too. A dying species. Together we have climbed the mountain. The meadows, valleys and lakes are below us. Our work is done. Sometimes our most obscure actions are closest to the truth of our being."

Azee's eyes hardened like cast iron and locked straight ahead. Only the whine of the jet engines covered the sudden silence. Henri began to shift and twist against his restraining shoulder harness. His hands reached down to release his seat belt and shoulder harness buckle. It wouldn't release. He tried again with no better results. He wiggled it and jerked at it. No luck.

Azee moved behind Henri's seat. His lips moved within an inch of the Frenchman's right ear. "You blew it!" Azee whispered. "You really blew it, you bastard!" His voice burst out furiously. "You are supposed to know explosives. That is why I pay you and the separatist so damn much money." Azee kicked the briefcase at his feet.

A terrified look appeared on Henri's face as all color drained from it. He could not find words to speak.

"Your assignment was to terminate the president. The first lady was not supposed to be hurt. But she was, and you know why, don't you, Henri? Your proportions of Semtex and gasoline were wrong, boosting the explosive power far above what was needed. Do you agree?"

"I don't... I don't know. I did it the way I always do..."

"Fifty feet from the limousine, where the Aqua Mole was docked, the shock wave should not have been severe enough to do that kind of damage. The bomb crater looks like a nuclear warhead went off. Henri, you used to be an artist of making bombs. Now you've lost your caution, all for a more spectacular bang so the news media will think the Front de Liberation Quebecois is still a force to be feared. But those days are long gone."

"It will never happen again, sir, I swear..." Henri shrugged his shoulders under the taut harness.

"Indeed, it will not. And do you know why not?"

Wide-eyed, Henri shook his head.

"Of course you don't," Azee continued. "Nobody does. You see, the first lady and I are lifelong friends. Many years ago, I took her virginity, and she took mine. Whatever has happened since, that makes us lifelong soulmates. This is a fact no one else must ever know. So, Henri, why do you think I'm explaining this to you now?"

"Because you know I always keep your secrets, Azee. I always do."

"No, that's not it."

Azee sat and flipped a pair of switches on the electrical panel hidden on the right side of his chair. They could both hear a generator starting in the cargo compartment below. Henri writhed.

Azee relaxed as he continued talking. "Your small diversionary strike could have killed me. It might as well have. You have left my dearest friend a total vegetable."

The lights inside the *Flying Mole* flickered and grew dimmer. Four-hundred-and-forty volts of electricity surged into the shoulder harness and raced through Henri's instantaneously rigid body to complete the electrical circuit in the chair back.

Azee pulled down a blue plastic tarp from an overhead bin and laid it out so he could roll Henri's lifeless body onto it and drag it toward the rear of the cabin, where he could perform oral surgery on Henri with a pair of channel-lock pliers. If the bomber's shattered, decomposed corpse was ever recovered, identification would be difficult. Such was his rage that Azee had contemplated beheading the corpse, as he and Kathy had seen in a museum of early Roman history in Bath, during their long-ago high-school field trip. Though a beheaded corpse might be more classically correct and more difficult to identify, Azee thought about the gruesome consequences to his plane's interior. Instead, as a parting symbolic token, he inserted an unmarked fragment of Roman lead that Kathy and he had excavated in their Bath archeological dig into Henri's now-bloody, edentulous mouth.

Once these messy unpleasantries were taken care of, Azee sent Taajud-Deen a coded signal over the intercom. The pilot descended over the deepest waters of Lake Ontario. At 5000 feet, a hydraulic trap door opened into a ramp in the floor at the rear of the fuselage. The trap door had come built into the plane when Azee had bought it from the Bombardier factory, where it had been preordered by a drug smuggler who, he suspected, had intended to use it to jettison bales of contraband into the sea to be picked up by Cigarette boats in the dead of night. By the time the plane was built, though, the buyer was in no position to take delivery in a federal prison. Azee had bought the plane thinking that the ramp would be useful for moving his laser equipment on and off the plane for his far flung construction projects. Only later did he discovere other uses for it.

Azee wrapped Henri's naked corpse in the tarp, dragged it to the ramp, and gave it a shove. The corpse tumbled like falling Icarus, arms flailing and legs akimbo, and was gone from sight before it struck the frigid, unforgiving surface of Lake Ontario.

The *Flying Mole*'s refueling stop in Quebec City was completed as quickly as the ground crew could work. Descending the narrow airplane stairs with one of the briefcases, Azee cautiously scanned the handful of people on the tarmac, hoping not to see any uniformed police officers. Everyone was wearing mechanics' and service technicians' oil-stained blue coveralls. Taajud-Deen, stayed outside to supervise the refueling and to sign the necessary government paperwork.

Carrying his briefcase, Azee headed into the small fixed-base terminal and entered the smelly restroom, where he locked the door behind him. He shut himself in the end stall. Immediately, a matching briefcase slid under the partition from the next stall. Picking it up, Azee determined that it was empty, or at least much lighter than the briefcase he was going to exchange for it. "Three million Canadian," Azee said quietly. "As agreed."

"*Merci*. The operation went off as planned?" the anonymous, heavily accented, voice asked from the other stall.

"Yes, but with bad results. Don't worry, I'm paying you anyway. The three explosives teams showed cooperation and teamwork. No one group alone could have achieved the same results."

"Is Henri still returning by boat?"

"He is, but he's likely to have a very slow, wet journey because of the storms on the lake. Henri must keep a low profile when he returns, which will be difficult for him. It's crucial for everyone that he hibernate for the winter. Please convey this message to him in the strongest possible terms when you first meet him. Stay seated and count your money. Give me time to get airborne before you leave the restroom."

The nonstop transatlantic flight to Ireland took about six hours. Azee didn't sleep but tapped his fingers on the armrest and occasionally rose to pace up and down the short length of the passenger cabin.

During their stop in Shannon, a popular refueling point for corporate jets crisscrossing the Atlantic, the briefcase exchange was repeated. The heavily brogued Irish accomplice asked Azee to wait while he verified that the amount in the briefcase was exactly one million pounds.

"My men in Corktown told me you have unmatched skills and cunning," the anonymous voice said as he finally clicked shut the latches on the brief case. "Who else could have engineered this total cooperation from such a disparate group of madmen?"

"Getting people to work together is my business. I hope your operatives didn't cut too wide a swath in Corktown. Your men showed admirable professionalism in setting off their diversionary bomb on the bridge. I'm sure that they'll use the same discretion in getting to Toronto for their flight home."

"Thank you for the compliment and also for the briefcase. It will help further our own causes. Money is the magic elixir for our organization. My people are car bomb experts. Be sure to contact us again when you need a precise surgical strike anywhere in the world."

"So I've learned—too late. The minor damage to the bridge is already being repaired. The limousine explosion rigged by the Quebec team was excessive. I wish I had used you for that part of the operation as well. Nevertheless, I will not be in touch with you for at least three months." Azee gave the flimsy metal restroom partition a goodbye knuckle rap as he reached down to retrieve the empty briefcase.

The three-and-a-half-hour journey over the alpine spine of Europe to Beirut was restful for Azee, as his unpleasant business was behind him for a few days. He eagerly anticipated the reunion with his children. His calm-after-the-storm serenity was interrupted only once by the phone. It was his old navy buddy, Bart Jameson, notifying him that the acting president had fired him from his top Treasury Department job because of the tragic events in Detroit.

"Don't worry. I'll speak with the vice-president about it," Azee assured him, "and if necessary I'll take it up with the president."

"Thanks, old buddy, but it's over for me here. I don't want to hang around waiting for my pension with everyone in the Secret Service whispering behind my back about my failure to protect the first family. That's the kind of screw-up you never live down. I'm going to return to my old Wall Street brokerage firm."

Azee smiled as Bart reminded him of their longstanding agreement that if Azee ever took GCT public, he would handle the initial public stock offering. Azee could not bring himself to dissuade Bart's preposterous notion of taking GCT public. That would be like Bart winning a multimillion-dollar lottery. Azee liked his friends in high places to dream the impossible dream. It kept them on his side. But Azee knew that opening GCT's books to public scrutiny by going public would be suicidal.

To the muted jet engine drone, bemused at Bart Jameson, Vice-President Taylor and the dream jobs they would never have at GCT, Azee drifted into a sound sleep until the pilot's voice on the intercom announced that they were beginning their descent into Beirut. Azee's glance out the small port hole window revealed the unmistakable shoreline of his adopted homeland

XVII

Azee's tumultuous welcome at Beirut was repeated whenever he came home. *The Flying Mole*'s engines were no sooner shut down than the aircraft was encircled by shouting and chanting friends and family members awaiting the arrival of the crown prince. Through the jet's small porthole windows, Azee could see his wife Hasnaa restraining Jamal and Saarah from getting under the plane's descending stairway.

He bounded down the stairs two at a time to the embrace of his family. Armed militiamen from Hasnaa's family escorted Azee and his family to their dusty black Mercedes limousines for the trip to their opulent seaside villa, Temenos. Due to Lebanon's relationship with Greece and the pervasive influence of their millennia of trading and commerce, Azee thought it fitting to use this simple Greek word that means "a land set apart" for his awe-inspiring sanctuary. Hasnaa and the children rode in one vehicle while Azee, and Shakoor, his alter ego in Beirut, were in a second.

"Does Hasnaa know that you will be departing in two days?" Shakoor asked as they bounced through the streets of Beirut.

"Not really. I didn't want to tell her on the phone as it would have ruined the homecoming party planned for tonight. I'll tell her tonight after the children are in bed. She's planning on my

staying for the whole two-week holiday, but I must return to the
States after stopping in Damascus to collect final payment for our
work in Iraq. Sadly, the children and I won't have time to go wadi-
bashing. I look forward to that four-wheeling in the dry riverbeds
as much as they do. Shakoor, I really wish that you would take
the children out in the Jeep and tear up some of these old river
bottoms."

"I've tried more than once, but Hasnaa always says no, that it's
too dirty and dangerous for the children."

"Dirty, I agree. It would be less dangerous if you take them.
You'll be more careful than me because they aren't your children."

"Probably so, but you must convince Hasnaa."

"Jamal especially needs the fun of getting dirty and challenging his young life. My mother and my grandmother would be
very upset when I came home covered with sand and dirt from
my daily explorations in the sewer pipes beside our house that
connected with the drainage system under a new expressway
being built. They were always happy when I was safely home.
Hasnaa will feel the same way. You must remember what Kahlil
Gibran refers to as the strings that tie a woman to her family:
they're like the fine silky strings of a spider's web, but they're as
strong as golden wires."

"I would be honored to be your substitute wadi-bashing driver.
But you must order Hasnaa to allow me to take the children on
these outings in your place."

"No one gives orders to Hasnaa, especially about the children.
But I'll speak to her about allowing Jamal to leave the compound
with you for a little adventure and some shopping at the souks.
He needs to develop bargaining skills by dealing with the traders
and merchants. He must be exposed to more than the family in the
compound to mature as a young man. It will be your responsibility, Shakoor, when I'm not here."

"I'll never be able to adequately substitute for you, Azee, even
though we are all family in this together."

"We celebrate Jamal's birthday tomorrow, so the most

important family obligation will be taken care of before I leave."

"Should I schedule a big meeting with all our partners who have come to Beirut to see you?"

"We must shun any suspicious contacts. We are probably under surveillance, so none of our non-family partners can come to the compound during this visit. You need to leave Temenos at your first chance and contact Andre in Russia on a commercial phone line. Leave a coded message that he is not to contact us for any reason. We will re-establish contact with him when it's safe. We'll be true to our heritage by publicly practicing a philosophy of postponement for this visit. We can get discrete messages to other partners as needed. Has anything unusual happened?"

"Ambassador Bailey stopped twice at Temenos. The first time he was alone. The second time he had two young assistants who were eager to view as much of the compound as possible."

"Did they get a complete tour of Temenos?"

"No, sir. We followed your orders, although Haasna wanted to be her gracious self and show everything for their admiration."

"I'll speak to her again about being too good a host. Did they have cameras or recording devices with them?" Azee was even more protective of Temenos than he was of Cripplegate because his family lived there.

"We did not want to insult your country's ambassador by searching them. His two associates held their briefcases the entire visit. They could have been using hidden cameras. Should we use the x-ray and metal detector on the ambassador if he calls again?"

Azee became silently pensive when the tall, ornate minaret overlooking his property came into view. Most thought that this minaret had religious significance, and it may have to some, but Azee had it constructed as a visual and electronic observatory to monitor the Temenos' environs. From the circumferential top balcony, instead of a call to prayer, you can gaze westerly over the seaside green holy cedars and lose the azure Mediterranean as it becomes one with the sky, or you could look easterly to the parched brown biblical mountains hovering over the dark shadows of Beirut. Closed-circuit television cameras were cleverly disguised by the multicolored, kaleidoscopic decorative tiles that veneered the facade of the solitary minaret. Azee's high-tech minaret fulfilled the oriental adage that "The eye is far of view and the arm is short of reach."

The slowly opening security gate of Temenos unlocked Azee's reverential silence, "In the future have the ambassador's entourage walk through the archway with the hidden x-ray and metal detector. They never need full access to Temenos. Sweep all the areas they visited for planted bugs. I must know if they are spying on Temenos so I can call Washington to have it stopped."

Azee's forty-eight hours in Beirut were the usual nonstop series of hushed phone calls and secretive meetings inside the fortified confines of his seaside compound. His demeanor resembled that of an admiral more than a billionaire businessman. He usually wore an old dress white navy uniform at the villa, proud that his trim middle-age physique could still fit into these relics of bygone glory. His service ribbons had long ago been stashed in his secure GCT vault in Detroit. The solid scrambled eggs on his hat bill and the weighty gold shoulder epaulets indicated that Azee had indeed been self-promoted to the rank of admiral, at least in his small, secure corner of Beirut. From the first day of their suddenly aborted honeymoon ten years ago, Hasnaa had grown accustomed to the business demands of her workaholic husband.

The pace of vacation business activity once lead Hasnaa, in a moment of rare independence, to remark to Azee, "You have more contact with the children when you are working in Detroit or anywhere else in the world than when you are vacationing with us in Beirut."

Hasnaa wasn't privy to the scope and magnitude of Azee's worldwide activities and how their Mideast family members were part of them. Even Azee's infrequent attempts to spend time with the children were a source of great concern to Hasnaa. He would let them eat hummus and ghuzi with unwashed hands at open-air food booths in the dusty souks. At the end of such an intense day in the public market, they looked more unkempt than the homeless people in downtown Detroit.

The wealthier Azee became, the more she had to struggle to schedule family time. She had no suspicion that her husband's "busyness" wasn't always entirely business-related. It came as no surprise when Azee told her of his need to return to the States in two days and not two weeks as she had hoped. She never doubted Azee's marital faithfulness, but she still felt like a mistress to another love. Azee spent more time communicating with her and the children in his daily transoceanic phone calls than he did when he was physically with them.

Jamal's day-long ninth birthday party was the highlight of Azee's abbreviated stay in Beirut. The arrival of all their aunts, uncles, nephews, nieces and cousins always energized Azee. Hasnaa and Azee were from two of the oldest and largest families in Beirut, so over two hundred family members were invited. Many of their families had emigrated to other parts of the world, most notably the Detroit area. Those remaining in the Middle East maintained close family ties as a means of conquering the harsh realities of daily life in the struggling Lebanon.

Screening the arriving guests was more comprehensive than the most stringent airport system. All guests had to show photo identification cards along with their party invitations. Hidden cameras monitored the fenced perimeter and every room of the impenetrable compound. Azee had always felt that the weak link in his security system was the huge expanse of the Mediterranean Sea at his back door, so he relied on his former naval experience to rig underwater motion detection devices in the shallows.

Azee's cousin, Junaid, who had suicidally driven an explosive-laden pickup truck into the United States Embassy compound eleven years earlier, had been a favorite of Azee. He had been the absolute ideologue in the family. For him, issues were always black or white, and no price, even death, was too steep to pay for his convictions. The loss of Junaid left a void in Azee's life that he was constantly trying to fill with ever increasing levels of nefarious

activities that recalled and even one-upped Junaid's heroic sac-
rifice. The family blamed the United States for Junaid's death.
The fact that eight out the seventeen Americans killed were CIA
employees, including the station chief, was post factum justifica-
tion to the radicals in their families that the bombing and the loss
of Junaid wasn't in vain. Lebanon wanted to be free to return to
its proud status as the crown jewel of the eastern Mediterranean.
Any foreign country perceived as meddling in their internal affairs
was viewed as an enemy to be driven out. The family still felt bit-
terly that if the United States had not been spying on Lebanon and
the whole Middle East, Junaid would be alive today.

When the children's birthday games and treats were finished,
Azee summoned the men into his private quarters. Azee's greatest diplomatic accomplishment was maintaining unity and cohe-
siveness in his politically diverse Beirut family. The reports proceeded around the table until everyone had updated the group on
their specific activity. Azee's final comments and instructions were
always presented to a hushed room. Tonight's briefing was especially poignant as he described the unexpected comatose condition
of his friend, the first lady of the United States and the survival of
the president. He informed his family war council that the discovery of the true perpetrators of these acts was highly unlikely, since
the three groups came from such disparate global backgrounds
and were unknown to each other. Uneasiness blanketed the room
when Azee informed the group that he was returning to the United
States tomorrow, via Damascus, to be closer to the situation. The
one contingency that Azee couldn't plan for was a successor. None
of his relatives or business associates was a citizen of the world
like himself with an understanding of what was needed to run his
wide-ranging empire.

Azee's early morning departure, with his final weighty briefcase
as his only traveling companion, was subdued. He didn't want to
awaken the children for a sad, final goodbye.

XVIII

When the presidential party was boarding their helicopters for the short trip from Andrews to the Bethesda Naval Hospital, the president waved Gleason away from his Marine One helicopter so that he could be alone with his sons, Jason and Eric, for the flight to see their mother. Gleason used this short break from his duties to call his boss, who had been fired or retired, depending on whose version of the ill-fated cabinet meeting one believed. "You still on board, Bart?"

"Barely. I haven't submitted my resignation yet. Don't want to give Taylor the satisfaction of resigning on his watch as acting president."

"We appreciate your waiting. Have we been able to uncover any solid leads?" Gleason did his best to disguise his angry guilt at the needless tragedy.

"Nothing substantive. It's obvious there was a brilliant mastermind quarterbacking this operation. The bridge explosion is puzzling. Though it was the first of the three explosions, it's like an afterthought without any obvious purpose. I've told the investigators to concentrate on the house explosion above the expressway catastrophe. This must have been the headquarters they blew up to destroy any evidence. How are you feeling after the swim in the river and the double blood donation to the president?"

"Physically fine but, like you, filled with rage and conflicting emotions. The limousine and the bridge explosions were too easy. Someone seems to have a real feel for the game, scoring first, but we will ultimately win."

"I probably won't be with you when the final horn sounds."

"We're starting our descent into Bethesda. We can talk later. Rip up that resignation letter!"

The ground level helipad, centered by the universal red cross, was a beehive of activity. White-clad personnel pushing medical carts were streaming from the adjacent ground-floor emergency room. A modified golf cart that would carry the first lady's stretcher was inched closer to her landing helicopter. Simultaneously Marine One landed on the hospital's rooftop helipad. This allowed the emergency room personnel on the ground level to transport the first lady into the hospital out of sight of Jason and Eric. The president proceeded, with Jason and Eric in tow, to the presidential suite awaiting the first lady's arrival. Jason, snacking on a cookie in the suite's sitting rooms, innocently asked, "Daddy, will Mommy be awake for my birthday?"

The pensive president chose his words to answer his son's primal question more carefully than at a White House news conference. The full impact of the tragedy and all that the boys would be missing while they were growing up pierced the president's heart like an errant Olympic javelin. He wanted to be honest with the boys. "All of us are praying that mommy wakes up very soon." The president was fighting back tears while choking on the lump in his throat. He realized that sometime soon he'd have to take away the hopes and dreams the boys had for their mother. He snuggled with them on the cold black leather couch in the barren anteroom of the presidential suite.

Fortunately for the suddenly aphasic president, there was a gentle knock on the slowly opening door. "Mister President, I am Doctor Nancy Schmidt. I have been assigned to treat the first lady."

"Yes, doctor, please come in." The president and his sons rose to greet the trim naval hyperbaric expert. "We've heard nothing but good things about your work in this rather obscure field of medicine." The president motioned toward an open door leading to an adjoining room. "Boys, we'll be right back, and then we can go see mommy."

"I'm sorry, Mister President, for the heavy load you must be carrying. It will be our job here at Bethesda to lighten your load and your sons' as well."

"I appreciate your kind intentions, but your main job is to do everything possible to resurrect the first lady. Is that clear, and will you give the same instructions to the entire medical staff?"

The nervous Dr. Schmidt tugged on the stethoscope hanging limply around her neck. "Mister President, I've moved into the room across the hall from the first lady's suite. I make myself available twenty-four hours a day to supervise her treatment. It's taken for granted that the best possible care is given to all our patients, but especially to our commander in chief's family. My naval personnel file, including a letter of commendation from the surgeon general, is current and available for your inspection."

"The surgeon general! She's the last person I'd talk to about treating my wife. She hasn't treated a patient in years."

"I'm sorry. I didn't mean to upset you. I am a captain in the Naval Medical Corps. They published my research on hyperbaric oxygen therapy while I was head of the Navy SEALs' medical bureau. I have undergone hyperbaric oxygen therapy numerous times to be assured of its safety. If you desire, sir, I can remove myself from the first lady's case."

The president prided himself on being able to intuitively size up people that he was meeting for the first time. He was regretting his hard line opening comments to the now distinctly attractive Dr. Schmidt. He was now the one groping for words. "Nancy, may I call you Nancy?"

"My friends call me Nan." She realized that the initial presidential reaction was his dysfunctional method of assuming control of a threatening situation.

"Thank you, Nan. I'm sorry for speaking so harshly. I didn't mean to question the quality of the medical treatment by the staff here at Bethesda. The boys and I certainly can use all the help available in surviving this horrendous tragedy."

"No need to apologize for events beyond your control. I'm sure that you and your sons are still in a state of shock. I also have taken my specialty training in psychiatry since my work in hyperbaric oxygen therapy overlaps into its effect on brain function. I can prescribe some tranquilizers to get you through the next few days. Also you might want to get some counseling for the boys and yourself. I would..."

"No, Nan, I don't want the pills. I need to keep a clear head for the important decisions that I'll have to make for the country and the first lady. But we'll accept the offer of your counseling. We'll take the boys to see their mother as soon as she's ready."

The president marveled that the childless Gleason always seemed to be Johnnie on the spot with whatever it took to entertain Jason and Eric. Somewhere in the uncharted labyrinth of Bethesda Naval Hospital, he managed to find a small box of toys and games to occupy and distract them. "What defenseless little boy did you take this stuff from?"

"It wasn't a problem, sir. The boy was in a full body cast."

"I hope you didn't tell him whom they were for. That could cost me in the election! They'd wonder what kind of father would bring his kids to the hospital without something to entertain them." The president always rationalized that he was too busy saving the world to be attentive to his boys and besides, it was the White House staff's duty under the first lady's direction to see to the family's every need. He didn't want to think about how this privileged lifestyle was now irrevocably changed and the clock could not be turned back to a happier time when Kathy was there to raise the boys.

Three mini-footballs with the Washington Redskins logo were flying around the presidential suite's anteroom, bouncing off lamps and chairs. The president's one-armed condition was a source of needed laughter for the boys. They would simultaneously peg their footballs to their dad, who even with two arms would have been athletically challenged to catch them. Dr. Schmidt signaled a time-out to the anteroom mayhem announcing that they could now visit their mother.

Hospitals frighten even the staunchest of people, and the president, with his own arm in a heavy cast, was anything but brave on the inside, though he knew that he had to maintain a calm exterior for Jason and Eric. He was grateful for the warm, reassuring presence of Dr. Schmidt as he and the boys cautiously approached the first lady's cluttered bedside. Children accept realities better than adults.

"Where did Mommy's hair go?" the innocent and trusting six-year-old Eric asked upon seeing his peaceful, comatose mother.

The president absent-mindedly scanned the institutional furnishings of the presidential suite on the top floor of Bethesda Naval Hospital while groping for any answer to Eric's gut-wrenching question. For a six-year-old, worried about his mother's once beautiful hair, life was wonderfully simple. "The nurses had to cut it off so they could fix the bad bump on the top of her head."

"Do you think Mommy will be awake for my birthday next week?" the animated Jason again wondered in a pleading tone.

The president wanted to be honest with the boys without deflating their expectations for their mother's recovery. "Dr Nan is giving Mommy some special treatments that will help her wake up as fast as she can," the president listlessly replied while glimpsing Nan out of the corners of his moist eyes.

Nan tried to force a motherly smile for Jason as she, too, pondered how much reality to inflict on the concerned children. "I wish that I could promise you this, Jason. It would be the best birthday present ever. We'll try our hardest to help your Mommy wake up for your birthday. You have to help your daddy and your little brother by being strong." The president noticed Nan furtively dry the corner of her eyes with a quick swipe of her delicate fingers as they led the boys away from their mother's bedside.

The president was grateful for the calming presence of Nan, as she could provide a loving, hopeful honesty that he found hard to communicate to the boys because of his own dysfunctional childhood. As a child he remembered always having to wait until tomorrow to do something fun with his father, whether it be going fishing for the ugly black whiskered catfish in the muddy river or simply playing catch in the front yard. Tomorrow hardly ever came.

Fortunately, his older brothers provided much of the male companionship he needed growing up, and his loving mother was always present to dress his wounds and bolster his deflated ego. Only in later years did he feel indebted to his brothers for "toughening him up." At the time, the way that he, the youngest, was never given any slack by his older brothers probably could have been judged cruel and unusual punishment.

His true talents gradually emerged as he progressed up the grade school ladder, skipping a grade and starting to take some high school classes while still in junior high. His older brothers often came to him for help with school projects or homework problems. He gladly accommodated them, forgetful of their fraternal knocks and bruises. Unfortunately all the todays increasingly became tomorrows for his father.

The relentlessly progressive ravages of alcoholism consumed their perpetually fledgling father-son relationship. Although he never discussed with Kathy this gaping paternal void in his soul, he was sure she knew of it intuitively. She did her best to shield Jason and Eric from their well-intentioned but often absent father.

He remembered that on their wedding day he'd made a promise to himself that he would be the best "today" father ever, should they be blessed with children. As a protestant he didn't have to worry about confessing his abysmal failure to keep this promise to a priest in Kathy's dark little confessional box, but tonight he would contritely drop to his knees and beg the almighty's forgiveness when he lead the boys in their bedtime prayers.

With Kathy's future uncertain today, he was again forced to

live with the hope of tomorrow, which he was still having trouble adjusting to. He didn't want to inflict any false hope on Jason and Eric for the tomorrow that might never come.

"Daddy, can we play more football?" the birthday boy Jason hopefully questioned as they returned to the anteroom.

"Of course. Let's do it right now." The president said as he flipped a mini-football at each of his sons.

XIX

Azee's business detour to Damascus did not attract any unusual attention. He had done it many times before. Upon landing and deplaning, he quickly switched his heavy briefcase for an identical empty one being offered by one of the uniformed ground crew before jumping in the waiting Mercedes limousine for the short drive to the small fixed-base terminal.

Last week Shakoor had made GCT's perfunctory final inspection of the large underground grain storage complex that was being turned over to the Iraqi military. This warehouse, 50 feet tall and 25 feet underground, was as large as three football fields side by side. A series of tunnels connected this warehouse with a number of more heavily fortified subterranean bunkers, where the crew lived and worked at multi-terminal computer stations. GCT's computer technicians were fine-tuning the electronic controls for the environmental and security systems of the huge labyrinth they'd nicknamed the "Mole Hole." The only security system that could not be tested was the doomsday scenario. Upon activation of the embedded explosives, the concrete floor would elevate from its footings, and the collapsing walls would bring down the ceiling in a total holocaust of people and architecture.

Azee and the finance minister Mustafeedh met privately in

the well worn fixed-base terminal to conduct their last and most important business, the final payment for services rendered at the Mole Hole. Mustafeedh presented Azee with a Bank of Zurich check for fifty million U.S. dollars. "Mister Finance Minister," the perplexed Azee began, "there seems to be a slight discrepancy of ten million dollars in your payment. Our agreement called for sixty million dollars upon completion of the project?"

"That is correct, Mister Azee. While all of your actual construction work seems to be satisfactory, the bungled operation in Detroit greatly concerns me. I personally approved the ten million dollar pseudo-construction overrun based on the successful outcome of the Detroit presidential termination project. My country, to say nothing of me personally, is in great jeopardy if the international community discovers the origins of this failed plot to rid the world of your warlike president."

The stunned Azee was paralyzed by a torrent of anger and betrayal. There's no honor among thieves, he thought. No matter how much money you have, ten million dollars is still a significant amount of money, especially since Azee also considered it as a good faith retainer for the pending nuclear arms deals. A degree of rationality returned to him as he quickly remembered that his initial dealings with Mustafeedh were his first breakthrough contracts with this oil rich corner of the world. This secretive, highly profitable Middle East segment of GCT's business portfolio was the impetus that had propelled Azee into the rarified billionaire status in a few short years. Pending contracts for the decommissioning of the former Soviet Union's nuclear power plants would continue to multiply his billionaire status.

Azee struggled to maintain his composure as he said, "I gave the briefcase with ten million dollars cash to your operative at the airport for appropriate payment distributions. There's no way, unless there's a breakdown within your own people, that this money and operation can be traced back to you. You knew that this final add-on operation was risky and uncertain, with no guaranteed outcome."

"I've been informed of the briefcase with the money. My men can now be paid in untraceable cash. All our business relations have been based on trust and performance. Both elements must be present. Unless the international media are deceived, your president is still alive with only a fractured arm and a vengeful heart."

Hardball became the name of the game as Azee defiantly glared at the squirming Mustafeedh. "Are you telling me that I paid your operatives ten million dollars cash without being reimbursed as we agreed? I am the one taking all the risks in coordinating the three dangerous incidents, while you are safely insulated in your sovereign country. You want me to take on even greater risks, supplying the Mole Hole with decommissioned nuclear material from Russian nuclear power plants, without any assurance of being paid?"

Mustafeedh nervously shuffled a stack of papers on his lap. "We view the supplying of the Mole Hole with needed armaments as a continuation of the initial project, which we have just paid for. It must go on! It will go on! You are the only party in the world that can facilitate the transfer of this nuclear material."

Azee did not achieve his elite status by being stubborn and stupid, at least not at the same time. He always knew that he held the final trump card regarding the Mole Hole—his secret and undisclosed ability to activate the doomsday system via satellite and collapse the Mole Hole in on itself.

The disputed ten million dollars wasn't a sufficient ante for Azee to play his trump card this soon, so he made an effort at reconciliation with the hope of the much larger future nuclear payoff. "The building of the Mole Hole was the easy phase. Supplying it with nuclear materials will require a level of expertise and finesse that, as you said, only I and my company can provide. We will continue to cooperate until this project is finished. I am returning to the United States to see what can be done about completing our joint venture there to get paid here. Maybe we can arrange a slow, painful death for the president, which will be even better than our failed quick death. In either case, I expect the final ten-million-dollar payment to be made the next time we meet, otherwise there is not much point in getting together."

Before Mustafeedh could reply, Azee bounched up from his chair and was out the door headed back to his plane smiling to himself over one of the higher stakes pocker game he was again engaged in.

XX

The sunrise on the morning of Kathy's first hyperbaric oxygen treatment was more spectacular than Homer's celebrated rosy-fingered dawn. The brisk fall sky was afire with every shade of orange, pink and red as Marine One landed at Bethesda Naval Hospital. A subdued president was greeted by a phalanx of reporters, military brass, and somber doctors in their green scrubs. The president's eyes darted from face to face until he located the warm visage of Dr. Schmidt. Standing next to her in his conspicuous black suit and Roman collar was a person the president could not immediately put a name to. As he approached them, his political computer brought the name of Cardinal Rourke to his lips.

"Good morning, Mister President," the entourage around Cardinal Rourke and Dr. Schmidt intoned in unison.

"Good morning everyone." The president shook hands with the doctor and the cardinal. "Are we still scheduled to begin Kathy's treatments this morning?"

Dr. Schmidt quietly mentioned to the president while walking into the hospital that Cardinal Rourke wanted a few moments with them before the first lady's hyperbaric oxygen treatments began. The president nodded his assent as they boarded the elevator up to the presidential suite. In an adjacent conference room

Dr. Schmidt began by giving an update on the first lady's overnight medical condition. "The first lady had a relatively stable night with no alteration of her comatose state. I was called only once during the night to help regulate her ventilator. There is no change in the condition of the baby. The baby's heartbeat is strong and steady, and there is intrauterine movement."

From his usual position at the head of the polished oak conference table, the president quickly scanned the dozen or so silent participants in this medical update. His heart ached for a chance to discuss his wife's condition privately, without making it an affair of state or just another session of medical grand rounds. "Could I ask that only Doctor Schmidt and Cardinal Rourke remain to confer with me for a few minutes?" The president's abrupt termination of the update caused a momentary silence that was harshly broken by the chairs sliding on the polished brown terrazzo floor. "Thank you."

The president noticed that Gleason was still seated in a corner near the door where he could monitor everyone coming and going. He thought of asking Gleason to wait in the hall also, but he hoped to assuage the agent's feelings of guilt by letting him hear all that was being done to save the first lady.

"Cardinal, please join us in the front pew," the president gently chided while motioning to the chair on his left. "This isn't Sunday mass, where everyone sits in the back of church." The cardinal's age and frailty betrayed him as he had difficulty pushing his heavy leather armchair away from the table until Gleason came to his rescue by helping to slide the chair back from the table. A deep inhalation followed by sighing exhalation relaxed the president as the three of them groped for the proper beginning to this impromptu conference. Even the usually garrulous cardinal deferred to the president to initiate the discussion.

"I appreciate the support of both of you," The president began. "The lives of my wife and baby are literally in our hands. I find this responsibility more frightening than having my finger on the nuclear button that can destroy the world. I'm sure, doctor, that you are accustomed to making life-and-death medical decisions based on scientific evidence. You, cardinal, make dispassionate life-and-death pronouncements based on the tenants of the church. I don't have the luxury of these positions. I feel rather alone and helpless in this near-hopeless situation."

The cardinal reached out to pat the president's casted left arm. "Mister President, you are not alone. The entire world is praying that these tragic events reach a happy and blessed conclusion. The pope has phoned twice offering his prayers and best wishes."

"Thank you, your eminence, for your kind words. Please convey my personal appreciation to the pope the next time he calls. Kathy has great affection for his holiness. She often proposed the dilemma to our sons: which one of you wants to be pope? The other one can be president. They were both fighting to be pope! I used to complicate the dilemma by saying that the new baby was going to be a girl and she would have her choice too. My Southern Baptist lineage might be slightly ahead of its time at least in one of those options."

Dr. Schmidt reported, "Mister President, I have personally consulted with leading medical authorities on our proposed hyperbaric oxygen treatments. They're in unanimous agreement as to the probable futility of our proposed treatment. The first lady has nearly a zero chance of a substantial recovery and less than five percent chance for any improvement whatsoever. The effect on the fetus should be negligible, but we can't be totally certain. Nevertheless, all are agreed that time is of the essence if this experimental treatment is going to be tried. We should begin immediately if you decide on the treatment."

"I know. I know. A few more minutes won't matter. I am just concerned that we are doing the right thing for all concerned. If I can be blunt, Kathy is dead unless a miracle happens. I've resigned myself to that. You give her less than five percent chance to show any improvement at all. In politics less than five per cent chance means you are dead."

"Mister President," the cardinal interjected, "if I may say, the power of God can rescue many hopeless situations. We must give

God and Kathy every opportunity to work. If it were you and not Kathy in this dire predicament, you would want every effort made to prolong your life."

"Bullshit," the president exploded as he momentarily forgot that he wasn't in a raucous political meeting trying to achieve a consensus on a political issue. "Initially in Detroit I was thinking like that. Hell, we probably should have summoned Dr. Kervorkian, who lives in Detroit. There is no clear political consensus in regard to this assisted suicide issue. I have a living will, and there's no way I want my life prolonged in a vegetative state. As a matter of fact, Kathy also has a living will with a medical directive."

"Mister President, I wish you had informed us earlier of Kathy's living will. Legally we can't override a living will. My medical ethics are already being compromised by continuing to render care in a hopeless situation."

"This was our oversight, Nan. However, the White House counsel feels that the pregnancy is sufficient grounds to temporarily override Kathy's living will."

"I am concerned about your use of the word temporarily. How long is temporary?" the cardinal questioned.

"Let me try to answer that, cardinal," Dr. Schmidt spoke up. "In short, until the baby is mature enough to survive outside the womb, even though we would be legally within our rights to terminate this pregnancy either by an actual abortion or by allowing the first lady's vegetative state to cease. The long answer is we don't know how long the first lady can be sustained in her present vegetative state. Even with the world-class medical care here at Bethesda, the first lady will gradually start experiencing total system shutdown. There are certainly medical precedents from the Netherlands, with their legally assisted suicide measures, that we could rely on to terminate Kathy's hopeless condition. Medically we don't have a lot of pious platitudes supporting our scientific projections. Doctors aren't gods, as some would believe."

The cardinal's complexion became the same crimson color as the small red patch visible under his Roman collar, signifying that he was more than an ordinary priest. "The president and I will not be part of any medical decisions based on the gross immorality in the Netherlands that result in the murder of the fetus or the premature death of the first lady. We refuse to allow doctors to play god by deciding who lives and who dies. The heinous acts of the terrorists would be more forgivable in the eyes of God than the taking of the life of this innocent baby or the first lady."

The president found himself in the familiar role of peacemaker. To avoid eye contact with the righteously angry, rapidly darting eyes of the now animated cardinal, who no longer appeared to be the superannuated has-been of moments ago, the president caught himself staring at Nan's sterile white clinic coat, which appeared to be resting on the conference table as she leaned forward. "Somehow we have become distracted from the issue at hand. No one is talking death of the first lady or the fetus. The political polls wiill drop if we do anything to harm Kathy or the baby this close to the election. "

"I agree, Mister President," a placated cardinal nodded, "that political concerns are important in the two matters at hand. As a country, we need another four years of your moral and political leadership, and I'll do everything in my power to see that it happens. My main concern is that these medical decisions are based on sound moral grounds and not on medical expediency or temporary political gains."

"Cardinal, be assured that medical decisions affecting the president's family and hence the whole country will be reviewed by our ethics committee with strong religious input from our priest ethicist. I don't recall his name, but I am sure your office has it. You can be in touch with him."

"Thank you, Doctor. I certainly will make connection with your ethics committee to help me monitor the condition of the first lady and the baby."

Another senseless turf war avoided, the president thought. "As a matter of fact, the prospect of a new baby in the White House for another four years is the main thing sustaining the boys and me."

XXI

Gleason spent most of his time between hospital visits talking on the telephone to the investigating agents in Detroit. Substantial rewards were being offered to the public to come forward with any potentially helpful information. Many of the early leads in the bombings were superficial. Well-meaning citizens called in to the newly established tip hot line, and their calls had to be catalogued and investigated on the off-chance that one could be the big break the investigators needed to move the multiple investigations forward. These cases would be solved only after much old-fashioned police legwork. The constant media attention was often a hindrance.

Chief Hawkins kept calling Gleason to remind him that he needed to return to Detroit to discuss important details face-to-face. Gleason was also getting calls from his Secret Service subordinates on the status of their protection of the vice president and those in the line of succession to the presidency.

Gleason felt uncomfortable when he had to personally approve the heightened security plans for Vice President Taylor's social luncheon with Azee at the upscale Sequoia, overlooking the Potomac in trendy Georgetown. Gleason was naturally paranoid about another incident happening on his watch. The vice president became livid when Gleason suggested that the lunch be rescheduled to the secure confines of his Naval Observatory home. The vice president claimed that he was suffering severe cabin fever. Thus his pleas fell on sympathetic ears as Gleason relented and arranged for extra security at the Sequoia.

Azee loved the kaleidoscopic fall views of the Potomac and rejuvenated yuppie Georgetown from the VIP corner table at the Sequoia in the swank Washington Harbor development. Azee gave the Sequoia the ornamental oriental screen partition that provided total privacy and security for his frequent power lunches. The imported silk screen was decorative and also bulletproof by virtue of the Kevlar layers sandwiched between the ornate, hand-painted panels. "Good afternoon, Mister Vice President," Azee said, "We certainly have a beautiful day for our lunch."

"I've been going stir crazy following all the extra Secret Service precautions since the bombings. No terrorist in his right mind would want to get rid of an old, harmless pensioner like me. There are times when I just have to see some non-beltway real people."

"Thank you, Hubert. I've always been honored to be counted among your friends. The problem with most terrorists is that they're not in their right mind, so you had better follow the Secret Service's recommendations."

"I don't have any choice but to obey them and my wife. They are working hand-in-hand to keep me off the streets until they get a better handle on who was behind this Detroit fiasco. Gleason was wavering about letting me off the reservation until I told him I was having lunch with you."

"I didn't realize that I had that much influence. You got rid of your crutches."

"That certainly helps the psyche and the armpits. I still had to use the elevator to get up here, as stairs are a work in progress. I hope the rehab continues to work as promised. Thanks, Azee, for making time in your busy schedule to continue our friendship."

"The pleasure's all mine, Hubert. I've been looking forward to this since I left Damascus. The solitude and cuisine on the *Flying Mole* leave much to be desired."

"How was your trip back home to Beirut? Weren't you going to stay two weeks?"

"That was the plan until the bombings. We celebrated Jamal's ninth birthday, so the shortened visit wasn't a total loss. I'll get back to Detroit tonight to check on the cleanup of the *Aqua Mole*. It sure was lucky that you changed your plans for the Detroit visit and missed the terrible carnage. You and I would have been casualties if we were in the motorcade as originally planned."

"Somebody must be looking out for us. This old body and tired soul wouldn't have survived the trauma. I probably would have been in the lead limousine with you where they were all were killed."

"It's painful for me to even remember back to that horrible scene." Azee used carefully chosen words, debating how much to tell the vice president in case he was wearing a wire to record their conversation. Azee wanted to believe that the vice president wouldn't knowingly wear a bug to record his friend and future boss. But the ever-vigilant Gleason could have put a hidden mike in the vice president's jacket without his knowledge.

"One of the reports said you went below deck to relieve yourself. It sounds like nature's call may have saved your life."

"You're right about that. I drank too much coffee at the NAFTA lunch. It probably saved my life. Unfortunately, the first lady used the facilities at the Ren Center before boarding the *Aqua Mole*. Otherwise she too might have been below deck, protected from the bomb's shock wave."

"Can't fault her for avoiding the trauma of your boat's rocking toilet seat."

"Speaking of trauma, what's the latest on the first lady while I've been gone?"

"Her condition hasn't changed. She's still in a deep coma, and the hyperbaric oxygen treatments don't seem to be helping. The female navy doctor reportedly is spending a lot of time at the White House, allegedly to help the boys and the president."

"Who's this navy doctor? Couldn't the federal government

afford to get an outside expert from Mayo's or Johns Hopkins to treat the first lady?"

"Her name is Doctor Schmidt. She's been doing hyperbaric oxygen research for the navy since her officer candidate days in Newport over twenty years ago. All I know about her is what's in the PDB. Her picture looks like she's a sharp chick. As you know, the CIA doesn't give you many details in the PDB."

"Excuse me Hubert, but I'm not familiar with the PDB."

"I assumed that you were at least aware of it because of your close relationship with the first lady."

Azee stiffened in his chair as he attempted to determine the intent of Taylor's innuendo. "Please enlighten me."

"It's the top secret President's Daily Briefing prepared every morning by the CIA. They print only 10 copies a day for the president, me, the speaker of the house, and his security advisers. I've only been a subscriber for a short time. When I was added to the list, I knew that the White House was going to ask me to be on the ticket again. So when the president finally got around to asking me to be his running mate, I had to act surprised. The president, or should I say his young punk advisors, don't think I know enough to come in from the rain. Sometimes it's easier to play dumb. People leave you alone."

"I don't have to play too hard at being dumb either. Someday I'd like to see a copy, just to be able to say that I've seen a top secret document."

"Just happen to have today's PDB in my vest pocket. You can look at it, but I need it back to return to the CIA for confidential shredding when they bring the new copy tomorrow. They're real bastards about getting the old copies back. They have hidden codes that show up on any xeroxed copy that can then be traced back to one of the ten originals. Your ass is grass if it's your copy that's been compromised. You still have your security clearance from the White House?"

"I had access to the White House with all the necessary security clearances, but I've no desire to return there. I'm sure the president feels the same way. This must be a picture of the hyperbaric doctor, N. Schmidt, who's treating the first lady. They don't even spell out her first name. I wonder if it's to save space or some obscure security reason. I hope the president didn't hire her because of her good looks. If she's as smart as she's pretty, Kathy should receive the best of care."

"Who knows why the White House does what it does. To be honest, I don't think the president knew what this Doctor N looked like at the time she was assigned to treat the first lady. But knowing the president, her good looks will certainly give her job security."

"This thumbnail resume shows she's a bright, tough cookie. After medical school she did her naval OTC at Newport about the same time that I was there. Her picture doesn't look familiar to me. You would think, young stud that I was, that I would have known every pretty female officer at Newport. Later she was a Navy SEAL medical officer and then she completed the CIA counterinsurgency training at the Farm. Somewhere along the way she became a psychiatrist, too. Very impressive."

"I don't have the time or interest to read all this CIA spy bullshit. It tends to upset the morning coffee. What do you know about the Farm?"

"I hate to think about the Farm because it opens old business rejection wounds. When I started GCT and began using the new laser alignment instruments, the CIA sent us plans for an elaborate, high-tech underground facility. Exact location unspecified. The specs for this football field size facility were unbelievable. They wanted more security features than our armed forces command center in the Pentagon. Without notice we had to return the blue prints to Langley before submitting a final bid. Their excuse was that this project was too sensitive for a civilian contractor."
Azee neglected to tell the vice president that a number of his business associates were Farm graduates.

"Here's your PDB for safe keeping. I'm like you. Who needs to know how many times Colonel Quadafi flushed his toilet? I hope this navy doctor knows her stuff. Everyone loves the first lady and the first baby yet to be born."

"The White House seems to think that Dr. N is the world's expert on this last-ditch treatment. I hope she confines herself to arousing only the first lady. The president doesn't need any help in that regard."

As the tuxedoed server discreetly brought their gold-rimmed luncheon plates, Azee politely smiled while inwardly raging at the vice president's reminder of presidential infidelities against the love of his life. His mind backpedaled through his own navy years until he remembered a young navy doctor at Newport that he mnemonically nicknamed Fancy Nancy. His memory of her was starting to clear. He remembered surprising her while she frolicked with a foreign friend in the hyperbaric whirlpool at Newport. He was locking down the facilities on the evening watch. Was this the same person who now has resurfaced as the first lady's doctor?

"I'm sure everything is top drawer," Taylor continued. "The president couldn't afford to have anything but the best for his wife, especially this close to the election. As you know, I'm just trying to ride out two more years before I resign. Then the president can handpick my successor. I'm beginning to entertain the thought of resigning after just one year, but I will have to wait and see how the current crisis plays out. The rumors are already flying about who will be appointed when I resign in midterm, and we haven't been reelected yet. I just need to keep my nose clean so that private businesses can offer me the moon. Azee, I hope you will be able to afford me when I start looking for a real job."

"As I've said many times, Hubert, there will always be a job for a person of your ability and contacts. The only caveat might be that I myself could retire or sell GCT by then. But I doubt that either will happen. I'm having too much fun jetting to all our projects around the world. That is, until this Detroit mess hit us. You know that I'm forever grateful for your intercession with the Corps of Engineers on GCT's behalf concerning the Potomac bulkhead that is supporting the whole Washington Harbor development and this fine restaurant that we're now eating in. Without your senatorial influence, GCT would still be trying to get the go-ahead to start this Washington Harbor Project."

"Yes, the Corps of Engineers can act quickly when I, as chairman of the Senate Appropriations Committee threatened to cut off funding for some of their pet projects if they didn't approve mine."

"I hated to ask you for that intercessory favor, but I could see the entire Marine Construction Division of GCT going under if this major waterfront Washington Harbor Project didn't get approved. It was hurting our credibility worldwide that we could not do a project in our own nation's capital."

"My feeble memory tells me that I only made a couple of phone calls to the corps for the permission you needed."

"Well, by then our attorneys had softened them up with hundreds of phone calls and reams of paperwork," Azee bragged.

"You're probably right, but that's still another IOU that I will collect when the time is right, like in two years."

"No problem. That's what friends are for. This Washington Harbor Project remains the most profitable contract that the marine division has completed. The extra add-on work of the wooden walkway parallel to and below the concrete bulkhead was just frosting on the cake, thanks to your intercession."

"Occasionally on a warm summer evening Mildred and I will come down here from our Observatory home for an evening stroll on the boardwalk with our Secret Service handlers. If these damn knees don't start coming around, they'll be pushing me in a wheelchair all the way from the George Washington University crew barn to the end of the boardwalk toward the Key Bridge. Azee, if I can get funding, do you think GCT would be interested in finishing the bulkhead and boardwalk all the way to the Key Bridge?"

"Hubert, for you, we would be glad to bid on this project to give you a longer coasting distance in you wheelchair." Azee halfheartedly laughed as his mind was filtering a hundred other items more important than the vice president's evening stroll. "As you know, most of GCT's international resources are pledged to helping the breakaway Russia republics build an oil and gas pipe-line so that they can get their oil and gas to Western markets for the needed Western currency. I've developed many important con-tacts in this newly developing corner of the world. There is one person in particular that you will have to meet once you are out of office. I have mentioned before that I am providing technical expertise in tearing down and decommissioning their former mis-sile silos and nuclear power plants. Thanks to your intercession with the United Nations, the door was opened for us to bid on this dangerous work. It has proven very challenging for a private firm like GCT to handle nuclear materials, even with the international supervision provided by the United Nations."

"Well, this boardwalk extension would be a pleasant relief for you from the stress of handling nuclear bombs I'm sure. I'd better get on this while I'm still in office," the vice president offered. "By the way, how are the nuclear projects going in Russia? Remember, I might be able to open a few more doors there to help you secure any contracts you are interested in."

"The best part of another boardwalk project would be get-ting back to DC to see you more often. What's the latest on the Detroit investigations? Any serious leads?" Azee innocently asked to avoid answering the dangerous Russian nuclear question.

"I'm getting hourly reports and briefings. Typical government pablum. The CIA's Counterterrorism Center is coordinating the efforts of all the agencies. The Global Response Center has been activated because of the uncertainty of how widespread the terror-ism threat is. The Secret Service and the FBI are being very tight-lipped. Everyone is proceeding with the notion that multiple ter-rorist groups, very well coordinated, are involved. No one group that the government is aware of has the resources to stage these three bombings."

"That sounds logical to me." Azee was content to listen, and the vice president seemed to need to talk to someone.

"The Royal Canadian Mounted Police are investigating how their limousine got wired. They are reviewing government employment records to see who had access to their limousine fleet. It shouldn't take them long to narrow the search down to a few suspects. When talking to Gleason about our lunch, he mentioned that he was flying to Detroit for a shake-up visit to spur our own investigations along,"

When the vice president finished this lose-lipped CIA like briefing, Azee immediately shifted the conversation to the long-oared collegiate crew shells that were racing on the shimmering Potomac below their window. Azee knew that he would have to immediately return to Detroit to search his private files from his Newport naval tour days for any information on this Dr. N.

XXII

The president's most important incoming call of the morning was from the medical office in the White House basement. "Good morning, Archie. Did you sleep well after we parted last night?" the familiar female voice asked.

"What a pleasant surprise to talk to you this early, Nan. A problem with Kathy?"

"I'm sorry. I don't mean to alarm you. Nothing's changed overnight. As I mentioned last night, I'll draw your blood specimen this morning and pick up your urine specimen so that the results will be available for your actual physical examination at Bethesda later in the week."

"I thought you offered to perform the physical at the White House. I've been practicing my coughing as you ordered," a guffawing president replied to his newly appointed chief White House physician.

"I'm coming right over to the oval office, so roll up your sleeve but leave your pants on for a couple more days," the spunky ex-Navy SEAL doctor retorted as she grabbed her tray of medical surprises to bring to the president. The silence on the suddenly dead phone line shocked the president back to the necessary reality of his annual physical, appropriately scheduled before the election for maximum media exposure of his excellent health. A clean bill of health would certainly be worth a two or three percent increase in the pre-election polls, he thought to himself as he went to the door to meet the smiling Nan.

"Why are you putting on gloves?" the president asked as she stretched the latex to its ripping point. "Are you going to do the prostate exam now?"

"That'll happen in a couple days at Bethesda when you drop your pants to demonstrate your coughing talent. We'll need a second and possibly a third opinion on the prostate exam." Nan's sly smile distracted from the needle poke in his only available forearm. "You mention these gloves. Surely you are aware that your own Occupational Safety and Health Administration could fine us ten thousand dollars for not using them when we work with blood. That kind of publicity would be just what you need. You don't have much support in the medical community. The growing number of OSHA regulations certainly aren't helping your reelection."

"You know how to kick a person when he's down. While you're attacking my only good arm, you serve as house lobbyist for the American Medical Association. These damn doctors should be grateful for all the publicity their profession is getting by prolonging Kathy's treatment. After the election we'll see how they feel when medicine won't be front-page news."

"I am going to play post office and deliver these samples to the lab at Bethesda myself. I don't want to take the chance of losing them in intra-governmental transit. What pseudonym do you want on the lab work?"

"Nan, wait! What's the hurry? Name me whoever you want. Can you come back this afternoon? The boys and I need another group therapy session. They're still having a hard time adjusting to their mother's condition."

"I'll call you later after the first lady's treatments." Slightly exasperated, she hurried out the heavy oak door before any more delays.

The familiar drive to Bethesda became a serpentine labyrinth as she took unnecessary detours, constantly checking her rearview mirror. The last twenty-four hours had been the mother of all nightmares for her with people coming at her from all directions. Suddenly her main job of keeping the first lady alive until the election was secondary. Last night's phone call from Gleason, when he ordered that she must drop off a vial of the president's blood to him at Andrews Air Force Base, left her in violation of her Hippocratic oath as a physician. He clearly implied that it was a matter of top secret national security so she had no choice but to comply.

"Here is the vial of the president's blood," she told Gleason in the parking lot of a fast-food restaurant outside Andrews Air Force Base. "I hope you don't need anything else from me that compromises my ethics like this."

"The Secret Service will be in touch with you soon. Until then, carry on your normal duties. I'm flying this sample out of town for anonymous testing so we can compare our results with your Bethesda results. Don't forget to use a code name on the blood samples at Bethesda. We cannot trust security at Bethesda with all the media hanging around."

"Already have that covered." Schmidt slammed her door and sped out of the debris-laden parking lot.

She went through her required medical duties like a zombie on the longest day of her distinguished medical career. If the president had not been her commander in chief, she would have discontinued the hyperbaric oxygen treatments and walked away from her navy career. However, she was enough of a realist to know that personally and politically this wasn't possible until after the election.

XXIII

Chief Hawkins, in the unmarked Buick, met Gleason's White House C-21 jet at Detroit Metro Airport. "Hey, Gleason. Good to see you again. You must be planning on staying awhile," the ever-observant chief commented as he opened the trunk for Gleason to stow a small suitcase and an oversize one that looked like a Goodwll store reject. "Usually you just have your presidential briefcase, which of course is big enough for your weapons."

"I had to bring a few things to help advance the investigation. I plan on returning to Washington tomorrow. The president needs me more in Washington than you need me here."

"I'm sure that's true, but we have other business to take care of here. How have you been feeling?" the chief asked.

"How should I be feeling?"

A tense, embarrassing silence was finally broken by the chief. "Gleason, we've been through a lot in the past, and we have to leave it in the past. Our focus has to be on the future."

"Easy for you to say. Your future is safe and secure here in Detroit. You aren't responsible for this first family calamity. Everyone loves you here."

"Not everyone. There's a lot of guilt and hate coming from both sides of the river. We have to wrap up the investigations so we can get on with mending our public image and our private lives."

"At least you have a private life, Jeff. The little privacy I have is over, or will be shortly. Where are we headed now?"

"We have to do both the blood things. Do you have the president's specimen with you?"

"Of course. I wouldn't be here if I didn't."

"By the way, my secretary gave me a message for you to call Mister Azee as soon as you can."

"I talked to him earlier. Where are we going for the blood tests?"

"For your test we're stopping at a clinic on Gratiot. Your appointment for the blood work is under the name of James Anderson. I'll wait in the car."

"Is this the same clinic where Misty was tested?"

"Do you think I'm stupid? She was tested first in Windsor and then re-tested in a suburban Detroit clinic. We'll drop the president's blood at Detroit Receiving Hospital just like a regular police specimen."

"Too bad you didn't orchestrate my evening with Misty as cautiously as this post factum medical testing," Gleason said as they pulled into the run-down clinic's parking lot. "Don't you think I'm a little overdressed for this clinic? Do they use sterile needles to draw blood?"

"Don't let the shabby appearance fool you. Leave your coat and tie in the car if it makes you feel more at home. This clinic is run and staffed by Wayne State University Medical School. They test a lot of auto company executives with the same need for anonymity. Don't use a credit card or a check. Do you have cash?"

Gleason threw the chief a go-to-hell look as he slammed the door. While Gleason was having his blood drawn in the seedy clinic, the chief checked his voice mail to find another urgent message for Gleason to contact Azee as soon as possible. The chief alerted the returning Gleason.

"For God's sake. All he's worried about is getting his damn boat out of Secret Service custody so he can start refurbishing it. Doesn't he know that his damn boat is the least of our worries? I can call the clinic later today for my test results. I have to remember to ask for James Anderson's results. Drop me off at the FBI office downtown."

"No problem, buddy. While we drive, maybe you can clear up the two questions you posed at the thirty-day meeting. I could have cheated and asked Agent Kozial for the answers."

"Refresh my mind on the questions. A lot has happened since that fruitless meeting."

"You mentioned a name like Leo Showgun and his connection to Detroit."

"Oh, shit! I forgot to get everyone's answers before all hell broke lose. No wonder the Motor City Blitz was a disaster. I lost the edge I need to protect the president."

"Don't go there, Gleason. No one could have prevented what happened. Just answer the questions so I can sleep at night."

"The name was Leon Czolgosz. He was born in Detroit. He shot and killed President McKinley in Buffalo in 1901."

"Why did he do it?"

"If I remember the history of presidential assassinations from our Secret Service training, he was an anarchist who attended socialist meetings. He was a grade-school dropout and susceptible to radical ideas."

"Any parallels with our case?"

"Good question, chief. Whoever masterminded these three nearly simultaneous attacks had to be highly intelligent, not a school dropout. I doubt if the motivation of our attacks was socialism. When this case is finally solved, that's what I want to know the most—the motivation."

"Whatever happened to this Leon? Sure haven't heard of him like Lee Harvey Oswald."

"For good reason. He was tried and executed in the electric chair 45 days after he killed President McKinley. All his personal belongings were destroyed to prevent future notoriety."

"Sounds like a good way to handle it. It will take years to bring this case to trial, and God only knows how long the trial itself will last."

"Couldn't agree with you more. I hope I live long enough to see justice done."

The two old friends silently drove the potholed surface streets through the dingy boarded up neighborhoods of inner city Detroit until the chief double parked in front of the soot blackened, once proud Federal Building. "I'll call you later. Push the trunk release so I can grab my bags."

"Where are you staying tonight?"

"I don't know. I certainly won't be in the presidential suite at the Ren Center hotel, you can count on that."

"Can I drive you to the airport tomorrow?"

"That sounds good to me."

XXIV

Gleason always appreciated the perks of his high-profile White House job because he never forgot his modest upbringing. The FBI office on the ninth floor was the command center for the bombing investigations. Gleason was given a closet-sized office with Salvation Army reject furniture for his use. After being updated on the slow, steady progress of the investigations, Gleason placed a phone call across the Detroit River to Azee's office. Not being on a secure phone line, they agreed to a meeting in Azee's office. Azee would immediately dispatch his helicopter to pick up Gleason at General Motors' heliport across the street from the Federal Building.

The short helicopter flight across the Detroit River carried Gleason past the Ren Center hotel within sight of the top-floor presidential suite. Through the curtainless 70th-floor windows, Gleason could imagine the misty steam billowing above the shadowy figures frolicking in the bubbling whirlpool. It was a flashback nightmare he didn't need to relive.

Azee's offer to pick him up in his helicopter for the sensitive meeting at Global Construction Technology's riverside headquarters was a continuation of the privileged life that Gleason wasn't prepared to surrender. Over the international boundary at the midpoint of the river Abdul radioed both Canadian and United

States immigration services to report his position and that he was transporting one passenger for a business meeting at GCT's headquarters. As usual he was given permission to proceed and instructed to report back on the return trip. Gleason thought to himself that this was a pretty slick way to avoid the traffic backups at the bridge or tunnel connecting the two countries. Abdul skillfully threaded the helicopter down for the rooftop landing in the modern forest of tall antennae and squat satellite dishes.

The Windsor GCT office was not officially notified of Azee's return although it didn't take long for the word to spread that "the man was upstairs." He had immediately descended to his private vault to research his latest concern. In a dilapidated cardboard box marked with a black crayon, "Early Years," he found a musty manila envelope labeled "Newport" that contained a number of faded black-and-white photographs. A penciled notation on the back of one of them said, "Nancy Schmidt—Andre Molodny."

Azee double-checked the program of the self-detonating explosives for their seven-day spontaneous activation to turn the vault's contents into a pile of ash. Azee was pragmatic enough to remove two cash-filled briefcases for storage in his private office safe upstairs while waiting for Gleason's helicopter to arrive.

Before the rotors completely stopped, Azee was opening Gleason's door. "Let's get out of the wind." Inside the polished gold Otis elevator, Gleason's trained eye noticed an aftermarket control panel with an alphanumeric touch pad. Azee pushed the one simple button that said, OFFICE.

"You know, Gleason, I wouldn't have insisted on you coming to my office unless it was extremely urgent—or should I say, top secret?" Their quick smiles ligntened the awkward silence in the confines of the elevator.

Gleason's mind was in a free fall with the descending elevator as he wondered how much Azee knew about his and the president's potential medical problem. But Gleason instinctively reversed the tables. "How was your lunch with the vice president?" The chess game was on.

"The stress of his job seems to be getting to Vice President Taylor. It was nice of you to allow him a little extra freedom to relax at the Sequoia, which you know is his favorite restaurant with its beautiful vista overlooking the Potomac. I think he'll be more relieved than the president when the election is over." The elevator opened directly into Azee's spacious private office.

Gleason quickly scanned the elegant office and the panoramic view of the imposing Detroit skyline across the Detroit River where the battered *Aqua Mole* was clearly visible bobbing at her Renaissance Center mooring.

The only wall that wasn't a window was totally covered from floor to ceiling with framed photos of Azee posing with dignitaries and heads of state, often surrounded by women too artificially put together to be their wives. He easily recognized a stylishly dressed Misty in a number of the photos., so he said, "from everyone's smiles in these pictures, a good time must have been had by all. Who's the beautiful blond in so many of them? Your wife?"

"Hardly! My wife and kids live in Beirut, away from my crazy business. The lady you refer to is a professional hostess. She is on a retainer with GCT for escort services."

Gleason was shocked to get such a forthright answer about Misty from Azee. Surely he knew of the agent's dalliance with her. Or maybe he didn't. "It looks like you work for the United Nations," Gleason commented while scanning the rich and famous on the wall.

"I guess this photo wall proves that it's not what you know, but who you know," Azee answered in a rare moment of self-deprecation, while pointing to a chair at the head of a long conference table.

"This is an interesting shot," Gleason mentioned as he pointed to a picture of Azee standing beside a camel that was tied to a tree. "Do you often resort to camels for transportation when you're in the Middle East?"

"At least camels don't get grounded by sandstorms, as has happened to me on more than one occasion when I'm trying to get in or out of our remote construction sites. I probably shouldn't let you see that picture, since it was taken in an off-limits country where I was traveling at my own risk."

"It's not that incriminating. It's hard to tell what desert you're in. Could be Arizona or New Mexico. I don't see any license plate on the camel."

"Before the picture was taken, the Savak changed the blanket on the camel, which would have been a dead giveaway of not only the country but also the actual village. Each tribe of Bedouin camel herders has its own distinctive symbols within the overall pattern of the blanket. Believe it or not, this smelly camel tied to a tree has an important lesson associated with it."

"And that would be, don't stand too close to a camel's rear end?"

"No. There is a simple, yet profound maxim in the Middle East, 'Tie your camel to a tree and trust in Allah.' Do I need to explain this metaphysics to your overly analytical Western mind?"

"Maybe I could get my ex-wife, the philosophy professor, to explain it to me." Gleason was thankful that Azee had just told him the country where the camel picture was taken. He first thought that Azee was disrespecting his intelligence by mentioning the dreaded Savak, which anyone in governmental security jobs knew were the brutal Iranian secret police. It was rumored that the Savak operated with even less inhibition than the KGB. On second thought, he realized that Azee wanted him to know where the picture was taken without being too obvious.

Pointing to another picture on the wall, Gleason continued the cat-and-mouse game. "Unless I'm mistaken, this old photo of you looks like it was taken in front of the Kremlin. It's a little hard to recognize anyone around you."

"You can thank the old paranoids in the KGB for that. I know that many of the people around me are KGB agents. The photo was taken with a government furnished disposable camera that our KGB guide confiscated from us at the end of each day. He returned the developed, highly doctored prints the next day, along with a new camera."

"You have an interesting collection of the rich and famous.

Even though I've met my share of celebrities during my White House years, I don't think my list can match yours."

"Perhaps sometime in the near future we can compare notes on who knows the most famous people. Meanwhile, I've some rather old but terribly pertinent pictures that can make someone you know rather infamous," Azee said, anxious to get Gleason away from the rouges gallery on the wall."

"Your pictures better be worth it. I left my Detroit office just when they need me." Gleason finally joined Azee at one end of the long conference table.

Azee slid the yellowing pictures over to Gleason. "I'm sorry I couldn't be more specific when I called. I was not on a secure phone. I didn't know who to contact but you."

"Given the problems that happened right across the river on my watch, are you sure about me? The quality of these prints is really bad. Do you have the negatives?"

"No, I wish I did. They were made over twenty years ago from a surveillance camera film, where the quality is marginal under the best of circumstances. Your FBI can probably enhance their clarity if needed."

"I can certainly identify Doctor Schmidt, even without her navy uniform. Who's her fun-loving partner?"

"His name is Andre Molodny. He was on a low security public relations assignment with the Russian government at the Newport Naval Base during the height of the cold war. I discovered Doctor Schmidt and Andre in this compromising situation while locking up the hyperbaric whirlpool on my nightly MP security rounds."

"Why did you save these photos for so many years? Are you into hardcore porn?" Gleason had to bite his lips to avoid smiling while Azee was on the hot seat.

"After I reported this incident to my commanding officer, he told me to keep copies because we didn't know how the Russian government would react when we deported Andre on the next flight to Moscow. The old military 'CYA.' A formal report was never filed by the Navy so as not to disturb the Russian government. I was told the original film was destroyed. I forgot I even had them until Taylor mentioned her name at lunch."

"Did the navy take any action against her? She obviously wasn't discharged, or she wouldn't be treating the first lady."

"I think the navy brass wanted to act like this incident never happened. These photos are probably the only record of this incident."

"Did you tell Taylor about them?"

"No. I wasn't sure that I still had the photos. Over the years I've learned that Taylor should only be informed about issues on a need-to-know basis."

"You seem to feel the same way about him as we do in the White House. Do you have any idea where this Andre is now?" Gleason wondered if Andre was one of the obscured shadows in the Kremlin picture on the wall?

"I don't know where he is. It was assumed that he was in the KGB while at Newport. Thus he didn't have access to any classified material. I've recently heard that he is a consultant to an international public relations firm at the same time that he is head of security for one of the breakaway Russian republics. GCT is submitting bids on the decommissioning of obsolete nuclear missile silos in these breakaway republics, so who knows, we may meet up again. This time fully clothed I hope."

"I'll check out Doctor Schmidt to be sure the care of the first lady is not compromised. I sure don't want the CIA involved. I agree with your wise commanding officer. Keep the photos. Personally, I'll act like this meeting never happened. If I take the photos today, I will have to show them to the president, and he does not want to hear anything bad about Doctor Schmidt. Her twenty-year-old affair should not affect her ability to treat the first lady. Are you sure that Andre is not one of the obscured persons in the Kremlin photograph with you?"

Azee got up from the conference table, walked over to his wall of shame, tore the Kremlin photo off the wall and dropped it on the table in front of Gleason, shattering the glass. "See for yourself. I don't remember all their names, but Andre is not one of them."

Gleason calmly brushed the splintered glass away from his place with the back of his hand. He held up a steamy whirlpool picture of Andre beside the now-glassless Kremlin group shot. He knew he could not make a positive ID by comparing the two poor quality images, but that was not the purpose of the prolonged stare."

"Well, what do you see?"

Gleason ignored the fidgeting Azee for a few more moments. "Neither one of these would win a prize for news photography, that's for sure. The FBI could probably enhance them enough to compare some facial features and help us make an ID, but ..."

"Take 'em both or any others on the wall. I've run out of wall space. Take the whole damn wall."

"No need to do that. At least not now. I've got my hands full with the investigations across the river. I don't see how these pictures could be even remotely connected to the bombings unless Andre has resurfaced as an international terrorist. By the way, we should be able to release the *Aqua Mole* in a day or two, as soon as the FBI gives their okay. Unfortunately, as you know, the interior is a total loss."

"I will just salvage the *Aqua Mole*," Azee replied sadly. "I could never enjoy another cruise on it after what happened to the first lady with me aboard, providing no protection for her."

"Make sure you send a bill to the government for all losses you have incurred. It's the government's obligation to reimburse you for your kindness in hosting the first family."

"Thank you, but there's not enough gold at Fort Knox to replace what I've lost. I'll file an insurance claim and let it go at that."

"How long are you staying in Detroit?" Gleason quickly scanned the picture wall one final time. "I do want to visit your forest preserve sometime. They say it's the nicest natural attraction in southeastern Michigan."

"You would be more than welcome to visit Cripplegate any time. However, I'm leaving shortly for Annapolis to visit one of our construction projects on the Eastern Shore. I also told Taylor I would see him again before I returned to Beirut to resume my interrupted family vacation. What is the best way to get ahold of you without going through the White House operator?"

Gleason handed Azee his business card on the elevator up to the helipad for his return flight to Detroit. "Let's stay in touch."

XXV

Dr. Schmidt's evening drive to the Watergate Hotel was mentally more tortuous than her earlier journey to Andrews Air Force base to drop off the president's blood specimen that Gleason had ordered for the unstated purposes of the Secret Service. None of her rigorous Navy SEAL or CIA Farm training had adequately prepared her for the unexpected role in the surreptitious intrigue unfolding around her. Wheeling into the Watergate Hotel's circular driveway, Nan didn't notice the person making a cell phone call in the decorative red antique phone booth imported from England in an attempt to add a little warming ambience to the hotel's sterile, contemporary design.

After surrendering her car keys to a parking attendant under the hotel portico, she nervously hurried across the highly polished marble lobby floor to the modest bank of two elevators serving the small, exclusive Watergate. She was too preoccupied to be suspicious of the sole lobby occupant, sunk into an overstuffed white leather couch, observing her every move from behind the day's *Washington Post*. She most assuredly did not see him whisper into what appeared to be a cigarette lighter as the elevator doors closed behind its solitary occupant.

The door to the Watergate's presidential suite opened just as

she raised her hand to knock on the heavy oak door. She had no
suspicion of the metal detectors concealed in the door frames or
the hidden cameras that recorded her every move as she was asked
to leave her coat and purse in the anteroom of the opulent suite.

"Good evening, Doctor. It's a pleasure to meet you in person,"
Azee intoned. Smiling, newly bespectacled, mustached and heavily
made up, he offered his ringless hand for a handshake. "My name
is Maxwell. I'm with Internal Affairs."

Schmidt withheld her hand and moved around to stand in
front of the desk where the disguised guest was seated.

"Sorry you feel uncomfortable being here, Doctor Schmidt.
This does not have to be difficult, and it won't take long. Unless
you want to stay for dinner."

"No dinner. I have to get back to the hospital to care for the
first lady. Why did the CIA summon me here for a secret meeting
in a fancy hotel when you have offices all around Washington?
Will you get to the point?"

"As you will see this meeting is outside of the usual scope
of agency activity, so it must be kept secret by all participants.
Especially you, Doctor Schmidt."

"Are you threatening me? I'm leaving."

"Please calm down, Doctor Schmidt. You have not even seen the
evidence yet. You may want to sit down before I show it to you."

"What evidence? What are you talking about?" Schmidt
snapped, her mind racing to get a step ahead of her accuser. She
immediately thought of the unethical and probably illegal transfer
of the president's blood specimen to Gleason for the needs of the
Secret Service in the fast-food parking lot at Andrews Air Force
Base. No attempts at concealing this exchange were made, so it
certainly could have been photographed. Was Gleason also part
of this bizarre turn of events, she wondered. "Can we get on with
the reason that you called me here?"

"As you wish, Doctor Schmidt." Maxwell opened the aging
manila envelope on the desk. "I'll show you these photos one at a
time to see if you recognize anyone. By the way, let me state for the

record that these pictures do not do justice to the participants."

Reluctantly she sat down in the large chair, which hiked her uniform skirt above her knees. Maxwell handed her the top black-and-white photograph with the corners bending in all directions. "You bastard! Where did you get this? Give me the rest of them!"

Maxwell gladly complied with her request, pushing the short stack of photos across the glossy desktop. Studying the incriminating photographs, Schmidt was speechless until finally asking, "Where are the negatives?"

"They're in a safe place for now," Maxwell lied. " You don't have to be so upset. We can work out this minor problem."

"I should tear these up, but that wouldn't do any good, would it? You perverts in the CIA would just make more, probably life-size, and put them on billboards or in the tabloids! You forget that I trained at the Farm. I know how the CIA operates."

"Please, Doctor Schmidt. Our agency is pledged to protect the safety and well being of the United States at any price. Our only concern is the security of the United States against foreign aggression. You must cooperate with us in this case under penalty of treason, as you were an officer of the United States Navy cavorting with a Russian spy."

Schmidt instinctively knew that her "fight or flight" instincts did not appy here, so she resorted to monosyllabic babble, "Where do we go from here?"

"Can you tell us the name of your fellow frolicker, or do we have to torture it out of you?" A big smile elevated and cracked the thick makeup on Maxwell's sardonic face.

"Why are you asking me his name? It's scribbled on the back of the photos, so you won't have the pleasure of torturing me, which I'm sure you would enjoy immensely."

"I was just checking to see how good your memory is. How recently have you been in touch with Andre? Before you answer, remember that we can check your phone records, credit cards and travel stamps on your passport."

"Recently? I haven't heard from him since these pictures. He was deported back to Russia immediately. Even though we thought we were in love, there has been no contact since that day. Don't condemn me without a trial. How did you get these pictures?"

"The hidden security camera at the hyperbaric whirlpool took them. You and Andre sure did some unauthorized after-hours experiments in hyperbarics, or whatever you want to call it. Obviously, the pictures have been saved, and we must deal with the international problems that they can create. Andre was a member of the Russian KGB, which you foolishly ignored."

"We were told that he was a cultural attaché to the Russian United Nations delegation in New York, on special leave to study the basic training methods of our junior navy officers at Newport."

"You had to know he was a spy, yet you got intimately involved with him. Very poor judgment. For your information, Andre Molodny has had a steady rise in the KGB hierarchy. As head of the KGB in Siberia, he presided over a brutal reign of terror, even executing some of our CIA agents. He is now in charge of security for one of the breakaway Soviet republics. He literally has his finger on hundreds of nuclear missiles still aimed at the United States. Though married with three children, he has proven himself to be ruthless and without conscience. He cannot be trusted. Are you sure you haven't been in touch with him since these Newport photos?"

"I said no. Any more questions and I insist on a lawyer being present."

"Fair enough, for now. No more questions. However, as a practical matter, we must do all we can to prevent the tabloids from getting these damming photos before the election. As the physician treating the first lady, their leakage could impact the election, to say nothing of your career in the navy.

"You fucking bastard, Maxwell or whatever your goddamn name is!" Schmidt hissed as she flung the photos back at him. "I resign immediately as the first lady's doctor. I'll gladly give up my navy commission to get away from this nightmare you have created. I've done nothing wrong. Is this what you want?"

"Absolutely not. Remember, it wasn't the CIA that created this nightmare. You did. On the contrary, you will not be allowed to resign, at least not until after the election."

"What do you want? A romp in a whirlpool? Current nude photos for your private collection? What?"

"Please relax doctor. We can and will work our way out of this troublesome problem."

"How come you know so much about Andre? Is he now one of your double agents, who will soon have an automobile accident, leaving a wife and three kids, just because he was once young and foolish and the CIA does not want to be embarrassed by twenty-year-old photos? Don't I know you from somewhere?"

"Doctor Schmidt, do I need to remind you that I'm the one asking the questions?" Maxwell quickly changed the subject away from their chance meeting in Newport twenty years earlier that she might be starting to remember. "My final observation, doctor, is that you recently released a specimen of the president's blood without his written consent. This is highly unethical, if not outright illegal."

"I was ordered by the Secret Service to give them the specimen for purposes of national security. I'm also having the president's blood tested at Bethesda under an alias. I'll have the results tomorrow. Do you want to know the results of these tests also, which of course would be illegal for me to disclose to you?"

"We don't have time to get into a Nuremberg discussion on the morality of following orders, or what's right or wrong in times when the national security is challenged. I will contact you tomorrow for your results so we can compare them to our out-of-town tests."

"Why the hell is everyone all of a sudden so interested in the president's blood tests?"

"You will be told the reason for the interest in these tests when it's appropriate. For now, just keep assuming that this is a still matter of highest national security. In spite of what you may think, we're not interested in the president's or your STD history."

"I know this whole scenario is a pile of bullshit, and so do you! I'll bet that your name is Maxwell Smart, like the TV spy, so you should have all this figured out without my help."

"What you and I think isn't important," Maxwell said, struggling to suppress a smile at her astute observation. "The only other thing that must be done is to postpone the president's annual physical until after the election."

"Why should I do that? The media will become suspicious."

"You're asking too many questions that cannot be answered now. The answers will be clear after the election. Carry on your normal activities as if this meeting never happened." Maxwell escorted the still livid Schmidt toward the door without again offering dinner, for which he was certain she had no appetite.

Outside the polished brass hotel entrance she gave the bellman a two-dollar tip for retrieving her car and told him to put any parking bill on the presidential suite's tab. She was tempted to park on the street around the corner from the hotel to see who might emerge from her personal all-time hell hole. If indeed this was a CIA operation, she was most certainly under their surveillance. On further thought, she didn't want to give them, whoever they were, the satisfaction of knowing that they had her overly concerned.

XXVI

A profound serenity engulfed Doctor Schmidt on the drive back to Bethesda as she remembered incidents of her torrid affair with Andre. Maxwell's photos to the contrary, her personal favorite memories of Andre were of the weekend they'd spent together in New York City. Andre wanted her to meet his brother Boris, a dental student at New York University in lower Manhattan. In typical male fashion, she thought at the time, Andre had not notified Boris that they were coming for a visit, so when calling upon their arrival, Boris informed them that he had his important licensing exams, the North East Regional Board of Dentistry tests. He would only be able to see them Saturday evening while he was working his waiter's shift at a restaurant in the theater district.

Andre had obviously been there before, as he gave the cab driver the location of Fifty-second Street and Eighth Avenue without mentioning the name of the restaurant. Because of Andre's attitude that the cost of anything on their big city escape is not a consideration, she had a mental picture of a posh pre-theater hideaway where they would meet Boris wearing his tuxedo to wait on their table. They could enjoy a leisurely dinner since they had no plans to attend a Broadway show. So when the yellow cab came to a screeching halt in front of the Cosmic Diner, she froze in her seat until Andre gave her a gentle prod. "Let's go, we're here."

Boris spotted them immediately when they entered the dated nouveau Vegas interior of scratched stainless steel bar stools and torn tan naugahyde booths and quickly steered them to a back table in his section before they were devoured by another hungry waiter trying to build up his tip bank for the evening.

She had a twenty-year-old faded recollection of Boris as handsome in a rugged sort of way, whereas Andre had fine features and carried himself like an aristocrat.

Boris bragged that the Cosmic Dinner, hardly bigger than a fast-food hamburger stand, had the largest menu of any New York restaurant and after flipping through the eight plastic covered pages, she wasn't going to dispute that rather dubious honor. Ordering today's special—two pork chops with boiled carrots and mashed potatoes and gravy—from the narrow plastic strip down the permanently sealed center of the menu, she settled in to enjoy the diner's distinctive Big Apple ambiance. Its diversity reminded her of the United Nations which she and Andre had visited that afternoon as VIPs with his diplomatic credentials.

While strolling in the United Nation's outside courtyard overlooking the East River, the plaque on the heavy cast plowshare, "Beat your weapons into plowshares," had elicited a hope-filled question from Andre. "Do you think this will ever happen?" She viewed the interior of the bustling diner as one small steep toward world peace, and she knew that Andre, by the gentle tone of his question, felt the same way.

The waiters and busboys spoke heavily accented English and seemed to be from diverse ethnic backgrounds. Boris mentioned that they were like the United Nations, with over twenty nationalities working at the diner. When she asked Boris what he was going to do when he graduated, he commented that if he passed the North East Regional Board of Dentistry tests, he would like to practice dentistry somewhere in the New York City area because of the large Russian population that would want a Russian-speaking dentist. As she remembered, Andre offered to assist his brother with a work visa and other required paperwork to expedite this desire to live in the United States, but that probably didn't happen, as Andre was soon deported. She made a mental note to check if Boris was living in the New York area as he had hoped to.

The big sign for Bethesda Naval Medical Center jolted her back to reality, but not enough to notice the dark sedan that had discretely followed her from her Watergate meeting.

XXVII

After his enlightening meeting with Azee, Gleason was occupied with a series of quick update meetings and numerous phone calls from investigating agents pounding the pavement twenty-four hours a day. But the phone call that bothered him the most was the one that he had not yet made.

Before going up to his room at the Omni Hotel near the tunnel entrance to Canada and across Jefferson Avenue from the fateful Renaissance Center, he found an old-fashioned pay phone near the elevator bank. He could not chance that caller ID would trace the call back to his hotel room.

Closing the warped, half glass door, he dialed the medical clinic on Gratiot that he had visited earlier in the day. When the nurse put him on hold so she could get a doctor to come to the phone, he knew the answer he was calling about without the need for verbal confirmation. In the gloomy isolation of the dark phone booth tears filled his eyes. He wanted to hang up, but he couldn't. He was in shock, and nothing worked except his free-flowing tear ducts. Finally he heard a faraway voice.

"Is this James Anderson?"

"Yes."

"Can you come to the clinic to talk to us?"

"No."

"It's very important and confidential. Why not?"

Click was Gleason's answer to the well-intentioned doctor. Gleason sobbed in the cramped phone booth until his chest hurt from being hunched over. When he finally got control of himself, he made a call across the river to Misty, trying to arrange one last fling in the presidential suite. Fortunately, she didn't pick up the call, so he lucked out by leaving the terse message, "Tonight. Same time, presidential suite. No dessert needed."

You can only catch AIDS once, he rationalized. He was terrified of what he would have said if she had answered the call. Giving no return number to Misty, he was left with the uncertainty whether she would show up for this reprise performance, especially since Chief Hawkins had told her no more fun days, at least in Detroit.

Gleason was able to duck unnoticed from the phone booth into the elevator. In his violated smoke-free room, where the posted warning sign on the back of the door had been altered to read SMOKE FREELY, he emptied the dubious contents of his large suitcase without worrying about dirtying the already stained bedspread. He needed to blend in with the natives tonight, so he picked from his Goodwill rejects the ugliest homeless person disguise he could put together for his self-ordered undercover assignment.

The flabbergasted bellhop, seeing Gleason's outlandish street person costume, warned him not to wander too far from the hotel entrance where he could keep an eye out for him. Earlier in the day Gleason had spotted a bench that provided a view of cars exiting the tunnel under the Detroit River from Canada onto Jefferson Avenue and then into the Ren Center if that was their destination.

Gleason did his best drunken swagger, wearing his old faded blue Tigers' baseball cap pulled down so far over his face that he could barely see, to the pre-selected bench beside a reclining wino, who fortunately was too far gone to engage in any conversation. His sole mission tonight was to get the license number of Misty's limousine to verify with total certainty that it was owned by Azee.

His best partner tonight was the sleeping wino slumped on

the park bench beside him and Gleason was hopeful that Chief Hawkins wouldn't be cruising Jefferson Avenue tonight to test his disguise.

As the cooling evening advanced without the anticipated results, he remembered an idyllic week at boy scout camp with nightly hide-and-seek games. One night waiting under the umbrella of a weeping willow tree on the bank of the White River, his scout-master uttered the now prophetic words of an old Indian proverb: "Sit on the banks of the river, and soon your enemy's body will float by."

Only minutes later a white limousine exited the tunnel from Canada and turned right on Jefferson, then immediately into the fortresslike Renaissance Center driveway. Gleason quickly noted the Canadian license number, feeling like a scout who'd just won the camp's hide-and-seek game. He sincerely hoped there were no residents in the presidential suite tonight who would be tempted to taste some fatal late night dessert like he did when Misty came knocking. Gleason felt no remorse for standing Misty up for an encore performance.

Returning to his drab room in the Omni and confirming what he already suspected about the limousine's ownership by tracking the license number, Gleason felt compelled to open a new channel of investigation when he talked with the Indianapolis FBI office to request that they dispatch agents to the Otis Elevator corporate headquarters in nearby Bloomington to inquire about the elevators in the GCT office building in Windsor. He impressed on them the need for discrete alacrity.

The morning briefings by the lead investigators were an opportunity to share information on the three bombings with the whole team. Maria Visconti, as head of the Detroit FBI office, was coordinating the Ambassador Bridge bombing investigation. "Police divers using underwater sonar detectors have not recovered any evidence from the fast-moving water under the Ambassador Bridge van explosion. The road surface was deeply pockmarked but not completely blown through by the blast. The owner of the destroyed van had reported it stolen the day before the bridge explosion. A background check of the van's owner revealed nothing suspicious. The explosion and subsequent fire destroyed any chance of physical evidence from the van. "

"So, what are your agents investigating?" Gleason questioned.

"Hopefully our door-to-door canvas of a three-mile radius around the bridge entrance will uncover something. The area now is basically a seedy warehouse district with Tiger Stadium at the outer limit of our search grid. This once-flourishing residential area near the Ambassador Bridge is still called Corktown in recognition of the early inhabitants' Irish heritage. It seems ironic that the Irish, with their penchant for bombings in their homeland, would now be under scrutiny in this country, where they have been accepted and have prospered."

"Let's not be too quick to implicate my native land," Gleason said to the laughter of the other participants.

"We are also concentrating on the surveillance cameras above the toll booths on the bridge approaches. Witnesses are reporting that the van was abandoned about ten minutes before the explosion, and our surveillance film roughly corroborates that time frame. We have located the van on the film and currently are computer-enhancing the vehicles that entered the bridge simultaneously with the van on the United States side under the assumption that one of these vehicles picked up the driver of the van."

"Are there cameras on both ends of the bridge?" Gleason asked to try to clarify Visconti's report.

"Yes, there are, and we…"

"Okay then," Gleason interrupted, "we can't automatically assume that the pick-up vehicle is going in the same direction as the van, toward Canada. If we can get the license numbers of the cars entering with or slightly after the van, these drivers should be located and questioned about what they saw. I assume you're working closely with Canadian customs in analyzing their film."

A frustrated Agent Visconti stood again to resume her interrupted report. "We are analyzing the films from both sides of the bridge. This is very time-consuming work since vehicles do not have front license plates any more."

Gleason was determined to shorten Visconti's slow-moving monologue. "Driving the speed limit, as the bombers would to avoid attention, how long does it take to drive from the explosion site to the toll booths on either end of the bridge?"

"It takes about three minutes to get to either side."

"Then do the math, Agent Visconti. If the van was abandoned ten minutes before it exploded, I would concentrate on vehicles arriving at either toll booth seven minutes before the explosion. This seven-minute window probably allowed them to get off the bridge before the explosion. Does this make sense to you, Agent Visconti?"

"Yes, sir. Those are the assumptions we are operating under. We know that the explosion was set off by a timer, because a simple remote control detonator, like was used at the *Aqua Mole*, wouldn't work at that distance. With our joint Canadian-American team working around the clock, it will take at least a week to decipher and time synchronize the films from both sides."

"Agent Visconti, we don't have a week. There are dangerous international terrorists possibly still walking the streets of Detroit." Gleason was doing his best to be complimentary and also to control himself since many of the people at this briefing had attended the ill fated thirty day prior meeting where General Hodgechis got the best of him.

Agent Visconti was still standing to make her final points. "New technology will help us solve this bombing. It will just take time. For example, the black-and-white surveillance film is being converted to color by infrared technology. This has to be laboriously done, frame-by-frame. The end result of a color film with various shades of contrast will make license plate reading possible. It all takes time."

"Make no mistake about it. I love new technology. Hopefully it will provide some ironclad evidence. But stop for a minute and think like a terrorist, not a scientist. If you were running this mission to pick up the van driver, how many people would you have in the pick-up vehicle?"

"I haven't really thought about that. I would say probably one person."

"Not probably. You would have one driver for each vehicle. The main credo of terrorists is that you never endanger more people than necessary to carry out a mission. The rest of the terrorists that helped rig the van were either back cleaning up the staging garage or they've already left town and probably the country. In the surveillance films, look for a vehicle that enters the bridge with one person and exits with two. Both would be sitting in the front seat to avoid arousing suspicion. Now that I think about it, putting myself in the mindset of a terrorist, I would probably exit on the Canadian side and be on my way back to where I came from without worrying about United States authorities. Since this three-pronged terrorist attack was so precisely orchestrated, they probably exited the bridge within the seven-minute window we discussed before the bomb exploded. They had to be off the bridge before the bomb detonated so as not to get trapped on the bridge if it was closed down immediately. Concentrate on the vehicles leaving the bridge on the Canadian side with two people."

"Yes, sir. Is there anything else?" Visconti half-heartedly asked.

"Have the Windsor Police Department and the RCMP been put on alert to look for abandoned cars within a short radius of the bridge? This terrorist operation is a lot like a bank robbery where the criminals switch to a new getaway car. The terrorist will know that someone going in either direction on the bridge would have spotted the pick-up vehicle."

"We have been monitoring our tip line for anyone who says they saw the actual pick-up of the van driver. The owners of the bridge have posted a one-hundred-thousand-dollar reward for information helping to solve this bombing."

"Nice work, Agent Visconti. The final thing I'm counting on is that the terrorists did not either darkly tint their pick-up vehicle's windows or use a stolen vehicle with tinted windows to prevent us from viewing them on camera."

"Sir, we are operating on the assumption that the pick-up vehicle wasn't stolen, in case customs and immigration agents pulled a random check on vehicle ownership. It could be a rental vehicle, and we're doing a search of all vehicles rented last week in Detroit and Windsor. This list will then be compared to the surveillance film breakdown of vehicle models when it's available. Also we are not discounting the possibility that the pick-up driver could be female, as it would arouse less suspicion than two males during a customs check." Agent Visconti was relieved to sit down, having saved a little face in front of her colleagues with her stolen car and possible female driver comments.

"I doubt that they would change drivers at the time of the pick-up on the center span of the bridge. If there are no additional comments on the bridge incident, I would like to move onto the other investigations."

XXVIII

Agent Yance, who was at the scene of the yacht explosion, was appointed to coordinate this bi-country investigation. Gleason began, "Agent Yance, I haven't thanked you for helping me out of the river. I was in shock and could have drowned without your assistance. I'm grateful for all your help that difficult day."

"Thank you, sir. I just wish this investigation was going as smoothly as your rescue. The evidence recovered from the river bottom around the *Aqua Mole* is interesting but mostly inconsequential. The divers can hardly use their underwater metal detectors because of the thickness of the sediment on the river bottom. They are sifting the silt-like flour to see what remains in the sifter. They have found an old Indian arrowhead, which we'll donate to the museum.

"Agent Yance, "can you get more to the point? We have a lot of ground and water to cover today," Gleason abruptly commented.

"Yes, sir. We have found the usual assortment of bottles and cans, a garage door opener," Agent Yance turned the page to continue reading from his long list of river bottom memorabilia.

"What frequency was the garage door opener set for?" Gleason hoped to get Yance away from his laundry list of river bottom refuse.

"The electronics people are checking that. The opener doesn't appear to have been in the river very long. We could still distinguish its original light brown color."

"Speaking of electronics, what was operable on the boat at the time of the explosion?" Gleason asked.

"All the usual marine electronics like radios, radar and depth finders were unplugged as we ordered the owner so as not to interfere with our White House communication systems. The marine ship-to-shore radio was operative. On your orders, Azee called the coast guard cutters to enforce the no-wake zone."

"I remember that. What about other household items like microwaves, police scanners, AM/FM radio receivers?"

"The microwave oven was being used to warm the catered snack food. No police scanners were discovered. The only conventional radio on board is the original built-in AM/FM receiver located near the galley. The rear plugs, antennae and speaker wires are accessible from a closet in the adjacent head. We called the Stephens yacht people, and they confirmed the original serial numbers. There are some scratches inside the closet, indicating it might have been removed for service at one time."

"Did you remove the radio to send it for testing?"

"No, but we played it and it worked fine on both AM and FM. We don't want to delay getting the boat back to the owner in its original condition by removing it."

"Original condition!," Gleason boomed waking up any sleeping participants. "We are running water pumps to keep it afloat. The *Aqua Mole* is a barely floating piece of criminal evidence. We can do whatever we want with it. Have the radio removed and tested. Perhaps we have been talking too much about the *Aqua Mole*, which is merely the innocent victim of the car bomb. What's the bottom line on this limousine explosion, Inspector Brightwell?"

"I'm happy to give the Canadian perspective on our limousine's explosion. You can be assured that the RCMP are working with all due haste to solve this ghastly crime. As a matter of fact, we have called on our long association with Scotland Yard to assist us. They have much experience with terrorists on their own soil and in Ireland. Although we are rapidly gaining our own dreadful experience in our Quebec province with the French speaking terrorists, who are intent on blowing the country apart."

"Pleasure meeting you, Inspector Brightwell. We certainly welcome and need your help and that of the esteemed Scotland Yard, as well as Interpol in solving the sabotage of your limousine on our soil. Since the two most prominent components, the boat and the limousine, are Canadian licensed, both countries have a vested interest in solving these crimes. As you heard me explain to Agent Visconti, time is of the essence. We still have deadly terrorist groups on the prowl. It concerns me that if too many agencies and countries get involved, the investigations will get bogged down in red tape."

"The Canadian government is in total agreement with you. It appears our losses are limited to the limousine, whereas you bear the heavy loss of flesh and blood. We are fortunate that the prime minister and his wife were not in the limousine when it exploded. We have narrowed our suspect list at the motor pool in Ottawa to two mechanics. One of them seems to check out okay. The other suspect seems to have disappeared off the face of the earth. He has friends and family ties in Quebec that we are investigating."

"This is the most encouraging news of the day, Inspector Brightwell. I'm sure you will find him as quickly as possible. If no other comments, let's adjourn to the Lodge expressway site," Gleason ended the meeting.

XXIX

The visit to the Lodge expressway explosion was mildly encouraging to the stymied investigators. New evidence was being discovered by the minute. The federal ATF explosives experts theorized that the explosion of the gasoline station across the street from the house was most likely accidental and not planned by the terrorists—an unexpected bonus for them, complicating the ATF's already complex puzzle. The primary explosion under the roadbed of the expressway triggered the underground petroleum storage tanks via fumes in the storm sewers connecting to the gasoline station. The investigators were encouraged to rule the secondary explosion merely coincidental, even though they were no closer to solving the total case.

It was becoming apparent to the arson investigators that the house probably was the key to unraveling the mystery. The sandy dirt nearly filling the basement of the leveled house matched the foundry fill that had been used as a filling and leveling subsurface to build up the roadbed. The industrial contaminants in the sand and dirt were consistent with foundry fill from the Ford plant in River Rouge. This rather coarse-grained molding sand came from a sand mine on Muskegon Lake that leveled the once-majestic 300-foot-tall Pigeon Hill sand dune. The raw glacial sand, formed by retreating glaciers 100,000 years ago, was shipped 500 miles by freighters and barges to Ford's River Rouge complex.

A hole large enough for a man to crawl through had been cut into the old fieldstone basement wall of the leveled house. This hole connected via a short excavated tunnel to a three-foot-diameter storm sewer that ran parallel to the house's basement wall. Sandhogs obviously carried bucket after bucket of this excavated sand into the basement.

A calculation of the excavated area compared to the remaining sand in the basement revealed that some must have been removed from the premises. Once access to the storm sewer was achieved, it was a relatively simple matter to trace and follow the sewer system labyrinth until you were under the actual roadbed of the Lodge expressway.

Agent Sandra Kozial anticipated Gleason's questioning of how the terrorist knew the layout of the storm sewer explaining that a set of "as built" blueprints was missing from the road commission office.

Explosives experts determined that simple dynamite had been used in the storm sewer under the roadbed. Perhaps a dozen detonators, perfectly timed to explode milliseconds apart, started the catastrophic chain of events that demolished the presidential motorcade. She postulated that the terrorists must have practiced somewhere because it was critical to get the right amount of explosive in the perfect location to achieve the desired result.

Gleason waited until everyone was gathered around the charred, explosive-smelling basement. "Who owns this property?"

"We've done a title search to no avail." It was Agent Kozial's turn to be on the hot seat. "It seems the last two or three owners sold the property for cash on land contracts that were never recorded with the registrar of deeds office. The owner of the property listed on the city tax rolls has been deceased for over ten years. The property taxes are current and were paid in cash. No one in the city of Detroit tax office has any recollection of the person paying the taxes. Unfortunately, there are no video surveillance cameras in the tax office to record business transacted there. Ownership of property in this inner city locale is nothing to brag about with all the crack and prostitution houses around. Real estate ownership can be convoluted and often untraceable here. As long as the real estate taxcs are kept current, the city of Detroit maintains a benign hands-off policy as to the actual owner of any piece of real estate."

Gleason was thinking to himself that this is the same agent who a month ago was uncertain about the first lady's luncheon menu. "Agent Kozial, there is the old expression, 'possession is nine-tenths of the law.' Who has possessed this property for the last six months or year? What have the neighbors been able to tell you? There must have been a lot of truck traffic here while the terrorists excavated and removed the excess sand."

"Residents of this inner city neighborhood tend to mind their own business unless they want to get shot or killed. We are following up on some rental truck descriptions that neighbors have provided with great reluctance. The excavated sand was apparently removed one pail at a time from the basement, as no heavy equipment was ever noticed. The neighbors, that aren't too high on booze or drugs to talk, assumed that someone was remodeling and bringing the house up to code. There hasn't been a family living here for two or three years. Only for the last two weeks before the bombing were lights on at night."

"Maybe Chief Hawkins can use some undercover detectives who know the area to determine ownership of this property." Gleason nodded in the chief's direction, who flashed back a confirmaory thumbs-up, so he continued, "you don't knock a three-foot hole in the basement stone wall, excavate a tunnel in the sand connecting to the city storm sewer system, move yards of dirt off the premises, and haul in a ton of dynamite unless you are sure that the owner isn't going to show up unexpectedly. The current owner of this property has a hand in this bombing. Knowledge of past and present owners of this property is critical to solving this case. Chief, can you give us a little extra help on this ownership investigation? Maybe reassign some people from the boat and bridge bombings? The international teams seem to be making progress in those areas."

"No problem," the chief said. "We'll do whatever it takes to restore the good name of the proud city of Detroit."

XXX

"Let's go somewhere quiet and private, away from all the nurses," the president suggested.

"Certainly, Mister President. Let's step across the hall to my one-room suite." Schmidt replied, flipping shut the first lady's bulging chart to bring with them.

"Nan, I have a simple request." The president closed the door behind them. "Please call me what my oldest and dearest friends call me—Archie, short for Archibald. How I've always hated that name, Archibald. In this hopeless situation it doesn't help to be president. I'm just like any other man. The first lady wouldn't be in her dreadful condition if I wasn't president. It helps me to forget for a few fleeting moments that I am president if you call me Archie."

"This will take some adjustment, sir, as you are my commander in chief," Nan said as she sat on the hospital bed with the first lady's chart beside her. "Archie, how have you been feeling?" Nan could hardly contain her smile at her own boldness in addressing the president of the United States by his nickname.

"See, that wasn't so hard was it? I've never been into all the formality bullshit that goes with the presidency."

"Archie, do I have to order you to answer my question?" Nan surprised herself again with her frankness in talking to her boss.

With the patient seated beside her on the bed, separated by the first lady's medical chart, the gulf of the doctor-patient relationship was slowly closing. Nan remembered the nightly ritual of her mother or father reading her a bedtime story and how comforting that special private time with one of her parents had been. She was getting a similar warm feeling as the president encroached on her space.

"I am sorry, Nan. My mind is on other things. I'm feeling fine. How did my blood tests turn out?"

"I haven't had time to check with the lab, but I'm sure that everything is okay."

"Probably so and the media would like to report my every bowel movement or sexual encounter. I guess there isn't much to report on the second area anyway." Archie's leg moved the chart closer to Nan's trim, athletic posterior.

"Speaking of the media, I think it would be a good idea to postpone your physical examination until after the election. The media is preoccupied with the first lady's condition, It looks like that's helping your reelection efforts, so we shouldn't distract them with the mundane findings of your annual physical."

"I don't think we publicly announced that I was having a physical before the election. The only real need for a pre-election physical is if there is some serious question about the president's health and the election appears close. Neither of these conditions is present. Let's wait until after the election. Maybe even until I get this damn cast off. I'm having a difficult time urinating with this cast. Did you ever try to work the zipper on your fly with only one hand?"

"Can't say that I ever had that problem. Let's take a minute to review the first lady's chart."

"Okay, but spare me all the doctor lingo, unless there are significant changes in the last twenty-four hours," he said, sliding closer to look at the chart on her lap.

"We really haven't discussed one of the test results from the Henry Ford trauma team in Detroit that we have repeated here. Do you remember them mentioning a Glasgow Coma Score?"

"I was so sedated for my broken arm, that I can hardly remember the hospital. It seems a long time ago. A really bad nightmare, except nightmares are supposed to end when you wake up!"

"That's right. Nightmares end. This is a real-life tragedy with no end in sight. After numereous hyperbaric oxygen treatments, the first lady still has a Glasgow Coma Score of three. Does that sound familiar to you?"

"The number three does ring a bell. I must have assumed that since it wasn't zero, it wasn't so bad."

"You have a lot on your mind. A Glasgow Coma Score of three really equals zero, which is as bad as it gets."

"Three equals zero?"

"The Glasgow Coma Score quantifies the level of consciousness following a serious brain injury. Each of three areas of bodily function is evaluated and given a numerical score, with the number one being the lowest, meaning no response."

"What are the areas checked for responses?"

"First area is eye opening: a score of one means no eye opening. Second is verbal response: one means no words or sounds. Third is motor response: one means no reaction to external stimuli. So three equals zero."

"It's obvious why I blocked it out after hearing it in Detroit. Pretty bleak assessment of Kathy's present condition—and I suppose her prognosis too."

"We haven't totally given up. We are monitoring the first lady's brain activity, which still shows no sleep-wake cycles. If this ..."

"This is nothing new, is it?" the president interrupted.

"I was starting to say that if this condition persists for four weeks, it's classified as a vegetative state. If the condition lingers another month, it's called a persistent vegetative state."

"So she's in a vegetative state?" The president's casted arm came to rest on Nan's thigh as he struggled to inch closer to alledgedly get a better view of the chart on her lap. "Call it what you want. It sounds like we are getting caught in a medical terminology maze."

"I know, Archie, but I thought we were trying to preserve the status quo until after the election. Are we changing directions in managing her case? Should I stop the hyperbaric treatments?"

"Not unless you recommend it. You're in charge."

"Then I say let's go visit the first lady. The nosey nurses know we're in here with the door shut."

"I forgot. You have a reputation to maintain. Presidents don't have that problem."

"That's for sure. We have neonatal doctors coming in this afternoon for a consultation on the viability of the fetus. Do you want to talk to them?"

"No, I wouldn't understand their medical mumbo-jumbo. Why don't you bring their report to the White House tonight?"

"That works for me, assuming nothing changes with the first lady." She stood to straighten her crisply starched and ironed uniform. The president was airborne getting off the bed. He floated across the hall with a bounce to his steps that was missing since returning from Detroit.

XXXI

"I don't know if I will ever be back to Detroit, Jeff." Gleason was fighting back his "Irish eyes" as they turned into Detroit Metropolitan Airport.

"What are you talking about, man? You can't leave me to do all the work solving these bombings."

"I think you know what I mean. Are you forgetting my lab results? By the way, please apologize to Misty for last night."

"You didn't do it again last night with Misty?"

"You know what I'm talking about."

The chief instinctively slammed on the Buick's brakes and the car skidded to a halt halfway up the drive to the fixed-base operation where the Secret Service jet was waiting. He twisted his massive bulk sideways as far as the impinging steering wheel would allow while reaching across Gleason for the door handle. "You can get out here and walk to your private jet if you like."

"Jeff, let me buy you a cup of coffee. We have things to discuss."

"This is my office. We can do it right here, right now."

"It's your call. You could get off the road so we don't get rear-ended."

"Is this how all our years are going to end?"

"Nothing's ending. I just need some answers. How long has

Misty worked in the casino?"

"She started at the casino when it opened recently. She knew her tabletop dancing days were over. It's a young woman's profession."

"Do you know how many white Caddy limousines there are in Windsor?"

"That's like asking me how many overpass bridges there are on our expressways. I'll find out for you."

"Do you know who owns them?"

"Let's catch a breath. Go back to the beginning. What difference does it make how long Misty has worked in the casino? What happened at the Ren Center was your business, not the casino's. What are you getting at?"

"How often do the tabletop dancers have to be tested for sexually transmitted diseases?"

"The law requires them to be tested every six months. The Canadian authorities try their best to enforce this, but the girls are always changing jobs, making enforcement hard."

"Do the hostesses in the casinos have to be tested like the dancers?"

"No." Jeff sensed where Tom was going with this train of thought.

"Then if my math is correct, it could have been over a year since she was last tested."

"That sounds right to me. As I said, Misty's current hostess job at the casino does not require her to be tested. I can get a three-year record of her blood tests, but the record-keeping for this testing program has been notoriously lax and fraudulent. What are you getting at?"

"Have you been tested?"

"If you weren't my friend, I would shoot you with the thirty-eight on my hip. I'm a happily married man. I don't fool around."

"Sorry, Chief. Didn't mean to insult you, but I'm concerned and angry that I may have been set up for this very costly one-night stand."

"If you recall when we were eating in the casino, you made all the arrangements with Misty without any help from me. You were hot to trot, as I remember."

"I'm not accusing you of setting me up. But there are other forces at work in Windsor and Detroit even thirty days before the presidential visit, reaching all the way into the swank bedroom of the presidential suite."

"I don't know how much you talked to Misty that night. She has two kids from an abusive marriage. She's their sole support. One of her kids is terminally ill with leukemia, and the medical bills are staggering. She's always needed to supplement her meager salary with outside work and probably a sugar daddy."

"Probable sugar daddy? Who?"

"You don't have to believe this, but I didn't know or care about a sugar daddy until the last few days."

"One guess. He owns a demolished yacht that was used as a floating whorehouse for visiting dignitaries from around the world."

"Bingo. My Windsor sources report that Misty was involved with Global Construction Technology even before they moved across the river. She's a survivor."

"Misty was a survivor. Her kids are going to be orphaned. She has to be taken off the streets before she destroys more lives besides mine."

"I've already talked to the police in Windsor and to Misty about her blood tests. Her fun days are over."

"Did you tell her about my tests?"

"I should shoot you again. I'm going to be running out of bullets if this keeps up. You must really think that I hate you. As if accusing me of setting you up with Misty knowing that she had AIDS isn't enough, you really think that I would now tell her about your AIDS. Some friend!"

"I'm not trying to place blame on anyone, especially you. I'm angry, mostly at myself for my carnal stupidity. The damage is done. The horse is out of the barn running wild in Detroit, Windsor, Washington, Beirut and around the world, trampling everything in his path."

"I didn't tell Misty or anyone else that you were coming to town. Since you tried to play Dick Tracy by calling her and then standing her up for a reprise in the presidential suite, I'm sure she knows you are here."

"I had to be one hundred percent certain how she gets to work. The license plate on her limousine was traced to GCT."

"That doesn't surprise me. GCT is an octopus. It entangles and strangles everything it touches, just like its owner. They're always chauffeuring VIPs around both sides of the river."

"The most recent pictures on Azee's hall of fame wall show Misty with many local and foreign dignitaries. This will turn into an international wall of shame if more AIDS surface among GCT clients."

"This is serious business. I never realized that Misty was so intimately involved with Azee and his company. I wondered how she always seemed to be with the high rollers. Azee needs a blood test just like you and the president. The Canadian authorities should get the names of everyone Misty and GCT entertained in the last two years and notify them to be tested."

"Does Misty keep a little black book? That would be the simple way to get the names without alerting Azee too soon that we are onto something."

"Her little black book might more resemble a telephone book," the chief prophetically answered.

"Any local clients' names would make it uncomfortable for some of the big shots around Detroit, besides the international fallout."

"If she has a little black book, she wouldn't have to give it to us without a court order, which won't be a problem since I know all the judges. Don't forget that your name could be listed, so we may not want public disclosure."

"It's too late to worry about me. Morally we have to notify everyone on his list of clients—black book or not. I have to get foolproof evidence on Azee before I go to the president. Azee was a soulmate of the first lady's, which I couldn't fathom if I was president. Azee is also close with the vice president, and somewhat with my boss at Treasury. So I have to use a little more discretion than usually suits me. I should call the CIA's covert op people to resolve this in their own unique way."

"Before you call the CIA, call me. I and some of my people would take great pleasure in seeing that Azee feels pain for what he has done. Promise?"

"Chief, just kidding! I'll handle Azee myself before I call the CIA or get you involved. As much as you want to help, I can't allow you to do anything foolish. You have grand children that need your love for a lot of years. This is my war, and I've nothing to lose by resolving it 'my way,' as Frank Sinatra says."

"Are you going to tell the president about your positive blood test?"

"Not until these bombings are resolved and the election is over. If Bethesda got the same inconclusive results on his blood work as we did, we still have some time. We were specifically looking for the HIV virus in his Detroit Receiving Hospital test, and they could not conclusively isolate it, maybe because it's too early to get a positive test result from my donated blood. My sources tell me there is nearly one-hundred-percent certainty that the president's blood will test positive for HIV like mine, since he received two units of my infected blood. It's just a matter of when. Sometime you may have to explain and clarify some of these issues with the president and my ex-wife. Azee should be out of the picture by then."

"You're talking in riddles, which really alarms me. Sometimes problems are bigger that any one person."

"Chief, let's get going. My plane is ready. You've been parked so long you're smothering the grass. Write yourself a ticket for illegal parking."

"I don't know what more to say. I would trade my blood for yours if I could." the chief wiped his eyes with the back of his massive hand.

"With the current cocktail therapies being used for AIDS, I should have some time left. Of course, I'll have to resign from the service, but I was going to retire soon anyway. One final thing. I'm not sure where the bombing investigations will lead or how they'll end. I want you to know and believe that I'm doing the right thing for the country in spite of what the media or the government may say. The finale may get convoluted, so I'm trusting you to believe in me regardless of what happens. Please relay this message to Cindy if something happens to me. I'm going to try meeting her tonight when I get back to D.C. and try to explain this whole damn mess."

The chief got out of the car to retrieve his friend's overnight bag. Gleason was returning to Washington with less luggage—but more baggage—than he arrived with. The two friends silently embraced for what both felt could be the last time.

Gleason looked forward to the solitude of the short flight to Andrews Air Force base to clear his head and conscience of all the personal and professional fallout since his ill-fated thirty day prior visit to Detroit.

The one idea that kept derailing his train of thought was that he needed to talk to Cindy. There was no one reason why he kept recycling this obsessive idea of meeting with her that made it impossible to squelch with hard logic. There wasn't anything concrete to confront, just his gut feeling that he needed to see her.

Beginning his descent into Andrews, he dialed her number on the plane's phone with the everpresent paranoid feelings that he didn't want to bother Cindy and risk her possible rejection. In reality he feared that he would lay bare his fragile soul to her as he had never done in their years of marriage.

Fortunately there was the sweetly unforgettable "Hello, Cindy speaking," that immediately focused his attention away from his fear that she would reject his invitation.

"Hi, Cindy, how are you?"

"I'm fine. You're the one I still worry about way too much."

"Thanks Cindy. I'm just landing at Andrews, and I wonder if we could do dinner tonight? It has been a long time since …"

"Way too long. I'm only halfway through a pile of Philosophy term papers. You remember those days. But I'll be ready for a break."

"That's super. I really need to talk to you. How about meeting at the usual spot at seven? I need time to get cleaned up at the condo and call the White House."

"That's perfect with me. Will you be able to drop me back home after dinner? I don't walk, even that short distance, after dark."

"Can do. As always, your wish is my command." Gleason hung up before hearing Cindy's parting shot.

"Not always, Tommy boy. Otherwise we'd still be married."

XXXII

He resolved that for once he would beat Cindy to the venerable Old Ebbitt Grill, their favorite courting, marital, and postmarital hangout. He was pleased to be able to reserve the intimate "White House corner table" hidden behind a row of sturdy brick pillars covered by ceiling-high fake foliage. He shaved and soaked in the hot shower until his fair Celtic skin turned pink to be certain that the last germy vestiges of his homeless disguise were gone. He wasn't a singer in the shower, but a thinker. Unsolicited thoughts came and went as randomly as the hot steam swirling above his head. Today as he scrubbed to cleanse his body and hopefully his soul, he could not rid his mind of the words of Lady MacBeth: "Out, damned spot! Out, I say!" He knew that even though his body was clean, the damned spot was still present. His body, but not his soul, was the perfect tabula rasa, the clean slate, for a post-confessional state of mind. Perhaps Cindy again would be able to right his soul with her loving knowledge of his inner needs, if only he would let her in.

Gleason could hear a slight rustle approaching his isolated garden corner. The familiar smell of Cindy's Channel No. Five perfume was simultaneous with her discrete arrival. He jumped to his feet to give her a heartfelt embrace. "You look especially nice tonight,

Honey. I'm so happy that you could make it on such short notice."

"Thanks for calling. I've been thinking, rather obsessing, about you since the bombings. How are you?"

"I'm fine. Maybe not as good as when we were first dating here at Ebbitts, but okay. Work's busy."

"Please, Tom, I'll ask again: How are you?"

Gleason hated that Cindy could see right through his macho façade and peer directly into his inner being. Probably better that he himself could do. "It looks like nothing has changed. You want to talk about me and not what I do. You know that introspection is hard, if not impossible, for me." Before the divorce similar attempts at penetration into his walled-off psyche would have simply forced Gleason to leave the table and go back to work. But fleeing Cindy again was no longer an option, as he was running out of second chances. Tonight would probably be his last second chance, although he really wanted to hide that dire possibility from Cindy. Reaching across the cozy table for two, he whispered, "Your hands are warm," in an attempt to thaw his own frigid demeanor.

"So are yours, and they're squeaky clean. Another tank-draining hot shower?"

"Lately the showers aren't long enough for all the thinking I need. My emotions are so conflicted by recent events that thinking of you and the love we had is still the rock I cling to. I hope my saying so isn't out of place."

Cindy could feel an emotional surge running up her arms from Gleason's strengthening grip, and she had to swallow to clear the tightness in her throat. "Tom, you are still my pillar of strength. We can still be there for each other if we remain open and honest with one another."

The ensuing silence was interrupted by the waiter's appearance to take their order, which was easy. They ordered "the usual."

"I do need to talk a little shop. Not Secret Service shop, but philosophy. The Detroit bombings may have a Zoroastrian connection. What's this big Z word all about?"

"Well, that's a surprise! A philosopher helping to solve the crime of a lifetime. Where do you want me to begin? Actually this is the general area of the slowly shrinking stack of term papers, the philosophical roots and similarities of Judaism, Christianity and Islam. If you help me grade these term papers, you'll kill two birds with one stone."

"You know me, Cindy. I would give everyone an A-plus since I wouldn't have a clue what they're writing about. It sounds like you are inviting me back to your apartment. I would love to reenter the inner sanctum, but I don't know if I trust myself. Maybe I can have a rain check on the invitation. By then the term papers should be graded."

"Okay, lover boy. We can schedule it later. That is, if you're still interested after you denude my brain tonight of what you need to know."

Gleason's heart ached as he realized that his thirty-minute one-night stand in Detroit was going to prevent him from utilizing Cindy's rain check and being intimate again with the only woman he ever loved. He had to quickly divert from that depressing train of thought. "Why don't you just give me the highlights of Zoroastrian beliefs that would make or allow a psycho sicko to do what he did in Detroit. I'm all ears, Doctor."

"I'll try to catch you before you go asleep, fall out of your chair and hit your hard Irish head on the floor. Better yet, I'll kick you under the table when you start to nod off."

"Sounds like old times."

"Many scholars postulate that Zoroastrianism is one of the world's oldest religions, starting about 600 BC in Iran. Today there are two main sects remaining: the Gabars in Iran and the Parsees, mostly in India. Do you want to know how their beliefs differ, or are you mainly interested in one of them?"

"Let's just deal with the Iranian connection. We can do the India sect at a later date, if I don't die of boredom at this first lesson."

"The Iranians have an interesting word, *taarof*. In relationships with others, this word means to devalue or lower yourself while elevating or honoring the other party. Thus all stratas

of a segmented society could get along. This allowed the early
Zoroastrians to function, as they had a dislike for rules, especially
the need for an intercessor like a mullah or high priest to know
their monotheistic God."

"It must work, as Iran and the Middle East have survived a lot
of good and bad in these twenty-six-hundred years."

"True, and some of their forbearance might be their religious
belief that there is a universal struggle between a spirit of good
named Spenta Mainyu and a spirit of evil named Angra Mainyu."

"Do they believe that the spirit of evil is still 'alive and well' as they
say, or was it discarded centuries ago with other outdated beliefs?"

"Both Spenta Mainyu and Angra Mainyu are still present in
today's world. Angra Mainyu rears its ugly head in the form of
evil leaders and criminal terrorists that upset the world harmony
between good and evil."

"This can be scary stuff, whether you believe it or not, if someone thinks that they're the spirit of good when they actually are
performing the terrible deeds of the spirit of evil."

"If you unite that psychic disconnect with the old Persian
proverb: 'Knowledge of self is the knowledge of God,' you have
the making of a super terrorist who answers to no one except
himself." Cindy perceived from the slight drop and opening in
Gleason's jaw that she had hit a home run. She was content to
silently savor Gleason's eureka moment as he nodded his head
three or four times, acknowledging his newly discovered insight.

"Thank you Cindy, more than you can ever know," Gleason
finally whispered as he gently stroked her delicate hands while the
waiter was flaming the chateaubriand at table side.

"Do you want more Zoroastrianism? I can go on for hours,
you know."

"The French food gods are telling us to eat. Thanks to your
philosophy for dummies lecture, I know all that I need to about
this Zoroastrian business."

"You looked shocked, or was it just the light bulb turning on?"

"You flipped the right switch, the big 'thousand-watter' turned on, bright and clear. I always like to know a person's motivation or thought process before I take them down, or in this case, out," Gleason grimly replied, breaking the Secret Service protocol of not discussing cases with anyone.

Cindy dropped her fork and reached across the table to embrace Gleason's slightly trembling hands. "Please Tom, be careful."

The waiter reappeared and offered to re-warm their meals, but they declined. Food was the least important item on their agenda.

XXXIII

"Mister President, I hope you don't mind me not wearing my uniform tonight. I stopped at the gym to work out on my way to the White House."

"Nan, you look great out of uniform in your sweats. Please call me Archie, especially here in my home."

The president and Nan sat on an oversized sofa in the White House upstairs family living room. She opened her briefcase on the coffee table and removed a stack of medical reports. "Where should we begin?" She shuffled the latest medical reports like a Vegas dealer. "We have yours, the baby's, and the first lady's."

"Can't we go over these later?"

"I've always believed in work before pleasure, Archie. Would it be too much trouble for the kitchen to fix something? I haven't eaten since breakfast."

"So that's the secret of how you stay so trim, eating only twice a day." The president clumsily reached around Nan for the phone on the end table. "Don't you doctors still recommend eating three meals a day? I hate to see you eat alone. Do you like lobster? I'll have the kitchen steam up a couple two-pounders for our late night snack."

"Ever since my officer candidate school at Newport I've loved lobster. It's just that as an underpaid naval officer, I can't afford lobster very often. Let's make the food fast. I work and play better on a full stomach."

"You can have lobster every time you come to the White House. It can be one of the many perks of being White House physician."

"No perk can be bigger than a two-pound lobster."

"You might be surprised. It will only take the kitchen staff a few minutes to steam them. Let's do our work. Start with the easy one, my test results."

"Change in plans. I'm in charge, at least of the medical briefing. We'll start with the most recent test results on the baby. I mentioned that we were going to consult with a group of neonatal experts. They were unanimous in their opinion that the fetus presently is healthy and viable with appropriate high-tech specialty care after birth. All the tests, including amniocentesis, are very favorable to the survival of the fetus. Every day the fetus remains in utero increases the final odds of survival."

"Can you put a percentage on the baby's survival chances if it's delivered soon?"

"I asked the neonatal experts that very question. They said that there is a ninety-five-percent survival rate with the best neonatal care available. That's as close to one hundred percent as they ever give in these circumstances."

"That certainly is good news. Kathy was so happy to learn that she was going to have a girl. She told us one night at dinner that she liked the name Melody, spelled like the music. So Melody it is, Melody Katherine. I added the Katherine."

Nan glanced at the president as he swallowed hard, trying to regain his voice.

"Are Jason and Eric excited about having a little sister?"

"They seem to be, but they won't have a mother. What a terrible price to pay for the privilege of being the most powerful man in the world." The president laid back his head on the soft pillow back of the sofa and silently stared heavenward through flooded eyes.

Nan silently held the president's hands until he sat up. "The children will have you. Things can only get better."

"The boys will be excited once they see their baby sister. Oh my God, how Kathy wanted a little girl, and she won't be here to enjoy it unless a miracle happens. Do you have any miracles in your little black bag, Nan?"

"Unfortunately, I don't, nor do any of the trauma experts we keep consulting. As a matter of fact, there have been some subtle deleterious changes in her condition that we're closely monitoring. We have to be on guard for any changes that can affect the fetus. There are some medical ethicists wondering if we aren't subjecting the first lady to cruel and unusual punishment with our hyperbaric oxygen treatments. This argument seems to assume more validity as the fetus becomes more viable and the Glasgow Coma Score remains at three without the miracle the whole country is praying for."

"Just what we need this close to the election. Everyone with a word processor will be second-guessing our decisions on the difficult political, moral and medical issues we're dealing with. Have you heard any more from Cardinal Rourke?"

"Not since our meeting with him. He seemed more concerned about the fetus than the first lady. I can call him and present a medical update on the condition of the fetus and the first lady. Mainly to satisfy him that we are still doing all we can to save them both."

"That's a good idea. We have to keep the mainstream religious denominations happy, especially the Catholics, who represent nearly fifty percent of the voters in some key districts. What's the latest on Kathy's condition?"

"It depends on how you look at it. The good news is that she hasn't deteriorated any more, even though some of her blood chemistry is starting to show a possible slow downward slide. The bad news is that the hyperbaric oxygen treatments aren't showing any measurable effects. It's probably even stressful for her fragile constitution moving her and getting her set up for the hyperbaric treatments. But we have no scientific way to measure this. Since we are seeing no improvement from the treatments and with the possibility that we're actually harming her, the time is approaching when we might want to say enough is enough. I'm relying as much on my psychiatric training as scientific evidence when I propose this."

"I appreciate your total view of this case, Nan. I certainly don't want to continue the hyperbaric treatment if it's harming her in the final analysis. I would like to formulate a game plan for immediately after the election in regard to when the baby will be delivered, when you will pull the plug on Kathy and how long she is expected to live without life support."

"If the situation stays as it is until the election, which I'm not sure it will, we'll have sufficient time to establish the game plan you desire and deserve. The delivery of the baby by C-section will be traumatic to her precarious balance between life and death. There will be no need of general anesthesia or even a spinal, since she won't feel anything, as the low Glasgow Coma Score shows. This life-giving C-section for the baby could well have the opposite effect on the first lady. Even though doctors are trained to make life-and-death decisions, it's never easy, especially when it involves a family that they have come to know. Are you sure that when the time comes you will be ready emotionally to okay this double-edged sword?"

"With you and the boys at my side for support, I'll have to survive. I don't see anything to be gained by waiting more than a day or two after the election. Do you?"

"No, except for how you feel about post-election public opinion. By doing it too soon after the election, people might wonder if you waited that long for political reasons and not a personal, loving family decision."

"To hell with public opinion. At that point I will be reelected for my final four-year term, and my place in history will be secure. Speaking of timing and the election, I still need to complete my physical. We could start it tonight."

"When's that food going to be ready? I'm starved."

XXXIV

The president was reaching across Nan again, this time brushing her amply filled out sweatshirt, to call the kitchen, when the phone rang. "How much longer on the food?" he asked.

"Excuse me, Mister President, this is Tom Gleason."

"Sorry, Tom. I thought it was the kitchen calling. I have some food ordered for myself and a guest. What can I do for you at this late hour of your busy day?"

Gleason immediately sensed that the president did not want to discuss business matters tonight. "I just wanted to give you a preliminary report on the investigations in Detroit. I can call in the morning."

"Certainly, Gleason, let's talk tomorrow. There's nothing we can do about anything at this hour of the night anyway." The president winked at Nan, knowing that Gleason wouldn't have cleared the White House operator unless his message was important. "Where were we, Nan?" The president brushed her sweatshirt again as he hung up the receiver.

"We were talking about your physical. We'll need to draw another blood specimen to update your lab work."

"Damn it. You doctors like poking people. I may issue an executive order forbidding any more pokes until other conditions are meet.

A tit for a tat would be a good way to describe the new arrangement."

"Let's talk about the present, not the future."

"They say the future is now."

"Don't you want to know if you are going to live to see the future? You need to look at yesterday and today to get a glimpse of tomorrow. Everything appears to be reasonably normal on your lab tests, but things can change in a month. Certain numbers of your lymphocyte cell count are a little low, but the lab wasn't overly concerned. Remember, you were severely injured and your bodily defenses are just starting to return to normal."

"How can I forget? I have this damn cast to remind me every time I get dressed or go to the bathroom or try to hug a pretty woman."

"Since you didn't have any success in calling the kitchen, let me go see what the holdup is." To Nan's relief, a chime rang to announce that dinner was now ready. The simplicity of the family dining room in the White House surprised Nan. Seated at the vintage Jeffersonian table, she thought of the countless family dinners that presidents must have shared in this homey room. First families' basic needs were no different than her family's when she was growing up on the Space Coast of Florida. She felt sorry for the children in the first families, who couldn't go to the beaches of Florida for a simple Sunday picnic. She felt that she and her sister had the perfect childhood, watching the rocket launches from the NASA employee observation area at the space center. Often their father, an upper level NASA rocket engineer, would let them skip school to view one of his big blast-offs. Occasionally, the president and his entourage would be there to view the launch from their adjacent VIP observation platform. She and her sister wondered why everyone always fussed more over the president than on the ascending spacecraft.

The one dark cloud over her idyllic upbringing was her sandy beach blanket mistake with the star football player. Her attempt to put more joy and happiness into her already full life failed. She resolved that never again would she do it unless she was in complete control and truly cared for her partner. Her last serious relationship, the affair with Andre, was 20 years ago. Its memory lay dead and buried until Maxwell and the CIA rudely ripped away all her rationalizations. She now felt as naked and defenseless as the salacious photographs had shown her. She was not ready for a one-night stand, even if it was with the president of the United States.

When talking to family and friends, she always blamed the demands of her busy navy career for not marrying, but occasional flashbacks to her teenage fling and the hurt of the Newport incident were the more likely explanation for her fast approaching spinsterhood.

After medical school she stopped dating fellow medical colleagues when she projected that the double-death syndrome—two married doctors dealing with death—would devour any romantic medical relationship. Fortunately, during her naval medical career she wasn't dealing daily with death issues. How she would react to her current deathwatch was yet to be determined. Outwardly she appeared confident, but inwardly she was terrified of the power of her own untested emotions.

With the president distracted ordering dessert on the phone, as they were dipping the last bites of lobster into the warm drawn butter, Nan slyly pushed a button on her omnipresent beeper. Momentarily her cell phone rang inside her purse. Nan was relieved that the rigid White House security was no match for the simple wireless telephone transmission of cellular phones. "Excuse me, Archie, while I answer this call. I'm sure it's about the first lady. She's my only patient ... Hello. Doctor Schmidt speaking. Is there a problem with the first lady?"

The president, who could not hear the muffled words of the calling party, watched Nan nodding her head in agreement. He immediately sensed that his personal plans for the evening would be delayed, if not totally abandoned. "I'll be there as quickly as I can," Nan closed her phone and put it back in her purse, which she kept on her lap.

"Any major problem?"

"Every change in the first lady's condition can be potentially serious. Presently the attending resident is concerned that the monitor is showing some erratic fetal movements. I don't think we are at a crisis situation, but I had better return to the hospital."

"Are you sure you don't have a few minutes to go back to the living room for dessert?"

Glancing at her watch, which gave the president a false hope for possible events to follow, Nan stood up. "The attending resident is quite nervous about the baby, so I'd better be the one to make any necessary decisions. Do you want to come to the hospital?"

"What do you think? I can arrange a police escort to speed us there. Let me get my shoes on. I'll go with you. Then we can return here for dessert if it doesn't take too long to get the baby and Kathy stabilized."

"I'll return to the hospital and call if there's a problem. Meanwhile you can tuck the boys in bed like a good father." Nan gave the still seated president a quick kiss on his wine-flushed cheek as she escaped out the door.

"Call me and let's try to get together later," the disappointed president shouted at his hastily departing physician.

XXXV

Before taking his gym bag into the restroom of an Annapolis fast food restaurant to change into his new work clothes, Gleason used his cell phone to play back his office voicemail, which contained a message from the president to call him. He also made a call from a parking lot pay phone to the District of Columbia Police reporting that his private automobile was stolen from his gated condominium parking lot and that he would be unavailable to file a written police report for a few days because of an unexpected overseas trip. This recorded and traceable call would pinpoint Gleason's exact location in Annapolis for later verification.

After slipping into a bulky sweatshirt and his specially modified metal-free jeans over a Neoprene sweat suit, Gleasons still felt naked as he tugged at his beltless waist. He had left his favorite belt with the large metal buckle in a perfect coil on his dresser top, a cryptic sign to Cindy that he was going away—on this occasion for a long, long time.

He put his holstered Secret Service revolver in the gym bag along with everything metallic from his pockets, including his credit cards with their magnetic strips. He also put a fresh bandage on his index finger, which he had injured last night sewing, using his thumb as a thimble to push a bending needle through thick denim. It bothered him to do late-night surgery on his favorite expensive designer jeans, but he had to remove the brass waist button and metal zipper on his fly and replace them with plastic substitutes. At times like that, he missed Cindy's domestic skills. As the memory of his failed marriage receded deeper into his subconscious, he had come to realize that Cindy was like a delicate flower that needed sunshine to grow and prosper. All he had provided was shade and darkness where only weeds and thorns can survive. Sleepless in bed when the tigers came at night, he often fantasized that he would get another time at bat with Cindy. His overwhelming fear, which paralyzed him from aggressively taking a second chance, was that he would strike out again and lose forever his newly re-blossoming friendship with her. At least he could still hold onto his twilight dream of reconciliation, which was now clouded by his hopeless medical condition.

Even though he wasn't particularly hungry, he ordered a double cheeseburger, fries and chocolate shake to eat in the car on the way to Lee Airport near Annapolis. Gleason never enjoyed eating in his own car or his government-issued sedan because of the mess it created. Everyone knew that neatnik Gleason never ate in his car, so the dated receipt, partially eaten burger and fries, empty cup and food wrappers would be clues for future investigators.

He circled the Annapolis Post Office until he got in the proper lane to deposit, without getting out the car, his thick envelope addressed to the president's private White House box number, which insured that the president personally would receive it. He also mailed thinner envelopes to Dr. Schmidt and Cindy. He was perspiring as he parked at the small fixed base air terminal for private planes at the Lee Airport. The short walk to board the *Flying Mole*, resplendent under the bright sun and clear blue sky, seemed like a marathon distance to the heavily sweating Gleason.

"You're right on time," Azee greeted him, extending his bejeweled hand. "You have different glasses. You look like a movie star."

"I've always prided myself on punctuality. We're on a rather tight timetable, aren't we?" Gleason ignored Azee's astute observation of his change in eyewear from his aviator-style metal Ray-Bans to the wraparound plastic Foster Grants. He handed the keys for his black government Ford sedan to one of Azee's workers. "Make sure that you pull into my assigned spot, 5A, at the condo." Gleason certainly wouldn't mention that he never parked his government automobile facing forward in his personal auto's space. He always backed his government Ford into space 5B so he could make a quick getaway for any emergency call from the White House.

Every one of his friends and Secret Service colleagues, and certainly Cindy, knew of his quirky obsessions, and he was now desperately trying to leave behind a trail of unmistakable clues as tangible proof of his mental unrest and final motives. He was sure the media would be quick to harshly judge him and thus the president by his attempted solution where he alone was judge and jury.

"It looks like you are traveling rather light." Azee reached out to take Gleason's only luggage, his gym bag, aboard the plane.

"You told me we'd buy my Mediterranean wardrobe in Beirut. I don't need my socks and underwear on board for the flight. My book and Walkman are all I'll need to pass the time on this Atlantic crossing. I hope I can sleep part of the way. Let's stow my bag," Gleason said, carefully placing his gym bag in the open small luggage compartment under the pointed nose cone with the long antenna proboscis. He momentarily delayed following Azee up the narrow stairs until the ground crew closed and secured the latch of the forward luggage compartment.

Azee sat in his customary starboard recliner chair. Gleason would occupy the only other remaining seat, a matching recliner on the port side. Before sitting, he bent over and picked up a small book from his seat. He also quickly stroked the fabric of the seat. It had a cold, rough feel, as if delicate metallic embroidery thread had been used for its construction. The small book only had the capital letters IC embossed in rich gold leaf on its oxblood cordovan leather cover.

"Your interior is outfitted a little differently than the White

House cattle cars I'm used to flying in." He surveyed the luxurious cabin appointments and fastened his military-style combination seat belt and shoulder harness.

"I spend so much time in the air on business that the *Flying Mole* is my home and office, so I want it as comfortable as possible. I hope you don't mind wearing the shoulder harness. The performance of this flying sled is like a F16 jet."

"No problem. I did some flying during my navy days. I enjoy high performance machines," Gleason shouted over the powerful test roar of the revving jet engines. He had opened the cover and read the title of the book—*The Broken Wings*. "I think I'll catch the next flight. Is it written by the same aeronautical engineer that designed your plane?" After noticing the author's name, Kahlil Gibran, Gleason's smiling countenance instantly turned solemn to match his traveling companion's stern visage.

"You have copy ninety-nine of my prescient biography that I always present to first-time passengers on the *Flying Mole*. I hope I'm not being presumptuous in assuming that you would like to read my life story of how a poor, rejected son of immigrant parents can achieve the American dream like no one else before him. I only have one copy remaining from the first printing of one hundred."

"I don't mean to be contentious, Azee, but didn't Gibran die before you were even born? How could he write your biography?" Gleason was thinking that he certainly could embellish Azee's life story with all the research he had done before this trip.

"How do you know about Gibran? None of my previous ninety-eight first-time passengers on the *Flying Mole* did. I only started giving out these mementos of flying with me when I got this new jet. Copy number one was presented to a very special friend of mine as an honorary copy for all her previous trips with me. Now she has her own plane. She's been the driving force of my life as well as the inspiration for these little token gifts when she was first planning to fly with me years ago. I think of her every time I present a copy to my first-time flyers. To answer your question, Gleason, I said prescient biography. Do you know what that means?"

Gleason's mind raced faster than the ascending jet, though it was cloudier than the *Flying Mole*'s vapor trail as he sought to fend off and temporally dissipate the deleterious combination of too much knowledge and too-loose lips.

He remembered seeing the first lady alone in her office, wiping tears from her eyes, reading a strange book with no title on the cover, only the large gold letter *I*, which now he realized was the Roman numeral *I*. "We had a philosophy teacher in college who burned a votive candle every day in Gibran's honor," Gleason fabricated. "He called Gibran the twentieth-century Socrates, blending parable with reality to create metaphysical perfection."

As Gleason opened the book and began reading the first paragraph, he was relieved to see Azee nod his assent to his spontaneous philosophical psychobabble. "I was eighteen years of age when love opened my eyes with its magic rays and touched my spirit with its fiery fingers, and Selma Karamy was the first woman who awakened my spirit with her beauty and lead me into the garden of high affection, where days pass like dreams and nights like weddings." Gleason looked up and graciously commented, "From just this first paragraph I can see why you feel so deeply about this book and its special meaning to you and your wife. It's beautifully poetic."

"I didn't meet my wife until I was in my thirties, as I am sure you discovered from your background checks."

The *Flying Mole* was still in a steep climb as it approached the Bay Bridge, which connects the Eastern Shore with the Maryland mainland. Azee picked up the phone intercom and instructed Taajud-Deen to level off so they could better observe the conflagration on the center span. "How long will it take your crackerjack investigators to realize that you didn't commit suicide by jumping off the bridge after blowing up your car?"

Gleason had an unpleasant flashback to when he was helplessly airborne off the *Aqua Mole*'s flying bridge. It rendered him momentarily silent. "I hope at least long enough for me to pick up my ten-million-dollar payoff in Damascus. I don't think I'll bother to file an insurance claim for this loss of my old Ford. I finally should be able to afford my dream Mercedes."

"You'll be able to afford one for every day of the week, with an extra one for your lovely ex-wife," Azee assured his new partner.

Looking down at his own auto in flames, Gleason became philosophical. "I've never visualized my own death. Have you?"

"I am too busy living today to worry about dying tomorrow. Besides, they say the good people die first, so I have a long time yet."

"To answer your question, as difficult a time as we are having with the Ambassador Bridge bombing, this Bay Bridge conflagration will take an even longer time to solve, since there are no security cameras at either entrance and obviously no customs and immigration records. But the similar modus operandi of the two bridge bombings will help tie everything together. Did you use the same people to destroy my car as the van on the Ambassador Bridge?"

There was a long pause as Azee nervously shifted in his seat and mulled his answer over in his conflicted mind. "I have many groups that I call on to help. Since we are now partners, I don't mind telling you that we hired foreign experts for the Ambassador Bridge job. Terrorism is getting to be like the medical profession. You need specialists to get a specific job done. I merely orchestrated the experienced workers imported from your motherland, the beautiful but oppressed island of Ireland, to create the bridge diversion."

"Let's not blame the Irish for the Detroit failures just because they were the first to go boom," Gleason said.

"I was negligent in not exercising more vigilance over the Canadian separatists in the amount of explosives they used at the *Aqua Mole*. I could have been killed by those fanatical bastards. The most important attribute of a successful terrorist is restraint, always living to fight another day. They might as well have killed me. They have created an unlivable dilemma. My love is dead to me, but the president is still alive, and we haven't been paid our ten million dollars. "Azee concluded while opening a small liquor cabinet in front of him. "My wife forbids me to drink while flying. What is your pleasure?"

"I don't like to drink alone. Why would your wife do that? Do you take the controls of the *Flying Mole?*"

"Occasionally, once airborne, I'll sit in the second seat if we don't have another passenger. Relax. I wouldn't endanger the life of my new partner by flying a plane that I'm not rated in. Mostly my wife doesn't want me to arrive home to the kids bombed."

"That's reassuring. I really need to catch a few winks so jet lag doesn't totally wipe me out." Gleason reclined his chair. He removed his most treasured keepsake, an 18-karat gold Omega Seamaster watch that was Cindy's wedding present to him seventeen years ago and stowed it in the left-side chair pocket that contained the current issue of *Scientific American* with a cover article on decommissioning old nuclear power plants. He put the earpieces in and adjusted his Walkman to drown out the engine noise. "Wake me when we are at the midpoint of the flight." The constant rustle of Azee doing paperwork and talking on the phone kept Gleason in the twilight zone where simply closing his eyes provided the mental quiet he needed to go over his final plans.

XXXVI

Alexander Graham Bell should be the patron saint of Washington, D.C., if not the entire civilized world, the president thought. No invention since the wheel has had a more dramatic effect on our daily life than the old-fashioned telephone, and the ever-changing cellular models. It can even be argued that the twentieth-century God, the personal computer, is an extension of Bell's invention. George Washington had to jump on his horse to talk to his vice president, John Adams.

"Taylor, have you been in touch with Gleason?" the agitated president barked over the secure White House phone line to the one person in his administration who would not be offended by his rudeness, his docile vice president. "His office doesn't have a clue where he is. The district police received a call from someone claiming to be Gleason, heading overseas and reporting that his car had been stolen. What the hell is going on?"

"I'm sorry, Mister President. I haven't heard from Gleason in a couple days. The last I knew, he was going to Detroit for a quick trip to spur on the investigations. Did you check with Andrews to see if he returned from that trip? It's not like Gleason."

"He sure as hell returned from Detroit. He wanted to see me last night, but I was busy entertaining someone. I was supposed to see him this morning." The frustrated president slammed down the receiver.

Vice presidents customarily do not seek out any additional duties not assigned by the U.S. Constitution or directly by the president. Hubert Taylor was living proof of the continuation of this tradition. But his curiosity was aroused, so he went to his Rolodex for the international number of his friend and future employer. Azee had always bragged that he was reachable anywhere in the world by dialing a coded number, which bounced a secure signal from satellite to satellite until it found its home in Azee's yellow phone. He had only used it sparingly for other urgent situations.

Gleason heard only the muted ring of a phone because of the Walkman earphones. He watched out of the corner of his nearly closed eye as Azee went into the aft head with his phone.

"Hubert, you will have to talk a little louder. I'm in the *Flying Mole* on my way back home to Beirut. I'm sorry we didn't get together again. How are you doing?"

"Okay, but I just talked to the president. He's very upset. Did you cross paths with Gleason in Detroit? The president's trying to locate him."

"I heard he was in Detroit, but I didn't see him," Azee fabricated loudly enough for the vice president to hear over the noise of the engines, but not so loud that his resting passenger could overhear. "I stayed at the office in Windsor the whole time to clear my desk so I could vacation in Beirut. I didn't even have time to go home to Cripplegate. Is there a problem?"

"I don't think so. The president is just uptight because he was supposed to meet with him this morning. Gleason called last night, but the president couldn't see him then. The only excuse that the president would have for not seeing his top Secret Service agent would be if he was entertaining a woman in his private quarters. I know. I've been rebuffed more than once for this same reason. The current female attraction seems to the first lady's doctor, Nancy Schmidt, who also was just appointed White House physician. She's had a distinguished navy career like you. Didn't I show you the blurb on her in the PDB at our Sequoia lunch?"

"That's right, I forgot her name. I have too much on my mind. My navy years were a long time ago, and I really don't have the time or interest to stay in touch with that part of my life. Have you or the president mentioned my name to her? I wonder if she would remember me?"

"I haven't had the occasion to talk to her, as I'm out of the loop on the first lady's medical treatment. The president said the strangest thing is that Gleason called the D.C. police to report his car stolen this morning. He could not come into the police station to fill out the necessary stolen car report for a few days because he was going overseas. They are now analyzing the nine-one-one tape to verify if it's really him who made that weird call."

"I sure don't know what's going on. I'll call in a couple days from Beirut."

"Sorry to bother you with the president's problems. Have a good visit with your family."

XXXVII

Azee picked up the intercom phone to his pilot, Taajud-Deen. "Has there been any unusual radio traffic?"

"Nothing except for some sporadic radio static, which we usually don't experience this far out over the Atlantic. It could be caused by radio frequencies outside the normal commercial bands that we monitor."

"Get the location of any ships, especially those with Libyan registry, that might be in our flight path until we reach land. Also be prepared to implement security plan 5A." Azee started to dial his home number in Beirut but stopped when he realized his children were in school. He had no need to talk to his wife, Haasna.

Gleason shifted and stiffened his reclined torso as he heard an abbreviated Morse Code signal on his modified Walkman radio. With three quick button pushes, he gave the prearranged acknowledgment to the trailing F16, piloted by his former navy colleague, Neil Gibson. Captain Gibson was the world's top expert at flying covert missions for supersensitive government agencies in his specially equipped fighter plane. Trailing at an undetectable distance, he was still able to monitor and record the events inside the streaking *Flying Mole* with satellite-enhanced electronics. Gleason returned his seat to the upright position as

Azee was returning from the head. "I managed to get a little shut-eye," Gleason said as he fumbled trying to balance the Walkman on top of his book. "I should be a little better company the rest of the flight."

Azee forced a smile as he adjusted his seat belt and shoulder harness and felt the control buttons beside his seat. "What are you reading?"

"Glad you asked." Gleason held up the ornate leatherbound book for Azee to read the gold imprinted title, 'The History of the Decline and Fall of the Roman Empire, Volume I. '

"This is really too coincidental to be happening by chance, Azee stammered. "Kathy and I studied this two-hundred-year-old classic by Gibbons both for our high school debate and then in more depth at the University of Michigan in a humanities class. It was the only class we shared at Ann Arbor. The professor was constantly drawing parallels between the decadence of the declining Roman society and modern America. Kathy and I resolved that we would do everything in our power to reverse these trends that were leading to our civilization's demise. Of course, she ultimately married the joke in the White House, whose main brain is below his waist. So I alone embarked on the road to make the world a better place, like the ancient Roman Empire that she and I so loved and admired. I wear the ring that the pope gave me as a reminder of that time."

"Can I look at the ring?"

"Sure, but I never take it off." Azee conveniently forgot his ringless Watergate Hotel charade with Dr. Schmidt. He stretched his hand across the aisle for Gleason to examine the sacred gift.

"We had a hard time identifying it," Gleason commented.

"What do you mean?"

"There are numerous home video tapes that show a hand opening the porthole on the *Aqua Mole* and dropping something into the river. The FBI was able to enlarge and enhance one video image until they could read the words Pontifex Maximus, which any Latin scholar knows refers to the pope as the greatest bridge builder. The Vatican informed us that you and Mother Teresa are the only contemporary recipients of this unique Vatican treasure. I don't think Mother Teresa is into bomb-building. Whom in the Vatican did you bribe to get this rare papal gift? You certainly didn't receive it because you were trying to restore the Roman Empire to its days of glory."

Azee quickly retracted his bloodstained hand. "The walls of the Sistine Chapel are standing straighter and sturdier because of my firm's extensive subterranean work on their collapsing foundations without so much as a crack in Michelangelo's priceless ceiling frescoes. Don't you think preserving these frescoes using my patented bridge building laser and expertise was worth this special papal ring?"

While opening the little brass clasp that held the covers of Gibbon's book closed, Gleason thought he should send the pope a thank-you note for his help in identifying the mastermind of the Detroit bombings. "Azee, maybe you could help me to translate my papal thank-you note into Latin."

"Give me your copy of *The Broken Wings*. I should have required you to read it before you boarded the *Flying Mole* so that we could intelligently discuss our youthful aspirations to save the world." Azee started to flip through the pages of the Gibran book looking for a specific answer to enlighten Gleason.

"I thought that you would be more interested in reading from your and the first lady's bible," Gleason said, holding up Gibbons' book that he brought aboard for the long flight. Opening it revealed a rectangular opening where the center pages had been cut out to create space for a device such as a small garage door opener. "So you tried to kill your unattainable love with this detonator that we recovered from the bottom of the Detroit River. Why did you do it? Didn't she share your distorted vision of a better world?"

He waited inordinately long for a response from Azee, who was still leafing through *The Broken Wings*. "I guess if your real reasons for attacking an eight-month-pregnant woman, aren't even known to you, I don't need to be concerned either." He was watching Azee, still flipping through the pages of his self-proclaimed biography in search of a salient passage to justify his unforgivable actions, for any hint of remorse.

"Do you remember what happened on April fifteenth, nineteen-eighty-six?" Azee finally broke the silence.

"I paid my taxes."

"It was a very important day in the history of the world."

"Why? Because you didn't pay your taxes? Certainly not because I paid my meager taxes."

"What about October twenty-third, nineteen-eighty-three?"

"Was that a Sunday?"

"Who cares if it's a Sunday? Surely your investigations have discovered my relationship to this date."

"If it was a Sunday, Cindy and I made love. We always made love on Sunday."

"You're just like the president. Relating everything to your base desires. The president doesn't spiritually love Kathy, or he wouldn't be chasing his dying wife's doctor."

"Who's responsible for Kathy's comatose condition and ultimately her death?" Gleason needlessly questioned.

"I didn't try to kill Kathy. The sex maniac husband, yes. Kathy, no. My orders were that she wasn't to be harmed, not even a scratch. The prime minister's limousine explosion was the separatists' chance to make a name for themselves. It was supposed to be only a slight diversion, like the van on the bridge, to demonstrate how close the separatists could get to the prime minster and his family. These two smaller explosions would distract the investigators from our main effort, the presidential motorcade. Nobody was to get hurt in the two diversionary explosions. I've already punished the guilty party. He's fish food in the middle of Lake Ontario." Azee blankly stared at the little hand-held surprise that Gleason was holding, knowing that there were no garage doors to open 40,000 feet above the mid-Atlantic.

"We didn't find one of these detonators in the rubble of the house explosion. Believe me, we tried. We sifted every ounce of ash and debris in the basement and found very little physical evidence. The most incongruous discovery was the partially charred copy of your patron saint Gibran's *The Prophet* found in an old tin box. The FBI lab was able to partially reconstruct the inscription: To Aabid. My alpha and omega. Love, Gran ..."

"Here's the passage I'm looking for: It's wrong to think that love comes from long companionship and persevering courtship. Love is the offspring of spiritual affinity and unless that affinity is created in many moments, it will not be created for years or even generations."

Gleason searched for an escape from the uncharted waters of Azee's distorted logic. "Are you talking of your grandmother's love, as she signed in your copy of *The Prophet*?"

"Please, Gleason. Don't play me for a fool and impugn my grandmother's love. It was very special to me as a child. But as you should have discovered in all your investigations, Kathy and I had a higher love, as *The Broken Wings* describes it: Love is the only freedom in the world because it so elevates the spirit that the laws of humanity and the phenomenon of nature do not alter its course."

"Are you implying that the first lady was a willing participant in this sick terrorist drama of yours? That the first lady was a willing participant in these acts of terrorism where her husband would be assassinated so she could take up with you, a married man with children and that she was so sucked in by your perverse charm that the fundamental laws of humanity and nature could be suspended? That's totally preposterous," Gleason said.

"How clear do I have to make it for you to understand our lifelong relationship? Have you ever deeply loved someone or something that you could not have? Your small Secret Service mentality doesn't function very well with abstract, metaphysical concepts or, as your fruitless investigation of the bombings seems to demonstrate, concrete matters either."

"Let me understand this. We now have the comatose, pregnant first lady implicated in a plot to kill her husband, the president, so that she can marry you and swim off with the sharks into the fading sunset. But in the process of carrying out this bizarre plot, she knocks herself permanently unconscious. Boy, will the tabloids have a field day with this."

"Sorrow linked her spirit and mine, as if each saw in the other's face what the heart was feeling and heard the echo of a hidden voice." Azee, oblivious to his companion's taunts, continued reading from *The Broken Wings*: 'She was beautiful in spirit and body. She was pulchritude personified.' "You and your hundreds of investigators didn't discover our secret," Azee boasted.

"The first lady had a piece of lead gripped in her hand at the hospital. We didn't know who gave it to her or what it meant."

"I also felt it in her hand at the hospital. It was the last and most precious gift I've ever given her."

"I wouldn't say that it's the last thing you gave her. You gave her one big headache as your parting remembrance."

"It's too bad that they won't bury our lead memento from Bath with her. Someday it will be on exhibit in the Smithsonian Museum with Booth's pistol and Oswald's rifle. It was a symbol of our love, not hatred as history will want to interpret it."

"You had to know that the president would discover it?"

"The appearance of things changes according to the emotions," Gibran continued through Azee's emotion laden voice, "and thus we see magic and beauty in them while the magic and beauty are really in ourselves." Azee broke a long reverential silence with the simple declaration, "Kathy and Azee had magic and beauty."

XXXVIII

Gleason looked at his watch and realized that things had to move along past Azee's delusional view of reality. "In every crime perpetrated to gain possession of an object, the nature of that very object should give us a hint as to the nature of the criminal. Looking at the magnificent first lady surely doesn't compute to you, Azee, international terrorist."

"That's because you don't know the real me. Perhaps after this trip abroad and a few more events around the world, you will come to know me as I truly am, as the first lady knew and loved me."

"I like the way you minimize these multiple terror scenes by calling them events, as if they were part of another routine day at the office. They were cowardly terrorist acts. I hope that someday I can come to a similar state of rationalization. How long was the exploded house in your family?"

"I was raised there as a child. It was my maternal grand-mother's home. I grew up there when it was a nice safe area of Detroit. She was always afraid that I would be buried by a sewer cave-in, as we were constantly playing in the Lodge expressway construction beside the house. She fought the city over locating a large storm sewer line too close to our basement wall. She was afraid the wall would collapse. Needless to say, this poor immigrant woman's loss was my gain. We were able to access the storm sewer network under the expressway roadbed from our basement. With our lasers and the storm sewer blueprints, we were able to determine the precise location for the placement of the explosives. Our biggest fear was the weather. A torrential rainfall would have caused us to scuttle the mission, as fuses and explosives don't work when wet and washed away. The mission was still a technical success."

"God bless your prescient grandmother. Instead of her basement walls, the expressway collapsed years later. The President of the United States was nearly killed because you remembered her valiant fight over the proximity of the storm sewer to her basement walls."

"I bought the house as a tribute to this wonderful woman. I had to use a surrogate purchaser, a local wino who as it turned out was not a very strong swimmer with cement blocks tied to his ankles. He was the first casualty of the Detroit event."

"We didn't find much evidence at the house site. No remote detonator like at the *Aqua Mole* tragedy."

"Of course you didn't find much. My own associates, not hired outsiders, removed all the evidence including the missing remote detonator."

"Thanks to your grandmother we found that small tin box containing The Prophet hidden near the furnace between the floor joists."

"She gave me *The Prophet* as a first grade graduation present because I had learned to read. She said that Kahlil Gibran should be my Lebanese idol, and he is to this day. I confess that I had forgotten about it until your lucky investigators disoverd it. I wonder what the chances are of having it returned to its rightful owner."

"We were stymied until we ran a computer check of your name, Aabid. It's not that common a name in Detroit, so guess who popped up at the top of the list? We can thank your loving grandmother for helping us solve this case. She considered you the First and the Last, as I interpret the Greek Alpha and Omega that survived on the charred page with your name."

"I was her first grandchild, and she thought the last until my parents adopted an orphan from Lebanon. Interpret it any way you want."

The CIA had furnished Gleason a top secret memo concerning rudimentary coded radio and phone messages emanating from Lebanon that contained the words alpha and omega. The messages were usually obtuse with no obvious references to current events, but one of the messages was picked up in Russia as the final message from alpha and omega.

"That's the last piece of the puzzle," Gleason exclaimed. He would have jumped out of his chair except for his restraining harness and seat belt. "Who's been sending messages out of Lebanon as the "alpha and omega'?"

"You tell me, since you seem to have it all figured out."

"What's the significance of you referring to yourself as the Alpha and the Omega. You already have Azee, which is pretty unique."

Azee realized that someone had been doing extensive surveillance of his surreptitious worldwide activities. Azee had reserved the use of alpha and omega as his code name for his most sensitive business matters, known to only a handful of his most trusted associates. These secret communications were routed through his alter ego in Beirut, Shakoor. Azee gave a short Greek lesson trying to divert discussion from the Russian message to Andre, his conduit for the pending nuclear arms deal. "It's the Greek translation of my name. The first and last letters of each alphabet are me. I have always been the first and the last in either alphabet. I use Alpha-Omega when I'm home in Beirut as a tribute to the Greek heritage and influence in Lebanon."

"The CIA code breakers were really stymied by this simple translation of the first and last letters of each alphabet being you."

"So a room full of CIA computer geeks couldn't break this simple two-letter code: A - alpha, Z - omega."

"I guess not. Maybe give us a month and we might eventually break it."

"The crazy part is that this didn't start as a code for me, as I was already the Alpha and the Omega."

Tom silently pondered if Azee had really elevated himself to divine status, as he had surmised during Cindy's Zoroastrian exposition, and how difficult it was going to be when he was brought back to earth. He was shocked at Azee's sacrilegious presumption of divinity. "The real Alpha and Omega guy might not like having such inferior competition."

XXXIX

"The first lady's toxemia is crossing the placental barrier and will be affecting the fetus," Dr. Schmidt informed a somber president.

"I guess we're at the point we all knew would arrive sooner or later. It just got here sooner than we would have chosen. Nan, are you and your staff absolutely positive that there is no reversing the toxemia? Can't we wait even a few more days, getting us closer to the election?"

"Archie, this is a dangerous situation, especially for the fetus. It's irreversible. We have discontinued the hyperbaric oxygen treatments because some of the medical consultants think it could be making the toxemia progress more rapidly. We don't have any more days to wait, only a few hours at the most."

"As much as you think you have prepared yourself for this terrible decision, you really haven't. I trust your professional judgment completely. As they say, do what you have to do."

"The situation with the baby is as straightforward as it can be, given the fetal pre-maturity. The neonatal experts from Georgetown Medical School should be arriving shortly. Do you want to meet with them?"

"That won't be necessary. I don't want to put any extra pressure on them. Will you be assisting with the C-section?"

"Not really. I haven't delivered a baby since my internship. I would just be in the way. One good thing is that they won't have to use any deep anesthesia, just a little local anesthesia to help control the bleeding from the incision. This is the only benefit I can think of from being in a coma. If you wish, we could be off to the side in the delivery room watching. Most expectant fathers seem to want to be part of the action."

"Not me. I prefer the action nine months earlier. Besides I can't stand the sight of blood. Put me in the delivery room and I'll probably pass out and break my other arm. We can find a quiet corner to wait. Nan, can I ask you a personal question?"

"How about saving it for the quiet corner? The final and probably most difficult thing you have to decide is the fate of the first lady. We should know your wishes before the C-section begins, as it's really one continuous procedure."

"What do you mean, her fate? Her fate's been sealed since the bomb went off!"

"I'm sorry Archie. I know that you have a lot on your mind. What I meant to say is that you must decide if you want to continue her life support, and if so, for how long? Until after the election, as we talked about?"

The irony of the simultaneous life-and-death decisions silenced the president more than his harshest critic ever could. He walked to the window and stared blankly at the passing traffic many stories below the presidential suite. Finally he turned toward a sobbing Nan and asked, "Have you ever been married?"

An unprepared Nan could only blurt out, "No."

"Have you ever been in love?"

"Please, Mister President." Nan struggled to regain her composure. "Let's deal with the first lady's condition and leave me out of it."

"That's what I'm trying to do. If you have ever been in love, you would know what I am going through. It isn't easy saying good-bye to someone you love."

"I've only been truly in love once. It was especially frustrating because we knew our love was dead-ended by the international political climate twenty years ago. We were painfully parted with both our lives still ahead of us. You are saying good-bye to someone already dead, as cruel as this may sound. I cannot decide for you the timing for disconnecting the first lady's life support systems."

"I will have a real void in my life, just as you appear to still have. Is your friend still alive? Maybe you can still get together with him."

"I try not to live in the past, although I've been recently rudely reminded of it by some of your people. I am very hurt that the government has resurrected one incident from my early training days at Newport and is trying to blackmail me with it. I've always tried to look ahead and not dwell in the past. You must do the same."

"I'm sorry if I've caused unpleasant flashbacks for you, Nan. I have not authorized anyone to delve into your past. Professionally, you came highly recommended by your peers, and by my firsthand observation you are an extremely competent doctor. Personally, I've come to know you as a kind and loving friend. I will not allow anyone to jeopardize our developing relationship or your stellar naval career."

"Thank you. I appreciate your support. One can't have too many friends when times get rough. But we still must decide on the first lady's condition. The doctors will be arriving momentarily to deliver the baby."

"I know. I know. I guess I've been trying to postpone the inevitable as long as possible. The country would like me to keep Kathy alive. My advisers would tell me to wait until after the election before pulling the plug. Do you have any idea how long she'll live if we simply turn off the machines after the baby is delivered?"

"There is no way of knowing for sure. It could be minutes, hours or days. My own guess would be less than twenty-four hours We could call in ..."

"I don't want any more doctors summoned. The boys and I have been through enough. There are people out there saying we should bring in Doctor Death from Michigan to hasten her death. If I weren't president, this whole ordeal wouldn't even be on the back page of the newspaper. The boys and I had a bedtime talk last night. Jason asked if Mommy is going to die when Melody is born. I didn't know how to answer. I cried. We all cried."

"That must have been hard."

"Harder than any decision sitting behind my desk in the oval office. The boys understood the answer contained in our tears. But I don't want the boys, in their impressionable young minds, to blame Melody's birth for their mother dying. For that matter, when Melody gets older, I don't want her to blame herself for her mother's death. Sure, as adults they will come to understand the true story, but there are a lot of years before then that can misdirect their feelings."

"I have never thought of it from the kids' viewpoint. There is a point in trying to disassociate Melody's birth from the first lady's death. Still, there has to be an end point for the first lady."

"All I'm thinking is, let's not abruptly disconnect her life support the minute Melody is delivered. If she hangs on another day or two with the same life supports we have been using, that probably is the best case scenario. I know that I'll be harshly criticized for postponing the inevitable. So be it. I'm thinking of the kids."

"Thank you, Mister President. You have made a difficult and courageous decision. I'll notify surgery that we can start."

"One more thing. Has anyone tried to visit Kathy or send messages that aren't in the Secret Service log?"

"I've been too busy with the first lady's medical condition the last couple days to monitor her visitor list. I can check it now on my way to meet the neonatal doctors if you want."

"That's not necessary. I just find it a little strange that Kathy's best friend hasn't made an effort to be in touch since she arrived in Bethesda."

"What's her name? I'll alert the staff to notify you immediately if she calls."

"I don't know how to tell you this, Nan. It's embarrassing, but I'm sure that you will understand."

"Understand what?" Nan, anticipating the arrival of the neonatal doctors, nervously glanced at the large black-and-white institutional clock on the wall above the president's head.

"My last twenty years in politics have not been easy on our marriage. Kathy has always given me the freedom to do what I needed for advancing my political career. I likewise have looked the other way as she maintained her friendship with her closest high school and college friend."

"That's nothing to be ashamed of. Don't politicians have a saying: Politics makes strange bedfellows?"

"I'm not talking about Kathy having a bedding relationship with anyone but me. The baby you're about to deliver was our final gift to each other for allowing me to run again. She always said that our kids were the only sanity in the White House."

"That sounds pretty normal. She must have loved you to have another child."

"We loved each other at least as much as a politician can truly love another person besides himself. It's just that she seemed to have a spiritual, platonic relationship with her high school friend that I could never achieve."

"Many couples in high profile positions seem to have a similar accommodation. You might be projecting more into this relationship than there really was."

"I found it frustrating that I could never possess Kathy completely. She was on his yacht when the accident happened. I don't understand why he hasn't stopped for a visit, or at least called. When he's in Washington, he always has time to get together with Taylor for lunch or dinner at the Sequoia or the Watergate."

At the mention of the Watergate, Nan felt her face flush and her heart rate double. She summoned every bite of composure she could muster. "It sounds like you may have some issues that we can talk about when the first lady is gone. I have to meet the neonatal doctors."

Nan silently embraced the president, drying her tear-moistened cheeks as she quickly exited, all the while pondering the swirling maelstrom she was trapped in.

XL

"Confession is good for the soul," Gleason reminded his unrepentant host on the *Flying Mole*. "Especially for a dying man."

"You are the only one aboard this plane dying, with AIDS no less. You're also the authority on confession, at least so my men tell me."

"You bastard, Azee! Is nothing sacred?"

"Now control yourself, partner, or you'll have to go to confession again, and there is no little box with a waiting priest over the mid-Atlantic, unless he's stuffed in your stowed gym bag."

"You'd be surprised what's in my stowed bag. You should wish there were a stowaway priest to hear your sins." Gleason was angrier than ever before in his life, even more that when Cindy told him she wanted a divorce. Azee had violated his most personal sacred space as he was preparing for his final days. Azee's men obviously had been trailing him, and Gleason was so preoccupied with developing the perfect solution and conclusion to the Detroit madness that he'd became careless about his own safety.

Gleason started to calm down as he thought back over his last confession, made under the outstretched arms of the Byzantine mosaic of the risen Christ at the National Shrine of the Immaculate Conception on the campus of Catholic University.

Gleason was momentarily confused on entering the confessional area beside the smoking banked tiers of flickering votive candles where arrows pointed in one direction for face-to-face confession and in another direction for private confession. The new face-to-face confessional option reminded him of his pre-divorce counseling sessions, where there was no place to hide when the heat started coming down, so he opted to take his chances with the darkened anonymity of his childhood experiences in the stifling confines of the confessional box unique to the Catholic Church.

Now he hoped that it hadn't been one of Azee's own men sitting in the center stall of the unforgiving confessional box. "Bless me father, for I have sinned. It has been years since my last confession." The long hiatus precluded Gleason from remembering the rest of the ritualized form he'd learned as a boy from the Baltimore Catechism. He started to feel the same anxiety and nervousness in the pit of his stomach that accompanied every childhood experience in a dark box like this.

The same weekly litany of disobeying his parents, fighting with his brothers and sisters and not doing his homework—the sins of his youth. How happy he would be to have only these minor failings to confess now as an adult in the same frightening "box to salvation," as Sister Regina, his saintly eighth-grade teacher, euphemistically named it.

"Pardon me father, but I can't remember what to say next."

"That's okay, my son. Just confess your sins to me and your risen savior."

"All of them? I was hoping for some form of general absolution without mentioning everything."

"You don't need to mention all the venial sins. I assume you get angry and tell a little white lie once in a while. Let's just concentrate on your major failings, the mortal sins that will condemn you to the fires of hell for all eternity."

Gleason could picture the priest sitting behind the curtained screen in his black cassock, rubbing his hands, waiting for all the juicy details to come spewing forth from his contrite heart. I'm sure he has heard it all before, so I won't be shocking him too badly, Gleason thought while fidgeting for the proper beginning.

"You can begin, my son."

"Okay, Father, but I'm nervous. I haven't been very religious, especially since my recent divorce, when I had a lot of hatred and anger. I think I'm finally over it. I'm very sorry for any hurt that I caused at that time, especially to my ex-wife."

"Very good my son, you are forgiven. Please continue."

"In my job I've done a lot that I am not proud of. Some very serious things ..."

"Yes?"

"I can't say it any other way. I am killing my boss."

"When are you going to do this?"

"It's not that I want to kill him. There is just no choice. It's too late to stop."

"Everyone has a choice. Christ made the choice to die on the cross so we could be saved. You will go to hell and to jail for killing your boss."

"I guess I need to give you more details."

"For God's sake, as well as yours, please do."

"I slept with someone after I was divorced."

"Was it your boss's wife?"

"Of course not. I see what you're implying: that I'm in love with my boss's wife, so I'm going to kill him. Oh, how I wish that were true! I slept with a prostitute. I had great pleasure that evening, but God is punishing me now and forever. I am heartily sorry for this mortal sin."

"You are forgiven, my son, for this sin of the flesh. As a man of firm moral convictions, you have been tormented unduly by your weakness of the flesh. May God lift this terrible guilt from your heart and soul. Is there anything else you need to confess?"

"We still have this problem of me killing my boss."

"The arrogance of the soul is the devil. You will not get away with this murder in the eyes of the law or the all-knowing God."

"What allowed my boss to live also will make him die."

"My son, you're speaking in riddles."

"My boss hasn't died yet. He doesn't even know that he's to die. I'm sorry that I'm killing him."

"My son, there is no forgiveness prior to committing a sin— and in this case also a serious criminal offense. Fortunately, not all sins are crimes, but your impending action is a nonstop, one-way ticket to both hell and jail. You can't go ahead with the murder of your boss."

"You don't understand. He is dying because I gave him AIDS. I am heartily sorry for this serious sin."

"Before I give you absolution, I need details on how you gave him AIDS. Perhaps you should be confessing a homosexual or drug relationship with your boss. In which case, the AIDS is not the sin, but the immutable outcome of the homosexual or drug relationship. Which one is it?"

The profoundly mortified penitent could only mumble. "Neither." The stupefying silence was finally broken by Gleason angrily repeating, "I said neither."

"Forgive me, but I'm confused. You need to explain this problem so that I can give you absolution."

Gleason realized that the priest would know his and his victim's identity once the news of the president's AIDS became public knowledge. He also knew this was his final opportunity to make peace with his God, and he probably would not be around when the horrendous news broke. "I gave him some of my blood in a transfusion."

"Did you know you had AIDS when you gave him your blood?"

"What do you think I am, a killer?"

"I'm sorry, my son. I don't think you are a killer. The question is, how did you get AIDS? Do you need to confess a homosexual relationship or drug experience?"

"I got it from the prostitute. Those few minutes of pleasure have destroyed my life and those around me."

"You are not guilty of any sin, since you didn't know of your AIDS before donating your blood to your boss. I'm sure it was an act of compassion when you gave him your blood."

"It was a matter of life and death for him."

"My son, what's done is done. *Quod scripsi, scripsi.*"

These same sterile words of consolation, allegedly spoken by Pontius Pilate at the trial of Jesus, offered little solace to the penitent Gleason. "I still feel like I'm committing a sin by killing him. It's a terrible burden to bear."

"The risen savior over the main altar forgives all sins, and he'll give you the strength to weather this storm. Does your boss know about his AIDS and how he got it?"

"Not yet. We are waiting to tell him after the ..." Gleason caught himself just before completing his thought that would have revealed his boss's identity. "I only have one way to repay my boss for what I've done, and for this I humbly beg your advance forgiveness and absolution."

"As I said, the church cannot give absolution in advance. I can exercise a form of pastoral confessional discretion, as we do with soldiers going off to war, where God only knows what will happen. The one condition is that in whatever you do, your intentions are honorable."

"Thank you, father, for your kindness." A profound serenity came over Gleason that he hadn't felt since exiting the confessional as a child with the weight of all his sins lifted from his slender shoulders. "When you read the papers in a few days, this confession will make sense to you. I'm going to kill a very evil person, hopefully in self-defense. This truly diabolical monster must die by whatever means it takes. In the process of doing this, I could be killed or have to kill myself. For these and all my future sins I'm heartily sorry."

"My son, this has been the most extraordinary confession of my fifty years sitting in this dark box. I forgive you for all of your sins now and forever. For your penance I ask you, before you do what your conscience dictates you must do, communicate your contrition to your ex-wife for the hurt that you have caused her. Do what you can do to make things right with your boss, as hard as it may be. Will that be possible?"

"Yes, father."

"Go with the forgiveness, love and peace of our omnipotent God. May God bless you for all eternity in the name of the Father, the Son and the Holy Ghost."

XLI

The memory of the dark confessional's sliding wooden window banging closed jolted Gleason back to the present, equally confining interior of the *Flying Mole*. He glanced across the aisle at a grinning Azee.

"Did you bring a copy of the president's blood test results to give to our business associates in Damascus? That little piece of paper is worth ten million dollars to you. I, personally, was to receive this fee for killing the president, but since you are the one killing him with your blood, you should receive the full ten-million-dollar payment."

"You know they're probably going to pull the plug on the first lady." Gleason wanted to change the subject away from his new partnership. "Does this change anything?"

"Why should it? It's too late for her, you or me to change where we're at today. Do you know why I didn't stop by Bethesda to visit Kathy? You are probably thinking I was feeling too guilty to visit her or that I didn't want to see her, my first and only love, in her pathetic, hopeless condition."

"All these rationalizations for not visiting her certainly could apply. Plus I'm sure you have an even higher ulterior reason for not visiting her on her deathbed. You always do."

"How did you know? I had a little meeting with Doctor Schmidt at the Watergate Hotel posing as a CIA internal affairs investigator. I couldn't take a chance that she would see the real me if I visited Kathy at the hospital. In her condition, Kathy wouldn't know if I was visiting her or not. I've looked at her many times and saw heaven. I don't need to look at her now and see hell. We have exchanged many wonderful good-byes. We don't need this final, tragic one. Fancy Nancy, as all the drooling guys called her back in our Newport days, didn't like the Newport photos of her and Andre naked in the hyperbaric whirlpool, when she viewed them at the Watergate. She was quite upset, probably rightly so."

"I suspected as much. Thanks for telling me your real reason for not visiting the first lady. You used Nancy's flaws to destroy her strengths, much like you did with the first lady. Like I said, confession is good, especially for a dark soul like yours."

"You go into your little box with your priest. I go into my big dark soul with myself. Who's right? Probably the one with the most might

Azee revealed the global kunstwollen that dominated his entire life.

"Poor Doctor Schmidt. Another innocent victim caught up in your personal theomania. She's now a member of your infamous victim-of-the-month club because she had a little fun years ago and you were perverse enough to keep the photos."

"Which politician, or was it an all-powerful Secret Service agent, who once said, 'When your true enemies are too strong, pick weaker enemies'? Fancy Nancy and the president will need some clever footwork once the media does their homework on the current activities of the KGB agent Andre, who had an affair with the doctor now treating the first lady."

"I'm sure you have a current file on Andre. You were anything but honest at your office when you showed me the old photos and claimed ignorance of his current whereabouts."

"I haven't needed to keep a file on Andre. Some things are better kept in the grey matter than on white paper, just as many things are better left unsaid at the first interview for a new job."

"So that is what my emergency visit to your office was, a job interview? You should have warned me, I would have shined my shoes."

"No problem. You obviously passed the interview test, as you are now working for me, about to collect your first big paycheck."

"You know, I would have been fired from my Secret Service job if anyone found out that I left photos with you that incriminated the White House physician in possible espionage activity. Your numerous calls to Chief Hawkins requesting an immediate meeting with me and my probably illegal international helicopter ride over to your office convinced me that you wanted too much for me to have the photos."

"So why didn't you take them like any good detective would have when I offered them to you?"

"Probably because I'm not a good detective. I didn't see how they were connected to the bombings, and I wanted to see what you would do with them. What sort of blackmail did you try to extract from the surprised and trapped Doctor Schmidt?"

"Blackmail? Do you think that I would stoop so low as to blackmail the doctor that has the only love of my life in her hands?"

"Don't make me laugh at your newfound morality. She could have remembered you from when you caught her and Andre in the whirlpool caper, so you must have had a very good reason to risk recognition when you tried your Watergate shakedown."

"I had to be sure that she's had no contact with Andre since he was deported. I'll ask Andre the same questions I asked her. If his answers corroborate hers, then our business dealings with Andre can go forward."

"What if their answers don't jive? What if they have been secret lovers all these years and you are just finding out about it?"

"All future deals with him will be impossible. He'll have a fatal auto accident, as Fancy Nancy tearfully suggested. He knows too much about GCT from our past dealings, and he could be a direct pipeline to the CIA because of her. That scenario could permanently ground the *Flying Mole*."

"What if they have been incommunicado for all these twenty years? Will she need to have an auto accident too because she's seen you?"

"Gleason, as my new partner, you're worrying about things that I'll handle at the appropriate time. Your hands will be clean if she has an auto accident."

"Why not just leak your information on Andre to his government? I'm sure that they would willingly arrange an auto accident or worse for someone profiting from the sale of sensitive government-owned property like decommissioned nuclear weapons."

"He's part of the oligarchy. They are just a bunch of thieves selling off assets of the emerging republics. I don't trust any of them."

"I thought there was honor among thieves. How do you deal with Andre? Making sure that you, or should I say we, get the merchandise that we pay for?"

"The good old American COD method of doing business. I give Andre just a token five percent prepayment to stimulate his new capitalistic appetite, and the rest of the payment is on delivery of the merchandise. Our nuclear contract with Iraq, which we are going to finalize when we meet in Damascus to collect your ten million dollars, is our most difficult one to fulfill—and hence the most lucrative. We have all our bases covered, but it's still a risky proposition. I wouldn't fault you if you opt out when you hear the details in Damascus."

"What are some of the details? I may not even want to go with you to Damascus."

"No Damascus, no ten million dollars for you. The ten million is nothing to me except a tether to Iraq for the bigger nuclear payoff later."

"When you put it that way, there isn't much choice. Maybe just a little guilt for the job that I'm being paid for, killing the president."

"In our business there's no room for guilt. Mistakes are made. Life goes on. Life is for the living. I suppose that as long as Kathy is still alive, I'll harbor a little selfish guilt for what I am going to lose."

"I hope I can achieve your level of detachment. Life would be a lot easier without guilt."

"Maybe I misjudged you. I figured you for one tough SOB. Sworn to stop a bullet to save the president. I could have turned the Newport pictures over to the FBI or CIA. It would have ruined Fancy Nancy's navy career, and Andre would be tracked down."

"I'm sure that you caused Doctor Schmidt much stress. Are you going to set the record straight with her, keeping in mind that she's the person trying to help the love of your life?"

Azee didn't take the bait of Gleason's well intentioned question about the first lady. "I can't be responsible for Fancy Nancy's feelings caused by her lewd behavior twenty years ago. Collateral damage is unavoidable and sometimes even desirable."

"Desirable?"

"If she's upset enough, she might do something stupid, like trying to contact Andre. The breakaway republics don't have extradition treaties with the United States, so he couldn't be brought to this country for a trial. There would be three entities, his own government, the United States and GCT, interested in Andre having that fatal auto accident."

"I have a feeling that GCT would have the most to gain by Andre's auto accident to bury the past."

"Astute observation, but not entirely accurate. I've done big deals with Andre, but the biggest is yet to come. Technically, he is no longer in the KGB. However, he has the title of chief of security for one of the breakaway republics. This mainly ceremonial position allows him to run his own public relations firm, which facilitates the selling of former USSR military assets."

"Like munitions, guns and tanks?"

"Those items are entry-level items to build a level of trust between buyer and seller before the serious purchases are even discussed."

"Have you achieved Andre's highest level of trust?"

"As my newest business partner, this important question should be reversed. Has Andre achieved my highest level of trust? He needs me more than I need him. There aren't two or three arms-dealing middlemen in the world with the contacts and trust levels between buyers and sellers that I have. The more sophisticated weapons are being bought and sold, or as I say, being relocated to new owners, the more the buyer and seller do not want to deal face-to-face, so that they can maintain a posture of deniability to the world community. The middleman assumes all the risk and must be highly compensated."

"Please excuse my ignorance, but I've a lot to learn about your business. How high does this highest level of trust go? As high as dismantled ICBMs with nuclear warheads?"

The conversation seemed to reach a dead end. Azee did not reply for what seemed to Gleason too long a time. He was obviously crafting a non-answer. "They want and need what only Andre and I can deliver more than they want the president dead. They won't admit this, but I know how they think, because I am a kindred spirit. The president's AIDS death sentence allows them to save face when paying the money before moving onto what they really want."

Gleason still wanted to get the truth of Azee's nuclear dealings with Andre recorded by the trailing F16 jet for a blockbuster CIA file. "So how many times have you and Andre been down this nuclear path? Too many to remember?"

"Never too many to remember. Their sky-high risk-reward ratio makes them the most profitable. This final transaction is going to be my biggest. If you want to continue doing these geese that lay the golden eggs without me, learn all you can from me this final time."

"Is Andre going to be in Damascus so I can meet him?"

"Please forgive me, Gleason, but that is a rather dumb—or at the very least an extremely naïve—question. If any of my purchasers meet Andre, they would have no need for me, I mean us, and we go back to flying coach class on tardy airlines."

XLII

Gleason felt that he had all the information Azee was going to divulge on his nuclear connection. Hopefully it was all recorded by the trailing surveillance jet. "Azee, you have taught me well." Gleason fingered the garage door opener, turned detonator, that he'd removed from the center of the hollowed-out book. "This is your remote detonator, recovered from the bottom of the Detroit River. It's now set to explode the plastique inside my gym bag in the sealed front luggage compartment. Would you like to hold it and see if it works a second time?"

Azee hesitantly reached across the narrow aisle to take back the detonator that had destroyed the thing he most cherished in life. "You Secret Service guys think you are so smart. Here I am, one person defeating your entire system. You are now bluffing me into believing this airplane will blow up with you aboard. You've been watching too many James Bond movies. I love high stakes poker in our Windsor casino. I've risked my life many times, and I'm still sitting next to you, the dying man."

"How long have you known that Misty has AIDS?"

"Not very long. It was never a personal worry of mine since I'm faithful to my wife in Beirut. Misty is still the best hostess we have for entertaining all our foreign dignitaries."

"You really have no conscience. Knowingly infecting your friends and business associates."

"I didn't force Misty on anyone. They all asked for some fun, like you. So maybe the AIDS is an earthly form of divine justice. I'm not the one dying because I slept with a high-class whore. I'm not the one killing his boss, a serial cheater on the love of my life. You still want to talk about who has a conscience?" Azee sat back in his chair with the smug confidence of the unwavering agnostic who never let the unfathomable existence of a possible heaven or hell influence his thinking.

"Azee, you're dying and so are your pilots. We are all dying. The bomb in my stowed gym bag has a timer for self-detonation besides the remote detonator you are now holding. It's set to go off in twenty-seven minutes," he solemnly said while picking up the Walkman and looking at his gold Omega Seamaster wristwatch.

Azee fingered the switches beside his seat that again would turn the passenger seat into the diabolical high-flying electric chair. Trying to buy a little more time to judge Gleason's bluff, he said, "I trusted you as a valuable partner. Why did you call the Washington D.C. nine-one-one operator to report your car stolen?"

"I wanted to erase any doubt that I willingly participated with you in the betrayal of my country. Every man has his price. Mine is much higher than the ten million dollars that you keep dangling in front of me."

"You want more money? No problem. How much more do you want?"

"That's why I set the automatic timer on the bomb in my gym bag, so I won't be tempted by your generosity. What I want, you cannot give me. My fate is sealed with the AIDS. All your money won't save me from myself."

"Maybe not, but at least you will be more comfortable during your final days than living on just your pitiful Secret Service pension. Give me your bottom line price."

"Azee, you don't get it! You never will! That's why I've resorted to my own justice system, with divine or at least priestly approval from the confessional box. With your influence, you would make more of a mockery of our judicial system than OJ Simpson—that is, if you ever came to trial. You may want to push the detonator button now so we don't have to go through all this morality bullshit that you don't understand. Do it now, or wait twenty-four minutes. The choice is yours. I do have one dying man's final question. How long has Chief Hawkins been on your payroll?"

"There was never any need for us to hire him. He was always eager to please everyone. He unwittingly cooperated with us at every turn because of my friend in the White House. Besides, he thinks Misty is in love with him, even though he has yet to bed her. I doubt if he is still drooling over her with her AIDS."

"I'm relieved to know that Chief Hawkins isn't working for you. The FBI initially might focus on him, but now that they have your recorded statement proclaiming his innocence transmitted by this Walkman to our satellite, he'll be left alone."

A stunned Azee pushed the switch that started the generator in the fuselage below them. Gleason smiled as he heard the distinctive high-pitched chatter of the revving exterminator. The lights in the cabin flickered as the cabin's electrical power diverted to fully electrify Gleason's chair. Azee pushed the diverter switch once more, to no avail.

Gleason lifted up his sweatshirt to reveal the 5-mil-thick neoprene suit that shielded him from the chair's high voltage. "A fishing boat found Henri's smashed body floating in Lake Ontario. The autopsy revealed that he died of electrocution before his water immersion. There were severe burns on his back, shoulders and chest. The fingers still provided a set of identifying fingerprints, but there were no teeth present to check against dental records. His job in Ottawa at the Canadian government motor pool and his association with the Quebec Separatist movement were readily established. His broken bones, were inflicted post mortem by a fast airborne entry into the water. The *Flying Mole* was the only plane in the area that night that could have dropped the body. Gleason was struggling to undo his seat restraint.

"Don't waste your energy trying to release your harness. It's electrically fastened like a deadbolt," Azee smiled at his own sick humor as he turned off the ineffective electrical generator. "Sorry, partner, but you are not going anywhere—except into space as vapor when the plane explodes."

On the plane's intercom phone, Azee told Taajud-Deen to radio their exact GPS location to the nearest Libyan flagged ship in the area and to immediately implement 5A survival procedures. He didn't inform Taajud-Deen of the *Flying Mole*'s remaining twenty-minute lifespan.

The plane began a rapid descent while Azee quickly donned a Kevlar survival jumpsuit and a helmet with a Lexan face shield and built-in transponder radio before strapping on his parachute. He removed a large survival pack with its inflatable raft and his own parachute from a rear storage compartment. While Azee was engaged in his selfish survival preparations, Gleason pushed a pre-arranged sequence of buttons on his Walkman to alert the trailing Captain Gibson of the impending events.

When the plane slowed to near stall speed and leveled off, Azee pushed the switch that opened the rear hydraulic trap door so he could perform his D.B. Cooper imitation over the dangerous Atlantic. "You won't be needing this!" he shouted to Gleason over the inrushing turbulence as he carefully put the remote detonator in his jumpsuit breast pocket.

Gleason could only smile, relieved that the detonator was now in the possession of its rightful owner. He was content to do his waiting aloof from the panic and chaos that would soon erupt above and in the turbulent Atlantic when Azee bailed out of the doomed plane.

With the confident arrogance of the damned, Azee pushed the large survival pack out the trap door and watched the attached ripcord open its billowing parachute in the pitch of the night mirrored off the Atlantic below. Azee was looking down toward the water to see his heaven, while Gleason prayed Azee's jump would land him in the depths of hell.

"Have a nice journey," Gleason hollered at the departing Azee. In the split second that Azee was being sucked out of the fuselage before his own parachute opened, he heard and saw the trailing F16 pulverize the survival pack and raft with a burst of cannon fire. He felt the remote detonator in the survival suit's breast pocket and pushed the button to even the score with his rapidly departing partner. Instead, Gleason's bombastic bluff was an explosive pocket rocket, hopefully transposing Azee's heartless heart into an ethereal existence with Kathy that was unattainable to him in this world.

Acknowledgments

Friends and colleagues enriched the experience of writing *The First Lady Sleeps* with encouragement and suggestions. Special thanks to: the late Aloysius E. Bernard, S.S., my first creative writing instructor, for telling me to learn how to write by writing; Reverend R. Louis Stasker, for things theological; Dr. Thomas E. Rinkevich for things classical; Ben Delphia, for things artistic; my brother, Honorable Neil G. Mullally for things legal; my niece, Shannon M. Mullally, PhD, for showing me that I could (and should) write this story; Angie Maloy for her reality check of needed Writing 101 pointers; Critical early readers Robert Keesen, John Schrier, Mike, Tom and Carol Whelan for keeping me true to the literary mantra that good can always become better; romance novelist Terri Brisbin, Dr. Paul and Rochelle Adler for providing a needed impartial perspective; John and Kathy Snider for humoring me with the question of how soon before the sequel is out when *The First Lady Sleeps* hadn't yet arisen from its prepublication slumber; Roger Rapoport and editor Richard Harris for early on bringing it all together.

The stunning cover photograph of the pink White House was taken by friend Gerald Martineau and Steven Demos, M.D. assisted in the graphics and cover design.

I extend a deep appreciation to you, my reader, for taking a chance on a new author. The "book people" have categorized The First Lady Sleeps in the political thriller genre. I hope that you have discovered in it a philosophical depth and breadth often not found in this genre.

Words cannot convey my love and appreciation to my wife Barb, our four children and their families, on how much it means for all of us to just be there for each other through all life's adventures. Love conquers all.

Please turn this page for the introduction to the surprising,
action packed sequel!

THE FIRST LADY
MEETS AZEE

BY JOHN MULLALLY

THE FIRST LADY MEETS AZEE

JOHN MULLALLY

The trap door in the floor of the Flying Mole's fuselage that the deluded Azee jumped out of automatically closed. Tom Gleason, the White House's senior secret service agent, rested his weary head on Azee's streaking Bombadier jet's seat back. With closed eyes he uttered the simple prayer, "Amen." Azee's treasonous bombings of the first family in Detroit were avenged. Gleason rationalized that the country would be better off without the protracted trial that would be necessary to convict Azee of the crimes of the century: the maiming of the first lady and the attempted assassination of the President. Gleason could feel the Flying Mole's steep climb regaining the lost altitude needed for Azee's hasty departure from what he considered a doomed plane because of Gleason's threatened self-detonating bomb in his stowed bag.

Gleason was relieved that the pilot, Taajud-Deen, did not

immediately put the Flying Mole into a steep dive that would have doomed him and the pilots to the same uncertain fate in the mid-Atlantic that Azee had chosen for himself when he parachuted out of the Flying Mole. Gleason, with his ex-wife's helpful philosophical profile of Azee, had gambled that Azee would elect to take control of his own destiny, trying to save his own skin by bailing out of the allegedly doomed Flying Mole rather than deal with the possibility of Gleason's threatened bomb. Gleason was wagering his own AIDS shortened life that mega-egomaniac Azee would take his chances on drowning in the mid-Atlantic over being blown apart by a stowed bomb that he had no control over. Gleason provided the final bait Azee needed to make his jump when he gave him a remote detonator that would supposedly blow up the bomb stowed in the fuselage as he evacuated the plane.

The one major variable crucial to his own survival that the control freak Gleason was unable to forecast was what would be the reaction of Taajud-Deem and co-pilot Abdul after their boss bailed out over the busy transatlantic shipping lanes. All Azee's employees had a fanatical loyalty to their boss, so Gleason's life was in the hands of highly professional, yet unpredictable, pilots.

Gleason was still restrained by his seat belt and shoulder harness that was electronically locked closed like a deadbolt preventing him from getting out of his seat and moving around the jet's luxurious but cramped cabin. During his life and death game of chicken with the ever manipulative Azee, Gleason had used a prearranged, elementary form of Morse code on his CIA-rigged walkman to secretly communicate with Colonel Neil Gibson in his trailing F16 CIA surveillance jet. However, now he had nothing to lose and perhaps everything to gain if the pilots of the Flying Mole overheard their conversation.

"TG to NG," he shouted into his walkman to overcome the Flying Mole's screaming engines. He realized that Gibson would be totally preoccupied piloting the most sophisticated piece of equipment in the CIA's arsenal of high-tech toys, so he repeated his simple salutation, "TG to NG. Come in NG."

"NG here. Nice to hear your voice. Thought you might be dead."

"Azee took the bait and bailed. I heard your cannon fire, just before he jumped."

"Affirmative. I blasted the survival raft and saw a small report flash of the remote detonator as his parachute was filling. I didn't want to risk losing you in the heavy cloud cover by circling back to destroy his parachute."

"Get the exact location where Azee jumped. He should be shark bait unless he crashes onto the deck of a freighter. I'm restrained in my seat and can't get to the cockpit."

"Got the location where I destroyed the survival pack. Since leaving Annapolis, we've been flying over the international shipping lanes, so there probably are ships in the area. Should I put out a SOS for Azee?"

"Hell no! He's on his own."

"Good point. I'm ordering your pilots to land at our Sigonella naval air station on Sicily. We don't have to notify the Italian government as we have carte blanche to come and go there. This will be the test of Azee's contingency plans if the pilots cooperate with my orders to land there."

"What's the ETA? I don't want to mess up this beautiful interior so you'd better radio the pilots to release my restraints for a potty break. I'm still wearing the neoprene suit to shield me from the electrical charge built into the seat, so I probably have sweated away most of my body fluids."

"Will do. Don't worry about the pilots. They see me on your wing and we have radio contact. They should follow international protocol and land at Sigonella in an hour."

"I hope you're right, but I'm sure Azee and the pilots have contingency plans for any emergency. Though our main objective is accomplished with Azee choosing his fate, my order to shoot down the Flying Mole if the pilots don't cooperate is still in place."

After too long a pause without a reply, Gleason felt compelled to summon Gibson, "NG, did you copy my last transmission?"

"Affirmative, but I don't agree with it anymore. There's nothing to be gained by shooting you out of the sky with Azee gone. We'll deal with it if the need arises."

Although Gleason felt that he was in charge of this bizarre, clandestine mission he recognized that Gibson had all the power. He wasn't sure why he reiterated this suicidal order. He knew that he was mentally, physically and especially spiritually exhausted and wasn't reasoning properly. Did he want to die a hero's death and not the slow embarrassing death caused by his AIDS? As he was pondering this morbid dilemma Taajud-Deen opened the cockpit door and stood menacingly over him, brandishing a pistol that Gleason recognized as a thirty-eight caliber police issue revolver.

Gleason had only said a polite hello to Taajud-Deen on boarding in Annapolis when he handed him his small duffle bag to stow in the forward hatch. Taajud-Deen's stern appearance conveyed the obvious message that he was not pleased that Gleason had snookered his departed boss with the now obviously false threat of a stowed self-detonating bomb. Taajud-Deen's hand slid off the pistol's grip to the black barrel. Gleason crouched down in his seat preparing to be pistol whipped into a state of unconsciousness or even death.

"I've been ordered by your pilot to surrender my sidearm," Taajud-Deen meekly proclaimed while pushing it into Gleason's restrained hand. Taajud-Deen sat in Azee's plush starboard side recliner and began clicking a sequence of switches that Gleason worried would restart the electrical generator giving him the high flying hot seat that Azee had futilely tried.

His perspiration saturated neoprene suit would probably offer little protection against the seat and shoulder harness' deadly 440 volts of electrical current. Instead, a loud click of the waist buckle released the restraints that had kept him prisoner while Azee did his Cooper imitation over the foreboding Atlantic. "What's our ETA at Sigonella?" Gleason asked the pilot as he was returning to the cockpit.

"Probably about an hour if your pilot doesn't shoot us out of the sky. All is now in the hands of Allah and your demon pilot."

Gleason tucked the newly acquired pistol under his soggy waistband and gingerly stood up while bracing himself on the chair backs as he shuffled to the cramped head to relieve himself and to peel off the life saving, but now moisture-laden suit. Even though no one else was in the passenger compartment, he closed and locked the bathroom door as he sought a hiding place for his smuggled on transponder that would allow the Flying Mole to be tracked anywhere in the world. Sliding aside the fiberglass service panel behind the toilet he was able to wedge it between two overlapping fiberglass struts.

"TG, you okay? I just heard this awful sucking sound."

"Sorry! I just flushed the toilet."

"Let's hope that's our only snafu before landing. I heard your pilot give an ETA at Sigonella of an hour to the approaching Tripoli control tower and that's pretty accurate if he doesn't try any funny stuff."

"I think he's going to be okay. He gave me his pistol and released my seat restraint, which is about all that we can ask of him. I assume his co-pilot also has a gun, but I don't think that I'll try to retrieve it."

"Good idea. Don't precipitate an airborne shooting incident. Remember the pilots are still loyal to their departed boss and his terrorist causes."

Feeling more comfortable and relaxed after his visit to the head, Gleason discovered a plush black velour robe with gold braiding running the length of the arms hanging in the small closet across from the head. He slipped it on over his sweat drenched tee shirt and boxer shorts after peeling off the life saving neoprene suit that had shielded him from the lethal electrical current in the passenger chair. His super charged personality was never conducive to airborne cat naps, even aboard the luxurious Air Force One, and today was no exception as he struggled to drift away for a few moments of surcease.

The cop in him wondered whether he should get up and conduct a search of the plane's small cabin to see what other surprises Azee might have tucked away. It wouldn't matter if he found another gun or two as he already had one too many for use while airborne. Finally his tired mind rationalized that anything found could be construed as evidence and was better left to FBI experts to handle and process after they landed. He opted to sit in Azee's starboard seat, just in case the pilots could activate the passenger seat frying pan from the cockpit.

Closing his eyes for a few moments of quiet nirvana to gather himself like his fifteen minutes of morning meditation during his seminary days, he jolted upright in a state of heightened awareness. Things were not adding up. The pilots were being too cooperative. By training and culture they should be avenging Azee's fate by killing him, even if it meant dying in the process.

Gleason was startled back to reality when his Walkman squawked, "NG to TG. I've been recording your pilots' multiple radio transmissions in a foreign language that need translation. One was on the emergency frequency like an S O S. Should I jam all transmissions or order radio silence?"

"Keep the status quo but record them. We might be able to learn their contingency plans. How long will it take to get them translated?"

"It depends if the proper language expert is on duty at Langley. I'll have to break radio silence with Langley. Okay?"

"Do it!"

"NG to TG," Gleason's walkman barked just as he was starting to doze off. "I have word from Langley about the translation of the messages."

"Let's have it."

"Didn't mean to get your hopes up - it'll be fifteen minutes before the translator finishes his work. This shouldn't be a problem as we still have an ETA of forty five minutes at Sigonella."

"Great! I was just about asleep when you roused me with this non-news. By the way, have you talked to the pilots to make sure our fuel supply is adequate?"

"Sorry. I can't sleep while piloting this Star Wars plane, so I figured the same for you. I'll call them about your fuel level. Your plane should be okay on fuel, probably better than this high-tech hog I'm flying. Azee had the Flying Mole retrofitted with auxiliary fuel tanks to fly non-stop transatlantic."

Gleason was trying hard to doze when the disconcerting message came through from Gibson, "The pilots aren't acknowledging my radio contacts."

Suddenly, the cockpit door flew open and a scowling Taajud-Deen emerged brandishing a pistol, similar to the one that he had earlier surrendered. "Hands up—behind your head. Get back in your own seat and click closed the harness." With the 38 police-special pointed at his face and his own pistol ripped from his waistband, Gleason quickly complied. Taajud-Deen sat in Azee's vacant chair and began fiddling with the bank of chairside switches. Gleason felt the distinctive clunk of his seat belt being electronically locked. He wondered if next he would hear the exterminating hum of the 440 volt generator in the cargo hold that would turn his seat into the deadly high flying electric chair since he was without his protective neoprene suit.

From his regained prisoner seat he thought, 'They must want to keep me alive. Otherwise, the electricity would be surging through me.' He couldn't figure out why Taajud-Deen allowed him to keep his walkman radio which allowed him to stay in touch with Gibson's jet. Taajud-Deen was too much in charge to have simply forgotten to take it from him. The pilots wanted him to talk to the escorting jet, Gleason rationalized, so he'd better speak cautiously.

"TG to NG. I'm restrained again in the hot seat. Otherwise everything's under control."

"I'd say that we have a problem developing. The plane is deviating from the flight plan to Sigonella. The pilots still aren't responding to my radio messages."

"Wish I could help you, but I'm pretty much just along for the ride. All I can do is pray… to whom? Allah, since He's the god of our deviating pilots?"

"This is no time to joke! I'm just getting back the translation of your pilots' messages. Give me a minute to get their gist... When Azee bailed out the pilots sent an SOS to the ships in the area and worse yet, they have requested permission to enter Libyan airspace for an emergency landing at Tripoli. This explains the change in your flight pattern."

"No surprise there. Azee has an office in Tripoli and is buddy-buddy with Quadafi. If I wasn't restrained in this seat I'd bail out like Azee, using the second survival pack and parachute in the closet. I'm sure that Quadafi has ordered all the Libyan flagged ships in the Atlantic to look for Azee. We should do our Emergency Plan One."

"We talked about this! Azee's off the plane, so E P One, shooting you down, isn't an option. We're only one hundred miles from Libyan airspace. I'm sure they're scrambling their jets to meet us."

"What's the problem? The Libyans fly old Russian Migs, don't they?"

"I probably could take them all out, but it would take a while. Meanwhile you would have landed in Tripoli. I can't land this top secret bird in enemy territory to extricate you when I wouldn't be allowed to take off. I have to decide real fast as Libyan air space is only fifty miles ahead and I don't want to give their jets a reason to fire on me."

"Agreed! Peel off! You have enough taped evidence of Azee's treachery to establish his guilt in the Detroit bombings. Give my love to Cindy and my sincere regrets to the president." He spoke these words with a profound melancholy not knowing if they would be his final thoughts for the two people that were his reasons for wanting to live.